TALK DIRTY, COWBOY

DIRTY COWBOY, #1

ELLE THORPE

For Tamara. Because almost thirty five years of friendship must earn you the dedication on a book, right? Love you!

PROLOGUE

BOWEN

Four Years Earlier

*R*ampage thrashed his solid body against the sides of the metal chute, thoroughly pissed off before I even took a step towards him. The enormous bull had a reputation for being a mean son of a bitch. He didn't like the noise of the crowd. He didn't like the ropes around his middle. He sure as hell didn't like people. Especially those of us dumb enough to try to ride him.

A slow grin spread across my face as the announcer called my name. I eyed Rampage, silently letting him know that this was happening, and who was boss.

He snorted and kicked out, his hooves clanging against the metal enclosure.

His way of saying "fuck you", I guessed.

"Fair enough," I muttered under my breath, quitting the silent standoff with the beast and climbing up the rungs of the chute to prepare for my ride. I grabbed the rope, handed it off to Jimmy, my rope guy, and waited for my spotter to grab the back of my vest. The air around me smelled of dirt and animal, earthy and familiar, and I sucked a breath in deep, pushing it into the very bottom of my lungs, letting them expand. For the briefest moment, I let my eyes close. I heard the roar of the crowd. I heard my guys talking. I heard Rampage thrashing around, refusing to settle.

I pictured the argument I'd had with Camille before I'd left for the airport. I saw her standing in the corner of our bedroom, holding our son's hand so tenderly but looking at me like she no longer knew me. I saw tears rolling down her face.

I saw me walking out the door.

I held my breath until my lungs screamed for oxygen, and then I let it out in one long whoosh. And with the new breath, I let everything fade away. Nothing else mattered. There was nothing but me, the bull beneath me, and eight seconds to glory. This was why I was here. Not just here at the rodeo, but why I'd been put on this earth. I was born to ride bulls.

I settled on Rampage's back, and for one split second, the vicious bull that had most cowboys quaking in their boots quieted. The rosin warmed, I shoved my fingers into the handle and wrapped the rope around and through my fingers again, pulling it tight, the same way I had a million times before. My chin tucked, I let my mind go blank. Nothing else mattered. I was ready.

I nodded. The universal cowboy signal for "let's do this thing".

The gate swung open with a crack of metal against metal and Rampage exploded onto the dirt floor arena. One hand gripping the handle ropes, I held the other up, well away from the massive bull. His back legs kicked out as he spun in frustrated, angry circles, rearing up, kicking out, twisting, turning, his breath coming in fast pants that matched my own. I mirrored his moves, gripping his muscled torso with my thighs and feeling that familiar rush of adrenaline that coursed through my veins. It was that high that all junkies chased. And I was addicted.

Rampage changed directions, bellowing his anger, but I'd anticipated the move and went with him. Five seconds... Rampage bucked into the air. Every muscle in my body worked to keep me on his back... Six seconds... I dug my spurs in, gripping the beast with everything I had. Dirt flew up around us in clouds, Rampage's deadly hooves churning up the ground... Seven seconds...

The buzzer sounded and suddenly the entire arena erupted into noise, the world flooding back in like a literal smack to the face. It was deafening, the pure intensity of it, and I breathed it in like I needed it to live. Because I did. I craved this high like nothing else.

The rope loosened and I pulled my hand free, then got the hell off Rampage's back. My knees hit the black dirt with a thud, a sharp pain curling up through my kneecaps and into my thighs and groin, but without wasting a moment, I pushed to my feet and pumped my legs, running to the side of the arena. I scaled the chute with Rampage's hot breath at my neck, his deadly horns inches from my back.

He shoulder-barged the fence, giving one last angry bray before turning and running down the tunnels to fresh hay and water.

The guys crowded me, thumping me on the back as a laugh bubbled out of my chest.

"He nearly got you, Bowen," Jimmy said, elbowing me in the ribs.

I shoved him off with a grin. "Nuh. Not today."

I stood on the side of the arena, waving to the crowd like the cocky bastard I was. They screamed my name and stamped their feet while I waited for my score. It flashed up on the big screen: 90.7. I whooped, taking off my helmet and tossing it across the arena. Ninety point fucking seven! I punched the air, and the crowd went wild.

"That puts you in number one!" Jimmy crowed, fist in the air right along with me. My eyes widened and I spun around to check the leaderboard. He was right. My name was there in neon lights. Bowen Barclay. Number one.

"Bowen Barclay with the ride of the night, ladies and gentlemen!" the announcer called and a pride like nothing I'd ever felt before spread through me.

This. This feeling. This was what I chased every time I got on the back of a bull. These were the moments I lived for.

I jogged back through the tunnels of the arena to the competitors' locker rooms, guys congratulating me and stopping me every few steps to shake my hand as I went. I stopped and laughed with Colby, taking his good-natured ribbing in stride, then shoved him off when Deacon, my best friend on the tour, grabbed me by the shoulder. He spun me round and I threw my arm around his shoulders and let out a whoop of delight. "Did ya see that ride? A ninety, Deac! Hell yeah!"

I couldn't stop grinning. My face was actually hurting from how hard I was smiling.

But Deacon didn't smile back. He didn't cheer or yell or pull me in for a semi-awkward hug like we always did when one of us nailed a ride. His face was grim, and my good mood faded.

"What?"

He shook his head, his eyes glistening. He opened his mouth to speak but nothing came out. He closed it again, coughing to try to clear his throat, but he looked away, unable to meet my gaze.

My heart froze over.

"Deacon, what? Fucking tell me!" I grabbed him by the shoulders and shook him, a sinking feeling in my stomach. "What happened? Did I get disqualified?"

He shook his head sadly. "It's Camille, man. I'm so sorry. Your dad just called. He was real choked up, asked me if I'd tell you. He couldn't do it. Not on the phone."

Ice spread through my veins, freezing over the hot-headed, arrogant blood that had coursed there just moments earlier. I shook him again but it was half-hearted, fear making my grip weak. "Tell me what?"

"Camille. There was an accident on the farm. She's... she's gone, Bowen. The doctors couldn't save her."

I stumbled back a step.

"What? No," I whispered.

Images flashed through my mind. Long dark hair. Smiling blue eyes. Her fingers trailing down my bare back. Her lips pressed to my neck. Her cheek on my chest while we slow danced.

I closed my eyes and saw everything. Saw the last five years of my life. Saw my past. My present and my future.

Then watched it all evaporate into smoke.

1

PAISLEY

Present Day

*T*he scratched kitchen table was covered in dirty dishes, cutlery, and food scraps. A plastic cup lay on its side, liquid slowly trickling out of it. Ugh. It looked like animals had eaten dinner there, not two small children. A long sigh fell from my lips as I watched the spilled drink drip into a puddle on the floor. At least it was just water, I supposed, as I fished around the sink for a sponge. At least it wasn't something sticky, and at least it wasn't dripping onto the carpet.

I made a mental note to check the state of the kitchen *before* sending Lily upstairs for a bath next time. If she hadn't been neck-deep in bubbles, I would have had her clean the mess up. I could hear her little girl voice belting out a *Moana* song from down here, and I smiled despite my annoyance that neither of my children seemed to know where the dishwasher was. Her singing warmed my heart. She took after me like that. I sang a lot too. Especially in, but not limited to, the shower.

Shoving aside the electricity bill that was two weeks overdue, I unearthed my phone and pulled up the Spotify app, scrolling until I found my favourite cleaning playlist. As Sir Mix-a-Lot's classic nineties hit, "Baby Got Back", poured through the speakers, I let the bass roll through me. I stacked the pile of dirty plates and danced them to the dishwasher. I couldn't help it. That damn song was infectious.

By the second chorus I was singing along at the top of my lungs, with my butt shakin' as I dropped forks into the cutlery holder and filled the sink with soapy water to attack the pots and pans. I attempted a quick little twerk, which went horribly wrong and I vowed to leave that one to the teenagers. Yikes.

"Muuuuuuum! Would you please stop that! Ugh! You're so embarrassing!"

I spun around, expecting to see my eldest child standing in the doorway with his regular preteen scowl on his face, but there was no one there. So I bumped and grinded the air as I danced towards the adjoining living room, wiping my hands on the back of my jeans as I went.

In the living room, Aiden was staring at the TV like a mindless zombie, his fingers flying over a controller while he played some game that looked suspiciously like a rip-off of *The Hunger Games*.

"You know, you should never tell someone to stop singing, Aiden. Singing means they're happy. Sad people don't sing."

"Unless you're Adele," Aiden muttered.

He had a point.

"Henry! Go to Sandman's Curse!"

I jumped at his sudden change in volume, then rolled my eyes, realising he had an earpiece in. A microphone dangled on a cord by the far side of his face. The kid was obsessed with this game lately. If I didn't physically remove it from his hands some days, he'd do nothing else.

"Henry! No, back me up. I'm going in!"

On the screen, animated figures moved around, locating supplies and shooting at their enemies.

"Who are you playing with?" I asked curiously.

It always slightly concerned me when he played online video games, what with all the cyber dangers. He mostly played with a few school friends, but occasionally a name I didn't know popped up and when that happened, I liked to check out the situation and make sure he actually wasn't playing with some sicko making out to be a ten-year-old boy. This Henry kid's name had come up a few times in the past weeks and I hadn't had the chance to decide if this online friendship they'd developed was appropriate.

"Henry. You know, my bestie."

I raised an eyebrow. "I thought Simon Herringdale was your best friend?"

Aiden shrugged. "He is. He's my school bestie. Henry is my gaming bestie."

I was surprised when he didn't add a "duh."

"Rightio then. Tell Henry I said hi." I made a note to thoroughly check out this kid.

Aiden shot me a dirty look and covered his microphone with his hand. "I'm not telling him that!"

I raised an eyebrow. "Right, of course not. Sorry to be so uncool."

He rolled his eyes and went back to his game. Oh boy. He was only ten and already I was dreading the teenage years if this was where this attitude was heading.

I jogged up the stairs as a Celine Dion song came on and sang *extra* loudly, just so Aiden wouldn't miss out on the off-key, high-pitched bits that I was *super* good at. I hadn't been blessed with much of a singing voice, and it was the true bane of my existence. I would have loved to front a cover band or something. But unlike most of the *American Idol* wannabes, I knew I was bad. So the only people who got to hear me sing were my two poor, unfortunate children. God save their little ears.

I busted in on Lily and her bathtub full of horses and scooped the giggling five-year-old up into a threadbare towel that really needed to be replaced. I hid my sigh while I dried her off and got her into her pajamas. I deliberately picked out a cute little onesie that made her look younger than she really was and wondered if she'd let me do her hair in pigtails tomorrow. She was getting big and was already in kindergarten. It made me sad sometimes. I missed her and Aiden being babies.

But then I shook my head. I might have missed them being babies, but I didn't miss the way my life had been back then. Full of stress and always lonely because my husband was a workaholic asshole who cared more about building his business than he did about his wife and children. I'd never sung back then. So now that I was asshole husband free, I made an effort to sing every day. Because he might have walked out of our lives with almost everything I owned and left me with nothing but my children, but it had really been the best thing that had ever happened to me. It gave me the kick up the butt I needed to get myself together. I'd let a man rule my life and left myself vulnerable in the process. I knew better now. Knew myself and what I wanted better too.

I lifted the horse quilt cover and motioned for Lily to jump in. She wiggled beneath the thick, warm blankets and I lay down beside her, reading her a story then waiting until she fell asleep.

I tiptoed back downstairs and crossed my arms over my chest when I noticed Aiden was still engrossed in his video game. "Bed, kiddo."

I held my hand up in a stop motion before he could even get his complaints out. He rolled his eyes, tossed the controller onto the coffee table, and huffed up the stairs in a funk of mumbled whining.

I pretended not to hear and called goodnight to him as sweetly as I could. Sinking down on the lounge, I let the pile of cushions envelop me in their fluffiness. I loved those kids to pieces, but I was always exhausted by the time they went to bed. I was looking forward to a night of watching Netflix and drinking wine.

But first, I had to clean the bathroom. I picked up a pillow and groaned loudly into it. Oh boy. Was my life ever exciting.

On the TV, Aiden's video game was still going, his computerized man standing still now that there was no little boy controlling him. "Ugh! Aiden!" I muttered. He was always doing this. Just leaving his stuff turned on for the battery to die. Or leaving his stuff on the stairs. Or basically anywhere but where it was supposed to go. I picked up his headset, looking for the power switch to turn the Bluetooth headphones off, and jumped a mile when a deep voice said, "Hello?"

I glanced at the screen. In the corner, a pop-up window showed a grainy webcam video of a man wearing a headset. My eyes widened. Where had that come from? I checked who Aiden was playing against, with dread rising in my gut —HenryAceIII. Oh no. No. No. No. This guy—no, this *man* —was not the Henry that Aiden had been playing with for the past few weeks.

And worse, the man was smiling, like me standing there gaping amused him.

Wait, *could* he see me?

Fury raged through me and I yanked the headphones over my ears. "You have got to be kidding me, you creep! How dare you start an online friendship with a ten-year-old boy! What kind of perverted animal are you?"

The smile immediately dropped from the jerk's face and he put down the controller he'd been holding. He raised his hands slowly in mock surrender, which only made my blood boil hotter.

"Woah, woah." He leant forward towards his camera. "Back the truck up. You're Aiden's mum, right?"

"I am, *Henry*. If that's even your name." I folded my arms across my chest.

"It's not."

I barked out a laugh. At least he was an honest sicko. "Of course it's not. Don't think I'm not reporting this. I will be—"

He laughed. The sound deep and rumbling. It made me want to reach through the TV and strangle him.

"Wait. Before you call the police, let me explain. I'm Henry's dad. You're the singer?"

I paused. "What?"

"You like to sing, yeah?"

His country accent reeked of small-town manners and long days on cattle stations. One I might have found attractive. But not when he was preying on my child and getting off on listening to me sing. Ew! Creep. Dirty, filthy creep. "I —no," I lied, unable to stomach the thought he might have been...oh god no. I couldn't let myself go there.

"Yeah, you do. I hear you singing it every day. The big butts song?"

My face flamed red and I suddenly hoped that our

webcam was as grainy as his. The thought that he'd been listening to me sing, maybe for weeks now, was downright embarrassing. I'd never considered that anybody could hear what was going on in our house whilst Aiden was gaming. That was naïve of me.

I studied the man's laid-back body language. He was relaxed on a lounge not that different to my own. He wore a checked shirt, with the sleeves rolled to the elbows, the buttons loose around his neck. His skin was tan, his eyes friendly. He didn't look like a pervert. But it's not like being handsome got him off the hook completely. After all, Ted Bundy was a handsome man as well.

"You really heard that?" I asked, a little of the fire going out of me. If he was Henry's dad, that possibly made sense.

He chuckled, the sound deep and rich. "I did. I've heard many of your, uh, performances while Henry plays. You're good."

I frowned. Well, that was a red flag. The man was a liar. Nobody enjoyed my singing. Except me.

"Do you really have a son? You're not trying to groom my child?"

He choked on the word "groom". "I assure you, I have a kid. I have the messy bedroom and a load of foul-smelling socks to prove it. And here, look." The camera fuzzed out for a moment, before focusing again on a photo of the man with a child that looked to be Aiden's age.

It was really a very sweet picture. And I could relate to the dirty socks. That was for sure. Deciding to give the man the benefit of the doubt, I stood up again. "Well, thank you for the singing compliments. I am sorry you had to endure that. I'll turn this off now."

I reached for the headphones.

"Wait!"

My hands paused in midair while I waited for him to elaborate.

"Do you want to play?"

I frowned, looking down at the controller in my hands like it was some sort of UFO. "Video games?" Please, oh please let him mean video games. If *play* meant something else, I'd be shutting down Aiden's gaming account quicker than you could blink.

On the video, Henry's dad held up the controller. "Of course," he said with a puzzled expression.

I let out a sigh of relief. "I can't. I've housework to do. Plus, I don't...game."

He scrunched up his face. "Me neither. But do you really want to do housework? I've got a load of dirty dishes to wash and I'm avoiding them. You'd be doing me a favour by keeping me from them. One game?"

I thought about the toilets that needed scrubbing. Then focused on the image of the handsome man with the cute accent on my screen. "One game," I agreed.

2

BOWEN

*A*s I invited a woman who'd thought I was a perverted creep to play video games, I decided I could blame my impulsive behaviour on the tossing and turning I'd done last night. Sleep had pretty much completely evaded me, as it often did. I was tired and scrubbing the pot I'd practically burned a hole in earlier wasn't very appealing. It would be a whole lot easier to sit on the lounge and play video games with a pretty woman.

I adjusted the microphone by my mouth. Henry always complained about how the headset gave him a headache, so he often played without it. It meant I had to listen to his gaming through the TV, but at least I could hear what was going on with the other players. And I could step in when the trash talk became too much. I always knew he was playing with Aiden when I heard singing amongst the one-upping of the two boys. Her voice was terrible, but she sang with such pure joy at the top of her lungs and it never failed to make me smile.

An actual laugh had escaped my chest when I'd heard her song choice tonight. The feeling foreign, but pleasant.

Henry had gone off to feed the dogs and get ready for bed, but I'd picked up the controller in the hopes of hearing her sing some more. I wanted some of that joy to rub off on me.

That plan had gone sideways when she'd mistaken me for Henry and assumed I was some sort of child predator.

But as she sank back down onto a seat I couldn't see well through the camera, I found myself pleased she'd agreed not to call the police, and instead, decided to have a match with me.

"I've never played this game before," she confessed.

I shook my head. "Henry taught me some. But I'm not good. He kills me within moments every time. So I'll share what I know, but we're probably both going to die pretty quickly."

She frowned. "Nope. Come on, what sort of attitude is that? We play on a team, right? I can't have that negativity from my teammate. Let's kill it."

I chuckled as I hit the start key. "You don't like to lose?"

"Do you?"

When she put it like that... "No. I don't." Though losing was all I seemed to do these days.

She smiled and even through the grain of the camera, it looked smug.

On the screen, my player dropped from a parachute, landing beside hers.

"Okay, we're on the ground. What now?"

"Well, ammunition. We have to find some. Or we have to build a fort."

"Right. Which way should we go? Aiden is always yelling about Sandpits or something. Should we go there?" She bit her bottom lip and held her controller up, her fingers moving over the keys. Her player took two steps forward and—

My screen went red.

"Hey!" she cried. "What happened?"

"Red screen?" I asked.

"Yes!"

"We died."

She looked into the camera and choked out a laugh. "Seriously? I only took two steps."

"Better than me. I hadn't even moved. Evidently, we took too long standing there deciding what to do."

"How did the boys get so good at this?"

"They're young?"

"Hey! I'm young!" she exclaimed, her voice full of outrage.

Heat flushed my cheeks. I hadn't meant to insult her. "Of course. Sorry. I didn't mean to imply you weren't." The words came out in a stutter, but she laughed.

"Relax, Henry's dad. I'm joking."

Oh. A little of the stiffness in my shoulders eased. Then I realised she'd called me Henry's dad, because I'd been too rude to introduce myself properly. I was really botching this up.

"Bowen," I said quietly as the screen reset. "I'm Bowen."

She nodded. "Well, Bowen. We're about to drop again. Let's wait at least twenty seconds before dying this time? Perhaps?"

I nodded, but I'd become distracted. "What's yours? Your name, I mean?"

She tucked a strand of blonde hair behind her ear. "Paisley."

Paisley. I'd never heard that name before. It was cute and sunny, and I suspected it suited this upbeat woman to a T. A flicker of interest rose in some male part of my brain.

"Bowen!" she scolded in a tone that reminded me of the way my mother had yelled my name when I was a kid.

The flicker of interest spluttered out. Just as well, because it made me uncomfortable.

"You just died. Again."

I turned my attention back to my red screen. "Shit, sorry. I'm not much of a partner, am I?" I winced a little at the words, because they were accurate in more ways than just one.

"Hopefully your wife doesn't agree with that statement."

I let out a long breath, then shook my head. Her thoughts had gone in the same direction as mine. "No wife."

"Oh, that's interesting. Divorced?"

"Widower."

She put the controller down and turned her full attention to me. "Really? I'm so sorry to hear that. You look too young. And Henry... Was it recent?"

In the years since Camille's death, I'd been asked about her over and over. Asked how I was coping with her being gone. How Henry was feeling about it. And every time, I'd shut those people down so swiftly it was like slamming a door in their faces. And I'd felt no guilt about it. Even four years later, I'd put up such a wall around her death that no one dared mention her name in my presence. No one but Henry and my therapist. I may not have wanted to talk about her publicly, but Henry was always allowed to speak of his mother. And after a year of drowning in my own sorrow, I'd sought the help of a psychologist. The public had no right to know how I felt. I still believed I was owed that tiny shred of privacy in my otherwise very public life. I might have processed the loss, but it wasn't something I wanted to discuss with anyone but my boy.

But I didn't know this woman from a bar of soap and I'd

likely never speak to her again. She had no idea who I was. I was hardly a household name outside of the rodeo circuit. "It's been a long time," I admitted. "People think I should have moved on by now." The admission slipped from my lips.

She shook her head. "There's no expiration on grief. Only you can decide when you're ready. I am sorry for your loss, though."

"Thank you."

A polite but firm rapping on my door jolted me. I twisted to peer through the front windows of the ranch-style house I shared with Henry but I couldn't see anyone.

"Hey, I'm sorry. But I've got someone at my door. I gotta go."

"Oh," she said. I could have sworn I heard disappointment in her voice. "That's a shame. We were just starting to get the hang of it."

I snorted. "If by 'getting the hang of it' you mean we got fifteen steps before being blown to smithereens, then yeah, sure. I guess we were."

She grinned. "Tomorrow then, hot shot. Same time? I can't just leave it like this. Now that I've started, I need to be good enough to win."

I raised an eyebrow. "Did I create a monster?"

"Perhaps you did."

Another knock came from the door, this one less patient than the first.

"Alright, alright! I'm coming!" I yelled.

She waved me away with a smile. I was just reaching for the power switch when, "Bowen?"

I lifted my head. "Mmm?"

"Sorry for calling you a creep and a weirdo."

"I think your exact words were 'creep' and 'perverted animal'."

She covered her face with her hands and shook her head. "I'm not a very good judge of character."

"Or perhaps I'm not much good at first impressions?"

She was quiet for a moment, mulling that statement over. Then she said quietly, "No, I think you do okay."

I bit my bottom lip, not sure what that meant or what to do now. Was she...flirting? I'd just wanted to have a game to kill some time. Once Henry went to bed at night, it was so quiet in my house, and it gave me too much time to think. Too much time to dwell. I hadn't expected to be chatting with a cute blonde about my marital status.

Not knowing what else to say, I gave her an awkward wave. "See you tomorrow."

I flicked off the TV and stomped across the room, unreasonably irritated by the interruption. She was cute, with her messed-up hair and fierce determination. But it was probably better that we'd been interrupted. If any of that had been flirting, I was too rusty to keep up my side of the conversation.

I slid the lock off the door; a force of habit even though my property was remote and the likelihood of someone trying to force their way in was slim to impossible. But for my own peace of mind, I kept it locked. I'd never forgive myself if someone rolled in here while I was sleeping and something happened to Henry. Not that I ever really slept, but it still made me feel better anyway.

The door slid forward without a sound, but I had to stifle a groan of annoyance when I saw who was on the other side.

"Hey, cowboy," Addie St Clair said in her sultry voice through red painted lips. Her dark hair curled around her face and down her shoulders, and she wore a pretty blue sundress with a plunging neckline, though I tried hard not to look. Instead, I kept my gaze firmly planted on her bright brown eyes, lined with black makeup.

"Can I come in?"

I hesitated. I didn't want her to come in. I didn't want her here. Not tonight. Not now. Not ever. "What are you doing, Addie? My kid is here."

She glanced over my shoulder, and I was grateful Henry's room was at the back of the large house. He was likely holed up in there, watching something on his iPad, but she didn't know that. And it annoyed me that she'd just turned up uninvited.

She took a step forward, running her finger down the centre of my shirt, before looking up at me. "I thought you might want a replay of the other night."

I ground my teeth together. The "other night" had actually been a few months ago. And it had been a drunken mistake. Henry had spent the weekend at my dad's place and I'd spent the weekend getting drunk at the only pub in town. Addie and I had hooked up, and I was still berating myself over it. I'd been lonely and feeling sorry for myself and she'd been flirting with me ever since my wife died. She'd been someone warm to hold on to when all I felt was cold. She'd known it. We'd both known it. But that was no excuse. I'd left her place the next morning feeling like shit and I wasn't keen for a repeat. It had all just felt wrong.

I took a step back and shook my head. "Not tonight. Sorry you came all the way out here."

I went to close the door but she shot her hand out to stop me. "Wait! Deacon said there's a bull riding charity event in a few weeks. You need a date?"

I shrugged. The invitation was sitting on my kitchen

bench. Bowen Barclay, plus one. Didn't mean I couldn't go stag though.

She huffed out a breath, losing the sexy coy thing she'd been trying to pull off. "Look, Bowen. I know what this is. I know you aren't going to fall in love with me. But you're a good-looking single guy and my options round here are pretty slim. We have a good time, don't we?"

No. But I couldn't say that. She was a nice woman, really. Young, but nice. It was me that was the problem, not her. All my friends had been asking about her. Even my dad had seemed enthusiastic about her when he'd cautiously asked if there was something going on between us. I'd seen the disappointment in his eyes when I'd shut that conversation down quicker than a whip crack.

Addie's fingers snaked around the back of my neck and into my hair, her warm breath misting over my skin. I closed my eyes. I couldn't deny that having a woman wrapped around me again felt good.

But then I untangled her fingers and took a step back, putting distance between us. She might have felt good, but she didn't feel *right*. She wasn't Camille. And stone-cold sober, that was all I could think about. Camille and the fact I'd killed her. I hadn't been there for her when I needed to be. When I should have been. I'd been her husband and I'd left her alone.

"I can't, Addie. I'm sorry."

She eyed me, then sighed, turning on her heel. "You've got my number, Bowen. Use it."

I didn't have the heart to tell her I'd already deleted it.

3

PAISLEY

*T*he sun had already lit up the early morning darkness in a dazzling display of pinks and vibrant yellows by the time I parked my car outside Stacey's house. I shot off a text message letting her know I was here, but when the door didn't immediately open, I sat back in the driver's seat and folded my hands behind my head. Normally, Stacey being late would have bothered me, since it was my job I was risking by having her tag along. But I'd been smiling since I'd woken up, and not even Stacey's tardiness could dull my shine.

The passenger-side door eventually opened and Stacey, my best friend and all-round crazy person, dropped dramatically into the seat next to me, her afro-style curls bobbing wildly. "I know, I know, I'm running late. I'm sor— Why are you smiling like that?"

I raised an eyebrow. "Like what?" I knew my fake innocence wasn't going to fool her for a minute, but it was fun to string her along before I spilled the gossip. I pulled out onto the road. Thankfully, the food warehouse I worked in and delivered for was only a few streets from my house so if I was speedy about it, I'd still get my van loaded and be on my way to my first stop before 7 a.m. The warehouse might have been close by, but delivery shifts took me all over. Out here, there was a lot of space between towns.

"Something's happened." Stacey stared at the side of my face while I diligently concentrated on the road.

I stifled a laugh. The woman was a hopeless romantic and lived for rom-coms and sexy books. She was forever telling me about something called meet-cutes, and I already knew she was going to die over my little story about Bowen. Not that anything had really happened. But neither of us had a dating life so any little blip on the radar was a cause for excitement.

"What did you do in the last twenty-four hours that's got you doing a Cheshire Cat impersonation? I only saw you yesterday and you were not looking this..." She waved her hand around in front of my face. "Rosy? Sparkly?" She narrowed her eyes at me, then they widened. "Oh my god, you got laid!"

I pulled into the driveway of Johnsons' Wholefoods and yanked up the handbrake with Stacey practically bouncing on her seat beside me. Unclipping my seatbelt, I wriggled my eyebrows at her before climbing out. "You're going to have to wait until I get back for that story." I climbed down from the van and shut the door before she could protest.

"Argh!" she yelled through the open window. "You're the worst!"

I chuckled as I strolled into the familiar building. I'd fill her in as soon as I got back but Stacey wasn't known for her patience. If I looked back over my shoulder, I was sure I'd see her pouting like a toddler.

"Hey, Diego," I called to the owner of the small family-owned company who had been good enough to give a high school dropout with no work history a job when her husband had left her high and dry. I'd been a loyal employee ever since.

"I'll just be a minute," he said in his lightly accented voice. He rubbed the back of his neck with a pained expression on his face. "I just want to check this order before I hand it over to you." He waved distractedly and I took the opportunity to duck around to the staff-only area to check this coming week's roster. I frowned when I found my name.

I walked back to find Diego already loading the morning's deliveries into my van. "Diego? How come my shifts were cut? I normally do five mornings on the road plus two nights in the kitchen."

He glanced over at me apologetically. "I know, but business has been slow. I just can't afford to have two drivers every day anymore. And Angelo was here first."

"Oh," I said quietly. I hated to hear that his business was suffering. Diego was a nice man who supported a big extended family. But at the same time, this job was my sole income. Jonathan, my ex, rarely paid child support, and I depended on this salary to pay my bills, pay for my nursing course and keep food in my kids' mouths.

"I saw the sandwich shop is looking for someone new?" Diego said sympathetically. "Perhaps you could apply there? Pick up some extra cash."

I forced a smile and nodded. "Sure. I'll look into it. I better go get these delivered before the bakery rings and starts yelling."

I grabbed the printout of delivery addresses and the last of my orders and slumped back to the van. Stacey pounced on me as soon as I opened the door.

"Well? What's the story, miss?"

She was practically vibrating with her excitement. I

pushed down my worry about my dwindling pay cheque and passed her the address sheet. "I just had a good night. I did something I've never done before."

"Skydived? Hot air ballooned? Oooh! Bought a pet monkey!"

And just like that, I was back to laughing. Stacey was good for my soul.

"Uh, no to all of those. I played video games."

Stacey stopped her bouncing and blinked. "Video games," she said dully. Then she slapped my arm. "Screw you, Ackerly. You got me all excited."

I shoved her shoulder. "Don't be like that. It was fun."

"But...why the sudden interest in video games?"

I pulled the car out onto the road, the sun rapidly rising behind us, and followed my GPS instructions to the first delivery spot. "Because a nice man asked me to play?"

That got her attention.

"What! Who?"

I shrugged. "His name is Bowen. He's the dad of one of the kids Aiden plays with."

"Hot?"

I smiled coyly. "Maybe."

She hooted. "Oh, he so is!"

"It's not like you can really tell from a webcam."

"Oh, I can tell. I have a hot guy radar. It's my superpower."

I chuckled, but then turned serious. "It was actually fun though, Stace. I...I think I needed it."

She nodded. "You do definitely need...something. I would have gone for dirty hot sex but Jonathan did such a number on you, I haven't seen you truly let go in years."

My ex-husband's name was like a glass of cold water over my head. "Do we have to talk about him?"

She frowned. "He really screwed you up, didn't he?"

I sighed. "We had another argument last night."

"About your child support?"

I nodded. Jonathan and I only argued about two things —the kids. And money. Or rather, the lack of money he provided for our children. And the lack of effort he put into raising them.

"That man makes my blood boil. Where does he get off not paying you? He's rolling in cash."

And that was the kicker. Jonathan, with my support, had built an empire when we'd been in our early twenties. I'd given up all my individual hopes and goals to support the dream we'd had together. And then he'd thanked me for my support by sleeping with his secretary while I stayed home raising the two kids he'd fathered.

"He's always been cheap. He actually told me if he gave me more, I'd just spend it on myself." I looked down at the hole in my Target jeans. The hole wasn't designer. The jeans were just five years old. "I don't buy myself anything. Everything goes to feeding those kids, keeping them in clothes, and making sure they have everything they need for school."

Stacey held up her hands. "Preaching to the choir, babe. I know how hard it is for you."

I spotted the street number I was looking for and pulled into their driveway. Stacey handed me the mobile device I used to collect signatures. I took it but she didn't let it go. Instead she looked me hard in the eyes.

"I know things suck right now. And they've sucked for a while. But as soon as you get through your qualification, hospitals will be beating your door down to offer you a position. And then you can give up the delivery gig. And you can tell Jonathan to go jump off a cliff. Because if any man deserves a push in that direction, it's him."

I snorted on my laughter. "That's the father of my children you're talking about, Stacey."

"Pfft. I love you. And I love those kids. But I'm just saying, if he's ever near a cliff and I'm around, he better watch his back." She mimed kicking someone and then turned to me with a satisfied look on her face as if she'd hatched the perfect evil plan.

I may have had a douchebag ex to deal with, and I may not be able to pay my rent next month, but I had the world's best best friend.

And I had a video game date that night with a hot guy. A secret smile lifted the corners of my mouth. That was all I'd concentrate on today.

4

BOWEN

"Again," I gritted out, dirt coating the insides of my mouth. I pushed to my feet, ignoring the ache in my bad knee, and stalked back to the chute. The sun was rapidly sinking behind the horizon, but I didn't care. It wouldn't be the first time I'd had to practise at night. I'd had floodlights installed for this very reason.

Jimmy looked at me warily. "Maybe you've had enough for today, hey? We can pick it up again tomorrow."

I glared at him. "I said again."

He sighed but clambered over and let a bull into the chute. Buck Off Bruce was a four-year-old I'd picked up as a calf. I put my foot on his back, letting him know I was coming. I didn't want to startle him because he sure as hell wasn't a calf no more and here, in my practise pen, it was just me and Jimmy, who acted as my rope guy and my gate guy. There was no spotter to make sure I didn't fall beneath Bruce's hooves. Jimmy also doubled as the guy who distracted the bull so I could get the hell out of its way when I came off, and he was the guy who'd call the ambulance if I cracked my head open. Not that he'd ever had to fulfil that last role, but you never knew when it might happen.

I nodded and Jimmy threw the gate open.

Bruce bucked his way out, and before I even knew what was happening, my ass was hitting the dirt. On autopilot, I scrambled out of Bruce's way and ran to the fence.

"Fuck!" I roared, pulling off my hat and throwing it in the dirt. "That was fucking terrible."

Jimmy didn't say anything. He didn't need to. We both knew it. I didn't even bother asking him how long I'd managed to stay on for. It was probably a new buck off record, and I didn't want to know.

"You're tired, man. Let it go for the day."

I shook my head stubbornly. "I can't. If I keep riding like this, I'm not even going to qualify for the finals."

Jimmy looked up at me from beneath the brim of his hat. "Would that be so bad?"

If looks could kill, Jimmy would have been dead a hundred times over.

"Okay, I hear ya. I just thought, you're thirty-four. You've been doing this a long time—"

"I suggest you stop talking now unless you want my thirty-four-year-old fist in your face," I growled.

He laughed, knowing I wouldn't, but he wasn't the first to suggest I retire lately. And I was getting pretty damn sick of hearing it.

"Go home," I told him. "But we're back out here at dawn, yeah? I've got the Townsville Opens this weekend. I need to practise."

He saluted me, then jumped the fence, striding across the yard to where his ute sat waiting for him. He spun the tires in the dirt before peeling out along the kilometre-long driveway towards the road.

I dragged my sorry, aching, thrown-too-many-times-today body towards the main house, making a beeline for the kitchen. A note in my father's blocky handwriting sat on the bench, telling me he'd taken Henry to his place for dinner and I could join them if I wanted to.

I glanced out the window in the direction of his place. I'd given my father a little cottage on my property soon after I'd bought it. He'd been on his own, ever since my ma had died when I was little more than Henry's age, and it had always been my mission in life to buy him a home of his own. A place we couldn't get evicted from. Bull riding had made that dream come true. His cottage had its own entrance from the road, and I'd had the land subdivided so even the plot was in his name. I'd wanted him close, but I'd wanted him to have that peace of mind that nobody was ever going to take it away. Not even me.

The lights in his little cottage were on and dim shadows moved in the windows. I knew I should make the effort to get up and go over there and have a meal, but I was in a foul mood after my useless training session. And I really needed a shower and an attitude check before I inflicted my personality on my family.

Instead of doing either of those things though, I cracked open a beer from the fridge and sunk into the couch. There was a ragged tear in the fabric where Henry's dog, Meatballs, had gotten overexcited and tried to dig. But I'd refused to buy a new one. This couch had memories. And besides that, it was the most comfortable, worn-in thing I'd ever sat on. I wasn't giving it up for anyone.

I eyed the controller for the PlayStation, still sitting where I'd abandoned it last night. Paisley had said she wanted to play again today. I wasn't sure if she was just trying to get rid of me or if she was actually serious. It was probably too early for her to be on, but I turned the console on anyway, trying not to acknowledge to myself how much I really hoped she was online.

"Henry!" Aiden shouted the second I connected.

I fumbled around, finding the headset so I could burst the kid's bubble. "Nope, try again," I replied, waving to the webcam and the pixelated image of Aiden.

"Oh, right. Hi."

Poor kid looked crestfallen. Couldn't blame him, when he was looking at my ugly mug on his screen. "Henry is at his grandfather's house."

"Oh, yeah. Okay... You want to play then?"

Paisley's accusation of being a child predator was too fresh in my mind to agree without seeking her approval. "Is your mum home? You'll need to ask her if that's okay with her."

"Mum!" he hollered into the mic.

I winced, pulling it away from my now probably ruined eardrum.

"Can I play with Henry's dad?"

There was some muffled conversation, then her blonde head popped onto the screen. I sat up a little straighter and nodded to her.

"Do you plan to lead my child astray?" Her voice was faint for being further from the microphone at Aiden's lips. She crossed her arms over her chest, but she smiled. She wore a bright purple T-shirt and her hair was pulled back in a messy bun, strands escaping, framing her face.

She'd probably fry in the country sun, with all that pale skin and hair. Women out here were rarely as fair as she was. But I couldn't help noticing how cute she was. Or the way her smile blinded me even through the TV.

I realised I'd been staring a beat too long and that I

needed to say something. "Scout's honour." I saluted her with the middle three fingers of my left hand.

She chuckled. "Wrong hand, but I like the sentiment. Carry on."

I dropped my hand to my lap, a little embarrassed I'd mucked up something so simple. She waved, and I found myself disappointed when she disappeared from the screen. I didn't really want to play video games with a ten-year-old, but he'd have to go to bed at some point.

"Okay, old man. Let's do this!" Aiden yelled in my ear.

"Hey now, I'm not that old!" What was it about today that made everyone remind me I wasn't twenty anymore?

Aiden peered at the camera with an analysing eye. I waited. After a moment, he seemed satisfied with his inspection and sat back. "Yeah, I suppose you aren't as old as my dad."

"Does your dad play video games with you?" I asked.

"No," Aiden said flatly. "He's never around. And even when we go to his house, he never has time."

"Oh," I replied, not sure where to go with the conversation from there. I hadn't meant to pry into their family life, and now I felt a little awkward about knowing something that Paisley might not have wanted me knowing. But I couldn't help being a little relieved she wasn't married. Which was ridiculous really, because we weren't doing anything wrong. But still. "Lucky you have Henry to play with then, huh? I know he likes playing with you."

A huge grin broke out on Aiden's face. "Henry's the best!"

A warmth filled me with the knowledge these two boys had formed a real friendship, even if they had never seen each other face to face. Henry was so isolated out here. Because of how much I travelled, I'd decided to homeschool him. Well, I'd asked my father to. As a retired teacher, he was qualified, where I was not. Even though I rarely took them on tour with me, it just worked better. It meant Henry didn't have to waste hours every day on a bus. Hours that he could be learning. Or playing. Or doing chores around the house. But guilt constantly gnawed at me over his lack of social interaction and friendships. The fact he'd managed to form this friendship with Aiden eased a little of the pressure. Single parenting was rough. I'd wished so many times that my wife was still around to help me make these decisions. Instead, I had Jimmy. And Meatballs. And my father. None were ideal candidates for help in making decisions about my child.

We played in silence for a little while but Aiden's comments about his dad not being around to play with him were grating at me. "You know," I said casually as I forced my player to build a fort, "you should ask your mum to play with you."

"She doesn't like video games."

Paisley's competitive nature and her challenge to play again today rang through my head. "You sure about that? I played with her yesterday. She's pretty bad though."

Aiden broke out in peals of laughter and I was glad for it. He'd looked so down when I'd mentioned his father. I'd definitely stepped into a sensitive subject there, so I was pleased to see him laughing again.

"Mum!" Aiden yelled. "Did you play *Light and Legacy* with Henry's dad yesterday?"

I didn't hear her answer, but then Aiden yelled, "He said you were really bad!"

Paisley's head popped back on the screen and I snorted. She looked cranky. She was too cute to pull it off.

"I'll have you know, Henry's dad, that I was better than you."

"Nah, Mum, he's really good. See the fort he built?"

Paisley studied the screen for a moment, then shoved her hands on her hips as she glared at me.

"You said you were terrible!"

I held up my hands in mock surrender.

She disappeared from the screen. I was disappointed. I kinda liked making her mad.

"I think your mum is angry at me," I laughed to Aiden.

He was laughing too. "Nah, she's smiling."

Good. I was glad I hadn't misread the playfulness of the situation. A thought occurred to me. "Aiden, why isn't she singing tonight?"

Aiden shrugged.

"I like it when she sings."

"Ugh, I don't."

He was so much like Henry. I embarrassed him on a regular basis lately too. I wasn't sure when the morph from little boy who adored me to preteen who kind of thought I was a dweeb had happened, but it had definitely happened.

"Mum! Henry's dad wants you to sing."

There was a pause.

"She said she's not singing because she knows you're listening."

I grinned. "Tell her I said please?"

Before he could relay the message, a blurred child sized figure raced across the screen, followed by a distorted Paisley-shape in a purple shirt. "Bed, Aiden," I heard faintly.

Aiden groaned. "Gotta go. Nice playing with you." He threw the controller on the coffee table in front of him and I found myself staring at their empty couch.

There were faint noises of general evening bustling

around, then everything went quiet. I debated turning the game console off and taking that shower I desperately needed. But I just didn't want to. So I worked on the fort I'd started with Aiden, but the whole time my gaze kept darting to the corner of the screen, hoping for a glimpse of purple.

I noticed the moment she returned. "Hey."

"Hey yourself. What's this about my singing?"

"I was just wondering why you weren't tonight. I missed it."

"I'm not singing ever again while he's playing PlayStation. Who knows how many people have heard my awful off-key wailing?"

I sobered as I remembered her voice belting out songs at the top of her lungs and the pure joy she radiated. It was the entire reason I'd turned the gaming console on. "I could really use a song today."

She'd been moving to pick up the controller, but she stilled, her hand frozen in midair. "Want to talk about it?"

"Talk about what? Your song choice?"

She shook her head slowly. "About whatever is bothering you."

Ay. She was perceptive. I'd been cheerful and playful and even through a TV screen she'd noticed something was wrong. Women and their superpowers.

"It's nothing, really. I just had a rough day. You could sing the big butt song. That would cheer me up immensely," I joked.

Half a smile lifted the corner of her mouth. "Or instead of listening to me warble, you could just tell me all your deep, dark secrets."

I cocked an eyebrow. "Do you really want to know?"

She leant forward, resting her elbows on her knees. "I don't know why, but yeah, I kind of do."

I paused. I didn't know why, but I kind of wanted to know hers too.

"You ever seen bull riding on your TV?"

She sat back, surprise flooding her face. "Um, yeah? I guess?"

"You've probably seen me then. That's what I do. For a living."

Her eyebrows shot sky-high. "Seriously?"

I nodded.

She leant forward again. "So if I googled you..."

"You'd find a whole bunch of videos of me getting thrown into the dirt and stomped on. Can I recommend one particularly amusing video of me being tossed straight into a barrier?" I laughed. "Believe me, it looks funnier than it felt."

She cringed, the smile falling from her face. "That doesn't sound very funny."

I shrugged and smiled at her. "It's no biggie. It's funny in hindsight."

"Did you ride today?"

I tossed the controller onto the lounge beside me, any thoughts of playing video games long gone. I ran my hands through my dusty hair. "Yeah, I practise every day."

"It didn't go well, I take it."

"Never does lately."

She lifted a hand as if she wanted to reach out to me, then dropped it to her lap. "I'm sure that's not true. I bet you're great."

"I was. Once upon a time."

She went quiet.

The back door rattled, making me jump. Faint conversation drifted back to me, my father's and Henry's voices easily distinguishable in the otherwise quiet house.

"I gotta go. Henry just got home."

"Oh, okay then."

I stood, then ducked back down so she could see my face in the webcam. "Hey, Paisley?"

"Yeah?"

"I can't play tomorrow night. I've got a rodeo."

She brushed her hands down her lap. "Right."

"But maybe we could play again when I get back?"

She bit her lip, then let a smile spread across her face. "Sure."

"I'll see you then." I didn't know what else to say so I reached for the remote.

"Bowen! Wait!"

"Mmm?"

"Is it televised? The rodeo tomorrow?"

A strange tightness spread across my chest. "Why? You gonna watch?"

I studied her hard, wishing like hell she were here in front of me instead of on the other side of a screen. I wanted her to watch, I realised. I wanted her to say yes. It had been a long time since I'd felt the excitement of knowing a specific woman was watching me.

She shrugged. "I'm sure Aiden would think it pretty cool."

Ouch.

I nodded. "Yeah, you can watch it through the WBRA website—that's World Bull Riding Association. Or on the sports channel if you have it. I, uh...hope he enjoys it. Henry does."

She smiled. "I'm sure he will. See you next week, cowboy."

Addie had called me cowboy too. And I hated it.

But on Paisley's lips, it sounded hot as hell.

5

PAISLEY

*S*tacey's heavy wooden door swung open and I gave her my brightest smile. "Hey, bestie!" I walked past her, ignoring her confused expression, and dumped a load of wine bottles and thigh-fattening snacks on her kitchen bench.

When I turned around, she had her arms folded across her chest, her eyes narrowed.

"What?"

"Don't give me that. What's going on? Since when do you turn up unannounced? That's my job. You normally schedule a visit at least a week in advance, send me a message to confirm the day before, then call before you leave your house, just to let me know you're on your way. You do not just appear on my doorstep without warning."

She eyed the wine, plucking one from the bag, then turned and gave me a dazzling smile. "Not that I'm complaining of course. You can crash my joint anytime if you bring wine."

I grinned. "I brought three bottles."

She laughed. "Are we having a party?"

I shook my head.

"Where are the kids?"

"With my mum."

She shoved her hands onto her hips. "You're being awfully cagey. You want to spill your guts sometime soon? What are we doing?"

A blush warmed my cheeks and I turned away, searching through Stacey's cabinets for wineglasses so she wouldn't notice. "Watching some bull riding?" I said into the depths of the cupboard.

I paused there, waiting for some sort of reaction, but when I was met with nothing but silence, I poked my head around the cabinet door.

Stacey had one eyebrow practically touching the roof. "Why on earth would we spend a rare child-free Saturday night watching sports? And not just any old sports, but the specifically odd sport of bull riding?"

"Because Bowen is competing?" I asked sheepishly. I couldn't even look at her. I cracked the top on a bottle of wine and filled my glass right to the brim.

Stacey slapped her hand down on the bench, the sound making me jump. A huge smile overwhelmed her face.

She picked up her phone and started scrolling through it.

"Uh, Stace—" She held up one finger, cutting me off. I bit my lip as I waited, wondering what on earth she was doing, when suddenly the sound of Big and Rich's song "Save a Horse (Ride a Cowboy)" trickled through the speakers.

I rolled my eyes as Stacey swung an imaginary lasso around her head, pretended to rope, then reel me in. "Howdy, Miss Paisley," she drawled, getting in close to me.

I couldn't hold back the laugh and shoved her away playfully. "Stop. You're the worst."

She shook her head as the chorus started up and grabbed a broom from a cupboard, holding out a mop to me.

"Stacey, no."

"Paisley, yes. You date a cowboy, you get the song." She straddled her broom and proceeded to dance with it like she was auditioning for a Magic Mike sequel.

I swallowed hard, trying not to spit wine all over the kitchen, but it was practically impossible.

"Come on, cowgirl. Get on that horse. Get your practice in now," Stacey yelled between singing and dancing and I couldn't help it. I joined in. The song was catchy. So sue me.

We gyrated around the kitchen, singing and laughing until the last chords faded away, and then we stood, trying to catch our breaths. But Stacey's comment was bothering me.

"I'm not dating him, you know. I don't even know where he lives. He could be on the other side of the country for all I know."

"But you *want* to date him," Stacey said with a knowing gleam in her eye.

"I barely know the man."

"But he's hot, right?"

"Is that all you need to date a guy?"

She shrugged. "Doesn't hurt." She wriggled her eyebrows at me suggestively. Then she grabbed my hand and a bottle of wine. "Come on, let's go see what your cowboy's got. He must be pretty good if he's on the pro circuit."

I grabbed the chips and followed her into the living room. We sank down on the soft grey leather and Stacey propped her boots up on the coffee table. I glanced over at them.

"What? Isn't this what cowboys do?"

I shoved her feet off and she laughed, straightening in her seat and placing her feet on the floor. I found the remote and flicked on the sports channel. "Oh good, we haven't missed anything."

On the screen an arena full of people screamed and cheered as the announcer talked about the riders and the bulls who would be competing that night. We watched for a few minutes in silence, but Stacey was quick to get bored.

"So, you gonna tell me about him?"

"I don't know much to tell. He has a son."

Stacey wrinkled her pixie nose in disgust and I swatted at her arm. "Stop it, you don't hate kids!"

"Correction. I don't hate *your* kids. All the rest of them... meh. Not my favourite."

"His son is the same age as Aiden."

Stacey waved her hand around. "Not the details I want, Ackerly. What's he look like?"

I opened my mouth to respond then abruptly closed it and pointed to the screen where Bowen strode out into the arena, his name splashed across the back of his shirt.

He wore boots and jeans and a wide brimmed cowboy hat sat low on his head.

"Oh my god, the chaps are ridiculous!" Stacey crowed.

I had to give her that. The brown leather chaps he wore over his jeans were fringed. But on closer inspection, all the riders wore them, so it was obviously part of the gig.

"Booooooowen Baaarrclaaaaaay," the announcer called in an overexaggerated American accent and Stacey cheered. But all I could do was stare. The camera zoomed in, filling the screen with Bowen's handsome face, and I sucked in a breath as he pulled his hat off and waved it to the crowd.

Beside me, Stacey slapped my arm, then wolf-whistled, but I barely heard her, too lost in staring at him. He gazed down the barrel of the camera and it felt as if he were looking right at me. "Handsome" didn't even begin to describe him. And the webcam certainly hadn't done him justice. His fair hair was cropped close to his head and his blue eyes were mesmerising. My breath got stuck in my throat.

"I can't believe *that* is who you've been playing video games with. I obviously need to get one of those PlayBox thingos and get me a cowboy of my own."

Startled out of my Bowen daze, I grinned at her. "It's the chaps, isn't it? They totally do it for you."

She snorted, and for the next thirty minutes we watched men ride bulls. The judges scored each ride out of one hundred—fifty points for the rider and fifty points for the performance of the bull. Stacey came up with her own scoring system, based on how good their asses looked in jeans. As the competitors ticked on, I grew more and more quiet, topping up my wineglass and sipping at it until I had a nice buzz going.

"Next up, Bowen Barclay."

I froze, watching as the screen focused in on Bowen preparing for his ride. He handed one guy his rope and then climbed over the rails of the chute and settled himself on the back of the beast. The bull shifted around a little but then settled. I let out a little sigh of relief. The bull didn't look too bothered at having Bowen on his back. Not like some of the others who had nearly unseated their riders before the gate had even opened.

"Are you nervous?" Stacey asked.

I shook my head quickly. "No."

She laughed. "Liar."

I didn't bother arguing. I *was* nervous. I didn't want to see the guy get hurt. I didn't want to see *anyone* get thrown to the ground, or stamped on, or gored by a wayward horn. But being injured seemed like a very real possibility.

The gate swung open and I found myself on my feet. The bull exploded into the ring, spinning to the right and bucking with all his might to get Bowen off. Bowen held on, one hand waving but he was being thrown around like a rag doll. Within the first second, even I, who knew nothing about bull riding apart from what I'd learned in the past thirty minutes, knew he was in trouble. I could see air between his ass and the bull's back, and his body jerked around. The other guys that had lasted eight seconds had a control that Bowen didn't. The bull changed directions, and Bowen slipped off, landing on his side in the dirt.

Stacey squealed and I squeezed my eyes tight, grabbing her arm, my fingernails digging in. My heart raced. I just couldn't watch.

But Stacey patted me on the arm reassuringly. "Paisley. He's fine. He's up and hanging off the railings."

I cracked open an eye.

"Think you can remove your claws from my arm too?"

"Oh, shit. Sorry. Yes." I forced my fingers to relax and took in Bowen's tense face. He didn't look happy.

"First ride of the night and it's a buck off for Bowen Barclay," the announcer said before a slow-motion replay started. I winced, watching it over again. It wasn't pretty.

Stacey passed me another glass of wine, and I shook my head. But she pressed it into my hand anyway. "He still has another ride. You might need that."

I glanced over at her. "I'm fine."

"Are you though? You didn't try to maim me when the other guys were riding."

"He's different. I know him. Sort of."

Stacey nodded towards the drink. "Then as I said. You might need that."

As it turned out, Stacey was right. Bowen's next ride came up and I was even more nervous than I had been the first time. Stacey squeezed my hand as Bowen was bucked off at the five-second mark. But at least this time, he landed on his feet and was able to run to the side.

"Bowen Barclay with his second buck off of the night. He's not going to be happy about that."

"You think?" I muttered angrily under my breath. The announcer was really starting to piss me off.

Stacey picked up the remote and switched the TV off. "You know, I think we've had enough of bull riding for one night."

I nodded, chewing thoughtfully on my chips. I'd definitely seen enough. I felt so bad for the poor guy, I hoped he wasn't taking it too hard. I suddenly wished I had his phone number to call him and just check that he was okay. With a start I realised that was ridiculous. I barely knew the man and here I was wishing I could console him? I didn't even know if he was single. I knew his wife had died a few years back but for all I knew he had a girlfriend. Who was probably wrapped around his body right now, doing all the consoling he could need. I squeezed my eyes shut as a stab of jealously speared through me.

Stacey was watching me quietly.

"I'm drunk," I announced.

She nodded slowly.

I wasn't really sure I was, but that was the only way to explain why my body was reacting like this.

Yep. Definitely drunk.

6

BOWEN

*D*ad and Henry were standing in the waiting area of the country airport when my plane touched down. Relief washed over me as Henry ran towards me. I scooped him up, even though he was really getting too big for that, and crushed him to my chest until he began to squirm.

I drew my head back and cast an appraising eye over him. "You good, mate?"

He nodded, a little wide-brimmed cowboy's Akubra bobbing on his head. I brushed my hand over his forehead in what I hoped looked like an affectionate gesture, which it was, but it was also something I did daily, checking for fever. My over-protective dad mode in full force after a few days away.

Dad came up behind him and folded his arms across his chest with a knowing look, as if he knew exactly what I was doing. The sympathetic gleam in his eye was telling, but I ignored it and one-arm hugged the old man hello.

"Sorry about the rodeo," he murmured, and I nodded.

"Yeah, me too."

"Doesn't matter, Dad. You've still got one more chance to qualify in Sydney, right?"

I dropped Henry back down to the earth and tapped the brim of his hat. "Sure do. Next weekend."

"About that..." Henry glanced up at me with puppy dog eyes, and I stopped in my tracks. I knew that look.

"What have you done?"

I glanced at my father.

He grinned. "Just hear him out."

"I want to come with you. To Sydney."

No. That was my first instinct. I opened my mouth to voice it but Dad cut me off with a look that said, *At least listen to the kid.*

I shut my mouth, considering my words before I responded. "You know I don't like you coming to watch me, mate. If I get hurt—"

My dad interrupted. "If you get hurt, I'll be there right next to him."

I raised an eyebrow. "You want to come too?"

He shook his head. He'd always hated my bull riding but after all this time, he knew it was just the way I was. Didn't mean he wanted to watch it though. It was a rare occasion that he came to the rodeo, preferring to watch me ride on TV when there was a delay and he already knew I'd made it out safely. It suited me. I'd never liked having my family there in the audience. Other guys on the circuit loved it. Needed it even, and their families travelled with them. But that had always been a problem for me. A distraction I couldn't have if I wanted to win. And I didn't just want to win. I needed to.

"Dad, please? There's a gaming con on the same day. We could go to that first?"

I chuckled. "Oh. I see how it is. You aren't really that

interested in bull riding, are you? You're just using me for a lift into the city?"

Henry shrugged while Dad smiled quietly at him. The two of them had grown super close in the years since Camille had died. It had been inevitable, with Dad living right there on the farm just a few hundred metres away. And it was nice. He was good about not stepping on my parenting toes but he quietly nudged me into line when I needed it.

And right now, he was giving me the look that said I was being nudged. "Let him go with you. That little friend of his he made, what's his name again, Henry?"

"Aiden."

"Right, Aiden. He wants to meet him there. I think it's nice they'll get the chance to meet."

I glanced between the two of them. "Wait, what? Aiden is going to the con too?"

Henry nodded enthusiastically.

I frowned. "Did his mum say it was okay?"

Henry shrugged. "I guess so."

I pondered that for a moment. "Look, if Pop wants to come along too so you've got someone to sit with while I ride, then yeah, you can come."

"And the con? Can we go?"

I ruffled his hair. "Sounds fun."

Henry cheered and scampered off to watch bags come out of the baggage claim area. It would be fun to spend a day with him in the city doing something different.

A big part of me hoped he was right about Paisley and Aiden being there too.

7

PAISLEY

"*A*re you going?"

I sighed and shook my head, watching Bowen on the screen. "I'd really like to. But it's a long drive."

Bowen's brow furrowed in that way it always did when I said something he found curious.

"It is? Henry said you lived close by?"

"To Sydney? No."

I'd never told him where I lived. We'd been chatting every day while we played but we'd never gotten too personal. I was overly aware that he was still just a man I'd met online. So I was keeping my cards close to my chest. After he'd opened up about his wife, he'd seemed to back off on the personal details as well. And that was okay with me.

"I guess to a ten-year-old boy from the country, everything else seems close to Sydney," Bowen said.

"So, how remote exactly are you? I kind of picture you to be living right in the middle of the country, millions of miles from anywhere. With tumbleweeds blowing by in the wind like some Western movie."

"But still with a good enough internet connection to play online?"

I laughed, and it came out a weird sound I wasn't used to. It was flat out flirty.

"Yeah, something like that."

Bowen chuckled. "We're not that remote. We're in country New South Wales. A little town called Erraville. It's about an hour from Lorrington. That's the nearest largeish town. It's not really very large though, by most people's standards."

I froze. My heart thumped harder.

"Did you say Lorrington?"

Bowen nodded. "Yeah? You heard of it?"

I laughed. "I've heard of it. I, uh...I live in Lorrington."

Bowen blinked. "Get the fuck out. You do not."

I shrugged. "Kinda do. Jimmy's Pub on the high street does the best pies around. There's a BP service station on the main road out. The school is on Jadek Drive...shall I go on?"

Bowen looked like a deer caught in the headlights.

"Bowen? You want to say something?"

He shook his head slightly. "Sorry. I just...I thought you were a city girl."

I frowned. "Well, I'm not as country as you are. I don't have a clue how to ride a horse. Definitely not going anywhere near a bull. We just live in the suburbs." I looked at my threadbare lounge, and the worn patch in the carpet. "Nothing fancy."

"How have we never met before?"

"I've really no idea." Lorrington was a small town. Not as small as Erraville. I'd only been there once and it was little more than a main street. Everything else was just acres and acres of farmland. "Henry doesn't go to school with Aiden then?"

"No, he does distance education. My father was a teacher before he retired, so that's kind of his domain. He lives here on the farm too."

"Ah. That makes sense then. I think I would have noticed you if we'd been at PTA meetings together." A blush warmed my cheeks as the words spilled out of my mouth. Ugh. That was too forward. "Sorry, I just meant..."

"I would have noticed you too, Paisley."

Oh my God. I felt like running from the room, flopping onto my bed, and squealing into my pillow like a teenager.

Bowen coughed to clear his throat. "So about the gaming con...do you...do you want to maybe meet us there? I know Henry is keen to go with Aiden, and the two of them do seem pretty into it. We're staying at the Park Hyatt."

It was on the tip of my tongue to blurt out "yes". Because taking a trip to Sydney, staying in a hotel, and taking Aiden to do something he loved so much all sounded amazing. But... "Uh, how much is it?"

"For entry? It's cheap. Twenty dollars for kids. Forty for adults."

I nodded. So that was eighty dollars just for tickets for Lily, Aiden, and me. I quickly added on the cost of fuel to drive there and back, which would be a lot, because it was a stupidly long drive. The cost of food, and accommodation for at least two nights...and had he said he was staying at the Park Hyatt? Wasn't that a luxury hotel? It probably cost a thousand dollars a night. But even a crappy hotel in the city still cost hundreds. It wasn't like the Lorrington Motel, though even that was pricey after the renovations they'd completed last year.

I came crashing back down to earth. I already knew Jonathan wouldn't be willing to chip in for a weekend away, even if it was for Aiden. And if he knew about Bowen... Who was I kidding? The man didn't give me enough money to even clothe my children. He wasn't going to help me fund a weekend away with some new guy I'd met. Even if there wasn't anything going on between us.

Bowen coughed. "If, uh, money is a problem for you, I'd be happy to cover—"

I shook my head rapidly, wondering if my concerns had been written all over my face. "Oh no, no, no. We're fine." My cheeks heated as I processed what he'd said. And then I wanted to crawl through the floor. How embarrassing. Had he really just offered to pay for us to go to Sydney? That was mortifying. Was it obvious I was barely making ends meet? I'd done my best to provide everything this family needed, without my ex's support. I never wanted my children looked down upon because they had less, so I scrimped and saved on everything from clothes to toiletries to food to make sure that didn't happen. But I obviously wasn't doing a good job if this man had noticed from across a television screen. He had to have money. If he'd been on the pro bull riding tour for a while... How much did those guys earn? He told me he competed overseas for half the year... Was he earning thousands? Hundreds of thousands? More? And here I was, a single mother, with barely any education and a crappy delivery job who were cutting back my hours.

"I should go." I suddenly felt raw. Like he could see right through my walls and into my deepest weaknesses. I silently berated myself for letting my guard down. For not being perfectly made up every time we'd chatted. For not making sure the stained couch cushion hadn't been in view of the camera, and for using the chipped coffee mug when we'd taken breaks to just talk. Had he noticed that? I'd never let the kids have friends over because I didn't want their parents judging our meagre belongings, yet with this man, I'd left myself wide open for his judgement. Basically giving him a front row seat into my home without a thought just because he wasn't actually bodily here.

Stupid.

Bowen's face fell. "You don't want to play tonight?"

I just wanted to escape from the intensity of his gaze. "Not today."

His voice was soft. "Paisley, if I offended you—"

"It's not that. I just have studying to do. I'll talk to you later." In a rush, I disconnected the console. The screen went black and I sucked in a few deep breaths, trying to calm my racing heart.

Then I flopped back on the lounge and stared up at the ceiling. In my heart, I knew he hadn't meant anything by offering to pay for us. But that meant he had money. Probably a lot of money if he could afford to throw it around like that. It all sounded too familiar for comfort. I'd fallen for a man who liked to splash his money around once before. I'd given up everything for him and it had taken me years to rebuild myself. I couldn't do that twice, so it would be better if I ended this silly infatuation with the man now. Before anyone got hurt.

B y Friday night, if you'd looked up the definition of "bear with a sore head" you would have found a photo of Aiden's scowling face. I gritted my teeth as he slammed his bedroom door and stomped down the stairs.

He threw himself into a seat at the dining room table, crossed his arms over his chest, and huffed out an overexaggerated sigh. His mood had gotten progressively worse as the week had worn on. I tried hard not to let the kid's moods affect me, but this week it was a losing battle. Aiden's sour face had me feeling down in the dumps too.

Or...I missed Bowen.

Which was utterly ridiculous. How could I miss a man I'd never even met in real life? It had only been a few days since we'd had that stupid, weird conversation about money, but I'd been avoiding the gaming console ever since.

Aiden laid his head down on the table and stared at me with sad eyes, his mousy brown hair swept to the side. "Did you ask Dad about the gaming con?"

My jaw clenched at the memory of how that little conversation had gone. I'd sucked up my pride and asked my ex about lending me the money to take Aiden to the city. Or even for him to take Aiden himself. I wanted Aiden to go, even if it meant I didn't get to see Bowen. But it was a flat out no with a rubbish excuse about having to work and Aiden needing to understand the value of money.

Like Jonathan knew anything about the value of money.

"Sorry, sweetheart. It's a no go."

I waited for the inevitable tantrum, but he said nothing. He just quietly turned his head on his arms so I couldn't see his face.

And somehow that felt worse.

The front door opened with a dragging noise because one of the hinges had popped a screw and I hadn't yet replaced it, and my mother appeared in the kitchen. Her casual pants and flowing jewel-coloured blouse weren't flashy, but neat and tidy. Her greying hair had recently been dyed its regular shade of blonde, a similar colour to my own, though mine was natural. She cast an eye over my uniform and sniffed in my direction before wrinkling her nose. "Did you already work today? I thought I was minding the kids tonight because you had a shift?"

"I do."

She recoiled a little. "Did you wash that uniform then? Because you already smell of grease and cheese."

I sighed, sniffing at the collar of my shirt. I *had* washed it, and the smells of working with food were barely noticeable. Or maybe I'd just grown accustomed to it. I shrugged.

"Muummmmm!" A pitiful cry came from upstairs. Instantly my mum senses flared to life. With kids, someone was almost always yelling my name, but years of practice had taught me which ones I could ignore, and which ones required my immediate attention.

And that cry had been one of the latter.

"Excuse me," I said to my own mother, pushing past her, and took the stairs two at a time to Lily's bedroom. I threw open the door to find her standing in the middle of the room, tears streaming down her face.

"Lil? What's wrong?" I knelt in front her tiny five-year-old body and scanned her for any obvious sign of injury. She seemed okay—no bleeding wounds or bones at odd angles. A little of my mumma panic ebbed away.

She shook her blonde head sadly, then whispered, "I don't feel so good."

I didn't even have time to flinch before she hurled her dinner up.

All over me.

I scrunched my eyes and mouth shut, whipping my head away just in time to miss the second wave, which landed all over her, the carpet, and again, me.

As her heaving was replaced with sobbing, I dared to

survey the carnage. And oh, as soon as I opened my eyes, I wished I hadn't. Because it was bad. So very bad.

"Sorry, Mumma," Lily whispered, tears rolling down her cheeks.

I gathered her shaking form up in my arms and recoiled when I touched her burning-hot skin. Woah. Where had that fever come from? I held her for a moment, debating my options, then decided that the first order of business was getting both of us in a shower.

She found a patch on my shoulder that was relatively vomit-free and laid her head down. I trudged out of her room, trying not to gag on the smell.

The doorbell rang when I was halfway down the stairs with my vomit-covered parcel. "Aiden! Mum! Could one of you grab that, please? It's probably the post guy, I'm expecting something!"

I shifted Lily's weight, peering over her and carefully watching the stairs to be sure I didn't fall. Because wouldn't that just top this evening off. A vision of Lily and me rolling down the stairs, spreading puke everywhere as we went, flashed through my mind and I almost laughed. It was either that or cry.

I took the last step, landing in the living room, right as Aiden screamed, "Henry!"

I whipped my head to the doorway, where Aiden was dragging a boy about the same height as him inside. My eyes widened as I recognised him from his pixelated form on the TV.

The two boys were jumping up and down in excitement and hugging each other while I was still trying to put the pieces together. My mind was refusing to process the situation. How was Henry standing in my living room right now?

My mother coughed with intention and I turned my

stunned gaze on her. She flicked her head towards the doorway. When I followed, my mouth dropped open.

Bowen, all six foot something of delicious, clean, and rugged man, stood in my foyer.

"Hello, Paisley."

8

PAISLEY

*M*y mouth had to be flapping around like some sort of fish or a demented bird while I tried to form words. I was sure I'd once known some, but the fact that Bowen and Henry were in my living room and not on my TV screen had effectively disintegrated my brain.

I couldn't stop staring at the man. I'd known he was handsome. But boy, those webcams and TV cameras were poor quality compared to the real thing. He was taller than I'd expected, his shoulders broader. A baseball cap covered his head, and his sleeves were rolled to his elbows exposing forearms corded with muscle and veins.

Oh boy. That was hot.

"Mumma," Lily wailed from my arms and I was suddenly jolted back to reality. The reality that I was standing covered in my daughter's regurgitated dinner with the most handsome man in the world saying my name.

"I...nope."

I spun on my heel and hightailed it to the bathroom. I closed the door behind me and locked it tight, double-checking it because I knew how much my kids loved just barging in whenever they felt like it. I did not need to add to the embarrassment of this evening by having Bowen see me naked in the shower.

The taps squealed as I turned them on and adjusted the temperature. "How you doing, baby girl?" I asked the curled-up ball in my arms. She didn't answer and I wondered if she'd fallen asleep. That wasn't good. Her bedtime wasn't for another hour, and normally she was still bouncing off the walls at this time. And this fever felt high. She was burning up. Despite the fact I'd just been rude to Bowen, I needed to get my daughter sorted out first.

Once the temperature was warm, but not too warm, I stepped into the shower, clothes and all. Lily flinched as the water hit her but then settled back against my chest. I let the water wash us both off before I stripped her of her soiled clothes and washed her hair while she sat drowsily on the shower ledge. I wrapped her in the fluffiest towel we had, then laid her on the thick bathmat. Her big eyes were fluttering closed as I returned to the shower to strip off my own ruined clothes. I scrubbed myself all over with soap and quickly washed my hair. My mind was a mottled mess of thoughts—worry for Lily combined with complete confusion over Bowen's appearance. How had he even known where I lived? Why was he here?

I had no answers by the time I stepped out of the shower, wrapping myself in an identical towel to Lily's. I checked her forehead. Still too hot. With horror, I realised I had no clean clothes in the bathroom. I sure wasn't walking out into the living room in just a towel with Bowen hanging around. If he was still there. The vomit scene and my lack of communication skills had probably sent him running for the hills. God. What a nightmare.

I was just about to crack open the door and yell for my mother when her voice filtered through the door. "Paisley? I've brought clean clothes for the both of you."

She may have had no qualms about telling me when I reeked of garlic and tomato sauce but at least I could count on her to know what I needed. I cracked open the door, making sure my body was concealed behind it, and peeked out. "Is he still here?" I whispered.

She nodded. "He seems very nice. He's concerned about you."

"About me?"

She nodded again.

"What is he doing here? Did he say?"

She frowned. "He said Aiden gave his son your address, and they were in town, so he just dropped by to say hello. Do you want me to tell him to leave?"

"I..." I had no idea what I wanted. "No," I whispered. "He can stay, it's okay. You can go though, Mum. I can't go to work tonight with Lily this sick." Mum looked past me to Lily sleeping on the floor and sympathy flashed in her eyes.

"You sure? You know this man well enough to be alone with him?"

No.

But my gut instinct told me I could trust him. And he'd brought a child with him. How dishonourable could his intentions be?

"I'll be fine. Go. See you later."

She nodded and I closed the door again. As I dressed myself and Lily, I heard the faint sounds of Mum and Bowen saying goodbye and the door closing. My heart sped up as I ran a brush through my tangled hair. Then I stared at myself in the mirror while I brushed my teeth. Twice.

Go on out there. You can do this. You cannot stay in this bathroom all night, even if you wanted to, I lectured myself.

I picked up Lily, who was a little more conscious now that I'd gotten her dressed in her onesie pyjamas, and carried her out to the couch. Bowen sat on the edge of an armchair, watching me intently. The boys had disappeared, and I could hear thumps and shouts and laughter from upstairs, so I had a pretty good idea of where to.

"I'm sorry. This is such bad timing. She's sick, huh?" he asked, nodding towards Lily, who watched him with big blue eyes.

I nodded. "A stomach bug likely. Or could be food poisoning." I suddenly remembered the vomit in the bedroom and groaned. "I'm so sorry, Bowen. This is the absolute worst way to meet you in person. But I have a mess in her bedroom to clean up." I went to stand, but he reached out and grabbed my arm. Sparks pulsed through me at his touch, stopping me in my tracks. Woah. His long fingers curled around my wrist, his skin warm, his calloused thumb resting over my pulse point. I wondered if he could feel how my heartbeat picked up at our sudden contact.

"Your mother already took care of it."

"Oh." I sat back down, but closer to his chair so he wouldn't have to drop my arm. I kind of wanted him to just leave his hand there for the rest of eternity because it felt so nice. But he let go as soon as he realised I was no longer making my way upstairs.

Drat.

His gaze remained trained on me, and that made a different kind of heat race through my body. Up close, his eyes were hazel, flecked with green and gold and absolutely mesmerising. For a long moment, I got lost staring at him, drinking him in. It should have been awkward, but it wasn't. He seemed content to do the same with me, though I knew my eyes were a boring grey-blue and not half as interesting as his.

A groan from the small body beside me reminded me we weren't alone. Lily's shoulders began to shake, and I realised with horror I'd made a rookie mistake. I'd gotten caught up in staring at Bowen and hadn't found her a bucket to keep by her head.

"Argh!" I cried, jumping up and racing for the laundry, where I kept a bucket for these exact situations. I sprinted, grabbed it from the spot beneath the sink, and raced back with such speed I was sure I could have qualified for the next Olympics.

In the doorway though, I stopped. Bowen knelt beside Lily, rubbing her back in slow circles while she heaved into his baseball cap. He murmured to her soothingly, in the exact same way I would have. In the exact way Jonathan never had. Jonathan didn't do vomit. Even when we'd been together, he'd completely disappear whenever the kids had been sick. And yet here was Bowen, a man I barely knew, stepping up to the vomit plate like a pro.

I knelt beside him and took the cap from him, dumping it into the bucket.

"I'm so sorry about that," I whispered, heat flooding my face.

But he waved a hand. "What's a bit of vomit between friends, huh?"

I wasn't sure if he meant he and Lily were friends. Or that he and I were friends. God, could anyone really be friends with a man who looked the way he did? I had to force my fingers to stay on the bucket handle when they really wanted to run through the short, sand-coloured hair on his head. Even before meeting him in person, I'd been pretty sure I didn't just want to be friends with this man. Even if he did wear ridiculous chaps.

Bowen touched Lily's forehead and when he finally turned to me, it was with a worried expression on his face. "She's burning up."

I didn't dare move the bucket from beneath Lily's chin. "There's a thermometer in the bathroom cupboard. Would you mind grabbing it?"

He nodded and pushed to his feet, striding through my small house and returning a moment later. I hoped he hadn't noticed the dirty mismatched plates and cutlery in the kitchen sink as he'd passed through.

"This?" he asked, handing me the gun-style thermometer, and I took it from him with a nod. I pointed it at Lily's forehead and squeezed the button. When her body temperature flashed up in red digital numbers my stomach plummeted. I'd never seen a number that high on any of my children.

"She needs to go to the hospital," Bowen said before I could get the words out. On the couch, Lily had stopped vomiting and had lain back down and fallen asleep. I shook her a little, but she didn't respond, and fear grabbed a hold of my heart. Was she sleeping? Or had she passed out?

"Aiden!" I yelled, a tinge of panic in my voice. I cursed myself for sending my mother home. "We need to go to the hospital." Lily began to tremble on the lounge, and I gazed around wildly for my shoes. The kids would need shoes. And jackets. It was getting cold. Bowen disappeared out the front door, but I had no time to wonder where he was going. I needed to find the car keys and—

Bowen returned and, in the doorway, caught me by my shoulders.

I glanced up at him, distracted by the huge to-do list suddenly unravelling in my head. "Bowen, I'm sorry, I can't find my keys and I need to get the kids down here and—"

"This is my dad, Alan."

"And I'm still here too," my mother called. When Bowen moved aside, I saw my mother and an older man, presumably Alan, standing on the doorstep.

I squinted at them both. Alan took pity on me first, stepping forward and squeezing my arm in a warm, fatherly manner. "I was waiting in the car, and your mother and I started chatting when she came out and accused me of casing the joint."

"Mum! You didn't!"

Alan squeezed my arm again and smiled gently at me. "It doesn't matter, we worked it out. Bowen said your little girl is sick."

"Dad can stay here with the boys while I drive you and Lily to the hospital." Bowen exuded calm and confidence. And God, it would have been so nice to just let someone...help.

But I shook my head. This wasn't his problem. "Oh no, I couldn't ask you to do that. I need to find my keys and my wallet and get shoes—"

Bowen ducked to catch my gaze. I stilled, my panic ebbing under his confident stare. "You didn't ask. I offered. Please, let me help."

Logically I knew I wasn't in any position to turn down an offer of help right now, and even though I felt like I needed to be in control of the situation, my panic over Lily was consuming. I needed to get her to a doctor.

"I can stay too," Mum called. "You know, just in case

Alan here really was looking to rob the place." She laughed, a tinkling sound I'd never heard from her before, and I had to shake myself back into action. My straight-laced mother giggling, because that was what that noise had been, was not only absurd but slightly disturbing. But that was something to ponder later.

"Okay," I said to Bowen. "Thank you." And I meant it. I really didn't want to go to the emergency room by myself. I'd had to do that a couple of times before and it was cold and scary and lonely.

He nodded curtly and I ran to the stairs to tell Aiden what was going on. By the time I turned around, Bowen had Lily scooped up in his arms, a blanket from the back of the couch tucked around her, and was striding for the door. There was nothing left for me to do but grab my bag and run after him. I passed Alan and my mother in the doorway. "I'm sorry about the vomit bucket," I said, but Alan gave me a reassuring smile and simply pulled up his sleeves before closing the door behind me. Relief filled me. I was a "get in and get the job done" sort of person too.

I stared at Bowen's back as he laid Lily on the back seat, then jogged around to the driver's side of a sleek black four-wheel drive. It wasn't the usual paddock bashers that most people out here drove. It was top of the line. I prayed Lily wouldn't puke on the expensive leather seats.

He stopped and stared at me over the bonnet. "Paisley," he said, and I realised it wasn't the first time he'd called my name. I snapped to attention, slid into the luxurious back seat beside Lily, and pulled the door shut behind me. Bowen started the car, and the engine kicked over with a purr so smooth I could have petted it.

"We'll be there in no time. How is she doing?"

I moved Lily's sweaty head onto my lap and stroked her

hair. She groaned but she didn't wake. I'd never felt anything like the heat that poured off her.

My eyes met Bowen's in the rear-view mirror as Lily's tiny body trembled violently.

"Please hurry."

9

BOWEN

*H*ospital waiting rooms were all the same, no matter which country you were in. Linoleum floors, uncomfortable chairs, and that unmistakable hospital smell of industrial strength cleaner, humans, and sickness.

It made my stomach roll. I hated hospitals. But I'd spent many Saturday nights either sitting in the hard chairs, waiting to see how bad one of my friends from the circuit was injured, or laid up in a bed myself, being inspected for broken bones and internal bleeding. No matter where I was, the smell and the worry and the ache in my tailbone from too many hours of sitting were all the same.

I watched the sunrise through the grimy emergency room window, waiting for news about Lily, and still Paisley didn't appear. I called my dad twice—once last night, and once this morning. The first time he'd assured me they'd gotten the boys off to bed after finding a pull-out mattress in Aiden's room for Henry. The second time I called, there was a cacophony of noise around him and he laughed as he told me they were all awake and he and Thelma, Paisley's mother, were whipping up eggs and toast.

"You behaving yourself, old man?"

He chuckled. "Don't I always?"

I wasn't so sure about that, but there was only so much trouble the old bugger could get into with his eagle-eyed grandson around, so I figured Thelma's virtue was probably safe until I made it back to collect him.

I hung up the phone right as a nurse strode over to me. I stood to meet her and went to take my hat off before I realised that my baseball cap was still covered in vomit back at Paisley's house.

"Sir, you came in with Lily Ackerly?"

"Yes, I did. Is she okay?"

"She's been moved up to the children's ward. Level 4, Room 22 if you want to see her."

I thanked her and she turned and moved on to the next person on her list. I headed towards the elevators, my muscles crying out in pleasure at actually moving again. When I got to the fourth floor, I found Room 22 and knocked quietly. Nobody answered, so I opened the door a crack and peeked through. Lily was propped up in a big white bed, with a mound of pillows around her. She was hooked up to a drip, and her blonde hair fanned out around her in tangled, dirty waves, but she was awake. She grinned when she noticed me. But then she put a finger to her lips in the universal shh sign and pointed to her left. I couldn't see what she was pointing at until I pushed the door open and saw Paisley slumped on a chair beside the bed, her arms folded on the mattress, her head resting on top. Soft snores fell from her open mouth. A weird sense of protectiveness washed over me. She looked young and vulnerable when she slept. And so incredibly beautiful.

"You're the prince!" Lily said, startling me out of my trance.

"Excuse me?"

"You're the prince from my dream. I was the princess and you carried me to the carriage." Then she frowned. "There were no white horses though. And the carriage was small...and black." Her confusion was written all over her face.

My lips quirked up and I leant in close to her. "You found out my secret," I whispered. "I'm Prince Bowen. So that must make you Princess Lily, yes?"

She nodded happily.

"You look much better this morning, Princess."

"She does, doesn't she?" Paisley's voice interrupted.

Lily giggled, then whispered to me. "Uh-oh, we woke the queen."

I winked at her. "I hope she's not an evil queen."

"Hey! I heard that!" Paisley faked insult but she was staring at her daughter with a huge smile of relief on her face. I could only imagine how she felt this morning. I was relieved to see the huge improvement in the girl, and I'd only known her twelve hours. It somehow felt longer after listening to Paisley talk about her for the past couple of weeks.

"Is Dad coming?" Lily asked suddenly.

Paisley's smile fell. She took Lily's hand, the one that didn't have a drip sticking out of it, and rubbed it.

"No, sweetie, I'm sorry. He can't be here. He said he loves you very much though, and he'll see you soon."

Lily shrugged and turned her attention back to the TV mounted on brackets at the end of her bed. Energetic cartoon characters moved about on the screen.

I moved to sit beside Paisley. She looked down at her

hands, but I could still see the dark circles beneath her eyes. She looked exhausted. Exhausted and sad.

"He must be a very busy man if he can't be here when his daughter is sick." Although I knew I was overstepping, she looked so miserable, I picked up her hand and squeezed it. I couldn't imagine anything that would keep me away from Henry if he was in the hospital, but I did my best to keep my judgement out of my voice.

Paisley gave me a tight smile. "I guess so." Then she pulled her hand away. Immediately, I wanted to take it back. I forced my fingers to remain resting on my thighs, but it took effort.

Paisley seemed to shake herself off and straightened in her chair, running one hand through her tangled waves. "I'm so sorry, Bowen. I can't believe you stayed here all night. I'm sure you're a busy man. Just let me call my mother and I'll let you get out of here."

She fumbled around with her bag, looking for her phone, but I shook my head. "It's fine. I can stay as long as you need. Or I can stay with her, and you can go home and catch some sleep and a shower if you need to? You can take my car if you aren't too tired to drive?"

Paisley's mouth formed a little O shape, and I couldn't stop myself from staring at the way her pretty pink lips looked.

"Why would you do all this?" she asked abruptly.

I frowned. "Do what?"

She waved her hand around. "Everything. You caught my daughter's vomit. You stayed all night with us at the hospital. And now you're here, offering to sit with her. You barely know us."

"Do you have to know someone well to be kind?"

Paisley's mouth opened then closed. "No. I suppose not."

"It's because he's my prince, Mama," Lily lisped, and Paisley laughed before smoothing back the little girl's hair.

"Is he just? I think perhaps you mean he's your knight in shining armour. But either way, you're a lucky little girl." Her gaze had turned to me as she said it.

Warmth spread across my chest.

"Thank you," she whispered. "I don't think I said that. You're a good man."

The words rolled easily off her tongue, and she closed her eyes again, so I knew she meant nothing by them. But they rocked me to my core anyway. *You're a good man.*

I wasn't though. And once I told her why, she'd look at me differently. She'd speak to me differently. The playfulness I'd come to know her for would disappear. Would she even want to game together anymore? Our daily chats and her attempts to beat me were the highlights of my week. I didn't want to give those up just yet.

Or ever, a voice whispered in my head. But that thought was startling and out of place. Completely ridiculous. I buried it by focussing on the here and now. When the doctor came in to talk to Paisley, I let the distraction wash away the thought completely.

10

PAISLEY

*L*ily was bouncing off the walls by the time Bowen drove us home late in the evening. She'd been given a clean bill of health after what seemed to just be a twenty-four-hour virus. She threw open the back door of Bowen's car and bounded down the path to the house, and I couldn't believe she was the same little girl who Bowen had carried, limp and unresponsive, just the previous evening.

"Whatever they gave her in the hospital, I want some," Bowen joked as we slowly followed behind.

"You and me both." We stopped on the doorstep, turning to face each other. I suddenly felt like I was sixteen again, being dropped home after a date. Our parents were waiting inside and everything.

"Well, thank you. For everything. That was really scary for me and you made it bearable." I dared a glance up into his gold-flecked eyes and caught him watching me. Something brushed over my hand, and then his fingers slipped around mine. Again. He'd held my hand in the hospital and it had been so overwhelming that I'd pulled away. I hadn't had a man touch me that gently in such a long time. Or ever, really.

"I'm glad I was here to help. Though I am still sorry for intruding on you the way we did. I wanted to call first, but I didn't have your number..."

"Oh, right." Because I'd been too chicken to ask him for his.

"I'd still like it, if you wouldn't mind me calling you sometime? I know Henry would like to see Aiden again. And maybe..." He looked down at his feet, his boots still dusty from whatever he'd been doing before he'd landed on my doorstep yesterday. "Actually, do you want to go to dinner? I need some decent food after all that hospital cafeteria rubbish."

I shook my head on impulse. "I don't think I can. I'm sorry. My mum has been here all day and night and I need to call my boss because I missed my shift and really, you've been too kind. I'm sure you want to get home."

"Oh. Yeah. Of course."

I was shocked to see disappointment flash in his eyes and I wanted to kick myself. Had I really just turned down dinner with the most handsome man who'd ever spoken to me? I must have inhaled something toxic in the hospital because obviously my brain cells were dying.

"My number," I blurted out, trying to rescue the situation. It was insane. I'd just turned down his dinner proposal, but I didn't want this to be the end. For weeks, I'd been wanting to ask him for his number so we could FaceTime. And here was the perfect opportunity, and I was botching it up.

He looked up, hope replacing the doubt that had been there a moment ago, and I almost felt giddy. For the life of me, I couldn't work out what that hopeful look meant. Had he really wanted to go out with me? Had it actually been a date he was asking me on? I was so out of practice when it came to dating, I just had no idea what the protocol was anymore. But my phone number. That, at least, I could do.

I held my free hand out expectantly. He eyed it for a moment, then placed his hand in mine. And while I liked that now both our hands were joined, I laughed and shook my head. "No, silly. I meant give me your phone so I can put my number in it."

He gave me an embarrassed grin, which I returned because had I really just called him silly? I was so used to speaking with children all day long I'd apparently forgotten how to hold a conversation with a man. Or maybe Bowen just made me forget words. Or maybe I was just delirious with lack of sleep. Probably a combination of all three.

Bowen passed me his phone and I saved my details before handing it back to him with a shy smile.

"I can call you then?" he asked in his low rumble.

I nodded. "I'd like that."

He stared down at me and I stared up at him, willing myself not to get lost in his eyes. His thumb rubbed over the back of my hand and my breath quickened. His gaze ducked to my mouth, and my heart stopped.

He was going to kiss me. I was suddenly sure of it. Is that what I wanted?

Yes! something deep inside me screamed. *Step in. Wrap your arms around the man and let his lips find yours.* My heart-beat thrummed against my chest as nervous energy filled me. Bowen leaned in ever so slightly, testing the waters perhaps, but that was enough to shock me into action.

I took a small step backwards. Suddenly, all I could think of was that I hadn't brushed my teeth or hair in twenty-four hours. I hadn't showered or changed my clothes. I reeked of hospital grime and probably stale vomit. And beyond the surface-level stuff, I wasn't ready to kiss him. Not with my children and our parents on the other side of the door. Not before we'd even had a single date. It was all too fast.

Bowen straightened but he didn't look upset by my rejection. He simply squeezed my hand. Then he nudged the door ajar and yelled up the stairs for Henry, who came bounding down a moment later followed by my tribe.

"Time to go," Bowen said to his son, starting off a chorus of groans and complaining from both boys.

I thanked Alan profusely as he herded Henry towards the car, with Bowen trailing after them. As he reached the car, he turned back and mimed talking on the phone with a questioning look on his face.

I couldn't help the smile that spread across mine. And I nodded happily as the most interesting, confusing man I'd met in a long time drove away.

11

PAISLEY

*M*y phone lit up with a text message before I'd even fully closed the door.

Just checking you gave me the right number.

I stuck my head back out the door and found Bowen sitting behind the wheel of his monstrosity of a car with the window down. He chuckled then looked down at something in his hand. In the next moment, my phone buzzed again.

Guess you did.

I rolled my eyes and waved as he put his car in gear and drove away. I closed the door and leaned back on it. I was just about to squeal like I was in some teen movie when I realised my mother was staring at me.

"What?" I asked defensively, pushing past her and into the kitchen.

"I didn't say a word." She sipped her cup of tea, watching me over the top of it.

"Like you can talk! What's going on with you and Alan? Hmm?"

One of her perfectly shaped eyebrows shot up.

I mirrored her expression. "Don't give me that. You were totally flirting with him!"

She huffed, putting her mug down in the sink. "Rubbish."

She kissed my cheek and picked up her bag hanging over the back of a kitchen chair. "I'm heading home now that you're back. I'm glad Lily is feeling better."

"Mmm-hmm." I couldn't help razzing her. In all the years since my parents' divorce, I'd never seen her so much as look at another man. And last night she'd been giggling at one. Pigs had to be flying somewhere.

"Oh, by the way, Diego called, and asked you to call him back immediately. He didn't sound very happy."

I groaned as I sunk into a kitchen chair. I'd completely missed my shift last night and didn't call to let them know. It hadn't even crossed my mind until we'd been on our way back home with a much-improved Lily.

I dialled Diego's number and cringed when his answering "hello" was frosty.

"Hey, Diego," I said as brightly as I could muster after spending the last day in a hospital, with little more than a nap in the way of sleep.

"You missed your shift. Without even a phone call. What am I supposed to do with that, Paisley? You cost me money last night."

I slumped in my chair. "I'm so sorry. I feel awful, but my daughter—"

"Yes, I know. You have children. So does everybody else. I've always been lenient with you, because I know you've been doing it tough, but there isn't enough work at the moment. I can't afford for you to not come in and cost me money in lost deliveries when Angelo is begging me for extra shifts."

I sat up a little straighter. "I...I know. You've always been really good to me. And I'm sorry about last night but—"

"Paisley, stop. Please. It's hard enough as it is for me to say this to you, but I've known for a while now that I was going to have to let either you or Angelo go. It has to be you. He's just more reliable. And more available. We're making your position redundant."

I bit my lip, feeling tears welling in my eyes. Angelo had a wife who stayed home to watch his kids. So of course, he was more available than I was. I had an ex-husband who couldn't be counted on for anything other than to be a pain in my ass. And a mother who helped as much as she could but had her own life too.

A mixture of anger and frustration clogged my throat. I wanted to yell that it wasn't fair and that I needed this job, but I didn't want to yell at Diego. He was a good man and was just trying to support his own family by making good business decisions. I was the weakest link. I did deserve to go. Goodbye.

"I understand," I said quietly.

On the other end, Diego heaved a sigh. "I really am sorry. You know I'll give you a glowing reference."

"Thank you. I need to go now." I hung up the phone, placing it down on the table before I could burst into tears.

---

*B*owen's texts continued to blow up my phone for the rest of the week. And every time one came in, I thanked my lucky stars, because his texts and talking to him each night while we pretended to play video games was the only bright spark in an otherwise crappy week. On the Thursday night, my phone lit up with a call from him around the same time we normally met on *Light and Legacy*.

I skittered down the hall, quickly checking my hair wasn't too much of a disaster and that there were no spaghetti sauce stains on my shirt before I answered the phone with a smile.

Bowen scowled back at me and I felt my smile fall.

"What's wrong?"

He sighed, the hard lines of his face softening. "Look, I did a thing. And you might not be happy about it. But just remember that I'm not very happy with you either right now."

My stomach sunk. "You're not?" I wracked my brain trying to think of what I could have possibly done to upset him. He was just staring at me through the screen and eventually I shrugged. "You're going to have to explain, because I've honestly no clue what you're so upset about."

"I'm not upset. I'm just...I thought we were friends? We're friends, aren't we?"

"Of course." I didn't add that being his "friend" was not really what I wanted but it was what I was stuck with right now so I'd been happy to make the most of it until I worked up the guts to maybe ask him out. I'd turned down his dinner invitation, so I felt like the ball had been left in my court. I was just too nervous to do anything with the ball. Or with the Bowen, as the case may be. The Bowen ball. Bowen's balls... Bowen's... Argh. I needed to get a grip.

"Then why didn't you tell me you lost your job last weekend?"

I paused, my mouth opening to respond and then closing as a new thought interrupted my immediate urge to deny his accusations. "How did you know I got fired?"

He shifted in his seat, like he was suddenly uncomfortable. "That's the part you might not be too happy about. I kind of called your work."

"What? Why?" For the life of me, I couldn't imagine a single reason why the man would want to call my work. Unless he was perhaps looking to talk to me, but I was doing deliveries most of the time anyway, and he knew that so why he hadn't just called my mobile made no sense.

"I wanted to ask your boss to give you a few days off."

"Okaayyyy. Want to explain more?"

His words came out in a rush. "Henry kept bugging me about seeing Aiden again and then my dad got in on the nagging and somehow made me think it was a good idea. And I said it was a bad idea but it also felt like a great idea because I'd get to see you again, and then he was calling, and... It was supposed to be a surprise. But then your boss said you didn't work there anymore, and I had to call you. Why didn't you tell me?"

I shrugged, frustrated, because I really didn't have a reason. "I don't know? Because it's embarrassing? What did you want me to say? Hey, guess what? I lost my shitty, minimum wage, no education required delivery job, and now I've no idea how I'm going to pay my rent, or pay for my kids' school clothes, or even how I'll feed them next week?" I blurted out the words, then immediately wished I could take them back. Bowen looked like I'd slapped him. I closed my eyes and took a deep breath, trying to paste a smile back on my face, but my words came out stiff. "I guess that's why I didn't tell you."

"I wouldn't have judged you, Paisley. I would have just been a friend. Been there for you. That's why I'm upset. I hate that you've been stressing about this all week while I yakked on about unimportant things like needing to find a new hay supplier."

I sniffed back the tears that were threatening to build in my eyes. "Hay is important...especially if you're a bull..."

He chuckled and I was glad to see him smiling again. I didn't want to be angry at him. And I didn't want him angry with me either.

"You still didn't really tell me why you rang my work. What was the surprise supposed to be?"

"Oh, right." He looked down. "Don't say no before you hear me out, okay?"

"Just so you know, Aiden has tried that one on me before and it doesn't normally end well."

"Yeah, yeah, I know. But really, just listen."

I said nothing and waited for him to continue.

"The gaming con is on Saturday. And Henry won't stop talking about all the things he and Aiden wanted to do there. And I know you said you couldn't go...but I booked a room, and I bought all of you tickets. I've already paid for it all and it's non-refundable, so come. I was calling your boss to make sure you could get the time off work."

As I processed all that information, I knew I should be angry with him and I was, sort of, but I was also focussing on the fact he'd booked a hotel room. "When you say you booked a room..."

Bowen's cheeks went pink. "I meant I booked an extra room. Henry and I already had one. My dad will be there too so I swear, I'm not trying anything..."

I shook my head. "No, no, of course not. I didn't think you were."

"Oh. Okay. Good."

Oh God, the awkwardness was so thick I could cut it with a knife. "Argh, sorry, I made this so uncomfortable, didn't I?"

He laughed, and I kind of wished he'd stop because it

was so deep and gravelly it made me want to do things I hadn't thought about in quite a while.

"No, I did. I should have just asked you about the whole thing, but I knew you'd say no, and..."

My fingers, wrapped around my phone, trembled slightly and I hoped he didn't notice. "And what?"

"And I really didn't want you to say no. I wanted—no, I mean, I *want* you to say yes. Especially now that you don't have a job to go to. Just come. Come for the weekend and hang out and have fun. I've got a rodeo in one of the big arenas in Sydney on Saturday night, but the rest of the time we can just hang out with the kids, and eat, and sightsee a bit if you want."

I paused, because God it sounded tempting. A weekend away to just forget all my problems. To forget the fact I had no income, and no job prospects and two kids who solely relied on me for everything. I imagined telling Aiden that we were going to spend the weekend in Sydney and he'd get to go to the convention after all. And I knew I couldn't say no. My heart wanted it. For Aiden. But also for myself.

"You've already paid for it? Really?"

He nodded quickly. "You won't pay a cent all weekend, I swear. I roped you into this and it's completely my treat."

I sighed.

"It's killing you a bit, isn't it?" He chuckled. "Just let someone be nice to you for once, Paisley. Please? Trust me. There's no ulterior motive here, other than I wouldn't mind some adult conversation at this gaming thing. I'm afraid I'm going to stick out like a sore thumb in my Akubra."

I laughed. "Maybe you should opt for a baseball cap?"

"Your daughter threw up in it, remember?"

"Oh my God. Please don't bring that up again. Fine. You

pay for the weekend away and I'll...I'll buy you a new baseball cap."

"Deal," he said with a gleam in his eye.

"Someone should really teach you about making deals. Because you totally drew the short straw there, you know?" I laughed, the words coming out light and playful, but Bowen stared at me seriously.

"I don't know. I get to spend the entire weekend with you. I think perhaps I'm the luckiest guy on earth."

I went quiet. If I lived to be a million, I didn't think any man would ever have a hope in hell of making me feel the way Bowen Barclay did in that moment.

12
———

BOWEN

I hadn't thought this through. Not at all. At seven o'clock on Friday morning, when I pulled into Paisley's driveway with Henry bouncing in the back seat, it had all still felt fine. The five of us—Paisley and me plus our collective three children—would make the eight-hour drive together in my Land Cruiser. Paisley's car was a gas guzzler, and I'd pretty much insisted she come with me. Petrol was so expensive, and I'd meant it when I said she wouldn't have to pay for a thing this weekend. It had been my idea to take the little trip, and I'd totally sprung it on her even after she'd said she wouldn't go, so I was determined that she wouldn't pay for anything while she was with me.

But thirty minutes into the drive, I was in agony. And it had nothing to do with the fact three kids made a hell of a lot of noise, and there had already been the dreaded "are we there yet" question. No. The problem was Paisley. And the way her intoxicating scent filled the cabin of my Land Cruiser, swirling around me, making it practically impossible to concentrate. She chattered happily from the seat beside me, and I tried to focus on her words, and the road, but I kept finding myself darting little looks in her direction. She had her golden hair loose, flowing over her shoulders, and she'd worn comfortable travelling clothes—leggings with an oversized knitted jumper. She'd pulled her hands inside the sleeves and I'd immediately leant over and cranked up the heat in the car, not wanting her to be cold, even if I was suddenly hot all over.

I didn't think any amount of air conditioning was going to help me.

By the time we reached Sydney, I was so distracted and frustrated, I was desperate for some space before I did something stupid like leaning in and kissing her. But the kids had spotted the Sydney Harbour Bridge from the hotel lobby and Paisley looked over at me and asked if I was keen to do a bit of sightseeing since we still had a few hours before it got dark. Her eyes were shiny with excitement and I found myself nodding even though what I really needed to do was go take a cold shower.

"Do you come to Sydney much?" I asked as we strolled along behind the trio of excited kids.

"No. Almost never. I haven't been for years."

I felt like even more of an ass for just wanting to go back to my room and take a break from her. It wasn't her fault she was so stunningly beautiful that I couldn't concentrate on anything else. I was here to show her a good time. She hadn't opened up a lot about her past, but I got the impression her ex had been more into his business than her. I couldn't understand that at all. If she had been mine, I would have struggled to even leave the house each day.

For the next few hours, we played tourist, stretching our stiff muscles by walking around the city, taking in all the major sights before stopping at a casual restaurant for some dinner. It wasn't late when we left, but Lily immediately started whining about the walk, so I lifted her onto my shoulders. Both the boys were dragging their feet as well, and when I looked over their heads at Paisley, I caught her yawning.

"An early night might be in order, hey?"

"I think so. Big day tomorrow. Especially for you."

I smiled tightly in agreement. She didn't even know how big the day was for me, or how important. I needed an early night just as much as they did. And I really needed some time alone to think and work out what I was supposed to do with this attraction I had to her. It had been a long time since I'd actively felt anything for a woman. The feeling was foreign, but not unpleasant. For the first time since Camille's death, it didn't feel wrong.

At her door, I watched her unlock it and shoo her kids inside before she turned back to me. "Nine a.m. tomorrow?"

"Yes, ma'am."

She giggled. "You do not really say 'ma'am'. Nobody here says that."

I shrugged. "I do say it. A lot of the guys on the tour are Americans. I guess I picked it up from them."

"Well then, cowboy. I'll see you tomorrow." She slipped behind the door, closing it gently after her, and I let out an involuntary groan.

Henry gave me a questioning look, and I straightened. I'd kind of forgotten he was in the hallway.

"Let's go, buddy. We need to sleep."

But sleep wouldn't come. Henry was out like a light the moment his head touched the pillow, but I tossed and turned, getting more and more hot and agitated the longer I stayed in bed. I knew I needed to sleep. I wouldn't be at my best tomorrow night if I didn't, but Paisley's scent still clung to me. And images of her smiling blue eyes, her long hair, and those tights moulding to her perfectly round ass kept playing through my head.

Eventually I got up and prowled around the room. I wanted to go knock on her door. I wanted to pull her into the hallway, where our kids wouldn't see us, and pin her against the wall and kiss her. God, I so badly wanted to kiss her. I wanted to know if her lips were as soft and gentle as they looked. I wanted to press my body against hers and feel her softness in the places I was hard. I stared at the wall that connected our two rooms and hated that drywall with a passion. She was just there, on the other side, less than a metre away.

I stalked to the door, my hand hovering over the handle as I imagined yanking it open and storming to her room. But as much as I wanted to do that, I couldn't.

I pivoted on my heel, changing directions and locking myself in the bathroom instead. I peeled my sweaty sleep clothes off and turned on the shower, not bothering to wait for the water to turn warm. The cold water stung my back, but I embraced it, needing it to cool my heated skin.

It did nothing to diminish the erection I sported though. I knew it wasn't going away without help. Reaching down, I slid my hand over my length and groaned. I'd been fighting it all day, like some lovesick teenager, but there was no fighting it now. I pumped myself in and out of my hand, trying not to imagine Paisley. But I couldn't help it. She was all I could think about. I moved my hand quickly, the pressure building inside me. I didn't want to draw this out. I felt like the biggest creep, standing in my shower jerking off while the woman I wanted was asleep in the room next door. But it was the best I could do for now.

My balls tightened and my hips jerked as I ran my hands over my cock again and again. I came hard, muffling a shout with my arm. The relief was instant, and I worked myself until I couldn't bear it another second. My breaths were pants, and I leaned my head on the cool glass of the shower screen. Fucking hell.

I washed up quickly and stepped out of the shower. Then tiptoed back into the dark room, found some clean pyjama pants, and slipped beneath the satiny sheets. They enveloped my bare skin like warm fingers tracing my back... like Paisley stroking down my muscles. I imagined her whispering in my ear as she did so, her hands travelling lower and lower until she found my cock, her tongue tracing a path over my neck and collarbone.

I groaned into my pillow as my dick began to thicken again.

It was going to be a long night.

13

PAISLEY

I dreamt of Bowen. I knew I would, after spending the entire day with him. I woke up breathless and needy, my core aching for relief I wasn't going to get. Because the alarm I'd set was blaring and my kids were stirring.

Pushing the last remaining shreds of my dreams away, I got up, staggered to the bathroom for a quick shower, then got the kids moving. Breakfast arrived at my door, briefly surprising me, but then I remembered filling out breakfast forms at reception when we'd checked in.

The hotel employee wheeled in a cart full of delicious-smelling food and my mouth watered. I thanked him profusely and closed the door behind him. I dished out meals to the kids and was about to take a bite of my own when there was a knock on the door.

I glanced at my watch. It was still too early for us to be meeting Bowen and Henry. "Maybe they have extra hash browns for us?" I asked the kids, but they ignored me, too busy scarfing down their pancakes. I pushed up from the little table and strode across the room to open the door.

"Yes?" The words died on my lips, replaced with confusion. "Mum?"

"Good morning!" she practically sang, walking past me. I dumbly turned, letting the door close behind her.

"What are you doing here?"

She grinned, then leaned a little closer like she was sharing a secret. "I came with Alan."

"What!"

She frowned at me. "Don't say 'what' like that, Paisley. It's unbecoming. We got in late last night. I thought you'd already be asleep, so I didn't want to bother you."

I grabbed her arm and tugged her away from my children and their flapping ears. "Did you sleep with him?" I asked in astonishment. If she said yes, I would actually die. I just knew it.

Mum pulled her arm from my grasp. "Of course not, Paisley. What kind of a woman do you think I am?"

"Oh good, good. That's good." I wasn't exactly sure why I thought it was so good. But that's what kept coming out of my mouth.

"I might though." Her grin had turned devilish.

My eyes widened. "I don't even know you right now. Who are you and where is my real mother?"

Her laugh trilled around the room. "You're so dramatic. Alan asked if I wanted to drive down with him. He couldn't go with Bowen because he had some suppliers to meet or something. But we wanted to get here in time to do the video game thing with you all today."

"You want to come to the convention?"

"Sure! Why not?"

"Because you normally tell me that I let Aiden play too many video games, then give me a hard time about how they're doing permanent damage to his young, impression-able brain?"

She laughed like I was being completely ridiculous then plonked herself down in my seat and took a sip of my orange juice. I just stared at the back of her head, wondering if she had perhaps gotten some last night, because I couldn't remember the last time I'd seen her so...breezy.

We'd just finished breakfast when another knock at the door startled me. I mumbled something about it being Grand Central Station in here this morning as I pulled it open.

Bowen's ridiculously handsome face stared back at me. "Howdy."

I laughed. "Stop it."

"I didn't say 'partner'."

"Thank God or I would have shut the door in your face." But I grinned at him to let him know I was joking. We stared at each other for a moment too long, but I just didn't care. I just wanted to drink him in.

"You ready to go?"

I nodded dumbly. I grabbed my bag and nudged my overexcited kids, plus my weirdly happy mother, out the door. Bowen caught the door and held it open for me. I smiled. "So polite."

"If I had a hat, I'd tip it at you."

"Oh! Speaking of, I bought you a new one to replace the...well, you know. The vomit hat," I whispered, not wanting to embarrass Lily. I rifled through my bag, pulling out the cap I'd stashed there before we'd left for Sydney.

"I love it," Bowen said sincerely, pulling it out of its pack-aging, folding the brim a little so it wasn't completely flat, and pulling it over his short hair.

I snorted. It was hot pink with the cowboy emoji embroidered on the front. Its yellow smiley face and brown cowboy hat was cute, but the hat was made for twelve-year-old girls. It looked completely ridiculous with Bowen's jeans and plaid shirt. But I'd seen it in a novelty store, and I couldn't resist teasing him. "You're such a liar."

"I'm not. You gave it to me, so I love it."

Startled by the sincerity in his words, I studied his face. "You really are laying on the gentlemanly cowboy thing today, aren't you?"

He feigned a look of innocence as we trailed our families to the elevator. "This is what I'm always like."

"Mmm-hmm. I bet the ladies love that."

I heard Alan snort and mumble something about him getting more ladies than Bowen did. Bowen shot him a warning look.

"Let's just do the convention, huh?"

We all piled into the elevator which took us to the ground floor and then we walked the few blocks to the entertainment centre the convention was being held in. Bowen handed over tickets for all of us, and I gazed around at the massive room filled with gaming paraphernalia. We were early, the gates only opening ten minutes ago, but a large crowd was already building. The ceilings were high and long banners fell from them with the convention's major sponsors. Booths lined the outside walls, and more were lined up in the centre of the giant room to make rows for people to walk between.

"This is amazing!" Aiden yelled, his eyes big. My heart swelled. Even though I still hated that I hadn't been able to bring him here under my own steam, I was glad I'd knocked my pride on its head and taken Bowen up on his offer.

Feeling brave in amongst the large crowd of people, and knowing that our kids were too preoccupied with all the noises and colours of the convention, I slid my hand into Bowen's and squeezed it gently.

He stopped and looked at me in surprise. "Thank you," I said quietly. He didn't say anything, just squeezed my hand back and turned around, tugging me forward to chase after our kids. He didn't let go until Aiden turned around to ask if we could get ice cream yet. I missed the warmth of his touch the minute he let go.

The morning flew by in a whirl of demonstrations, photos with cosplayers, and Bowen forking out money left, right, and centre whenever any of the kids so much as looked at something. He was truly going all out and spoiling them, and completely winning them over in the process.

At lunchtime, the kids were all getting whiny and it was clear to me that my mother and Alan had had enough of walking around.

"Why don't Alan and I take the kids to get some food?" Mum asked, as if she'd read my thoughts. "I think we could all use a break."

I nodded. "That's a good idea."

I started to head towards the fast food area when Alan put his hand on my arm. "Why don't you and Bowen go eat somewhere proper? He won't get another meal before the rodeo tonight so he should eat something more substantial than a hot dog that might give him food poisoning."

I narrowed my eyes at the older man, and he winked back at me.

Bowen rolled his eyes. "We see what you're doing there, old man."

Alan simply held an elbow out to my mother and called

to the kids that he was buying fries and burgers and who wanted one? The five of them ran off, Alan winking at us over his shoulder.

When I looked up at Bowen, his cheeks were pink. "So, uh. That was subtle."

I laughed. "About as subtle as a Mack truck. But is what he said right? Should you eat a proper meal?"

Bowen ran a hand over the back of his neck, his fingers brushing over the bright pink hat and making me smile. "Yeah, probably. Do you...do you want to go somewhere else? Get a real meal?"

I nodded quickly. He wasn't exactly asking me out, but this was as close to alone time as we were probably going to get, and I was going to take it while I could.

We fought against the crowds heading to the exits, but there were so many people, and Bowen and I kept getting separated. After the second time that happened, he slipped his arm around my shoulders. Sparks raced across my skin, straight into my heart, making it flutter. "So we don't get lost," Bowen said with a smug grin.

I just grinned at him and snaked one arm around his waist. Outside the convention centre, when the crowds had thinned, neither of us let go. Instead we strolled along like we were a couple, and I had to give my heart a stern talking-to about getting carried away. So the man had his arm around me? That didn't mean anything. Friends did that too.

We found a table at a nice little steakhouse and Bowen ordered half the menu. I ordered fish and salad and Bowen gave me a confused look. "We're at a steakhouse and you order fish? What kind of country girl are you?"

"The kind that doesn't particularly love red meat?"

Bowen sat back in seat, clutching his heart. "Blasphemy."

I laughed. "I'm surprised you do eat meat. How are you sure you're not eating one of those bulls you ride?"

"I've been bucked off a few that I wouldn't have minded serving up on a plate instead. Mean assholes, some of them."

"You'd probably be mean too if I tried to ride you..."

I closed my eyes as the words fell out of my lips. When I opened them, Bowen was laughing.

"Please stop. That did not come out the way I intended it to."

He winked at me, nodding in an exaggerated fashion. "Sure, sure. But for the record, Paisley. You can ride me anytime you want."

My face flushed hot and I dropped my gaze to my plate. I wasn't sure whether I wanted to leap across the table and straddle him right then and there or die of embarrassment. Both seemed viable options.

"You're cute when you're embarrassed."

I couldn't even look at the man. "You're not helping!" But I glanced up at him through my lashes and my heart just wanted to scream with giddy joy. He looked so relaxed. So sexy sitting back in his chair with his arms folded across his broad chest. I could only imagine the muscles he had hidden beneath that shirt.

He held my gaze and after a moment, I realised it was going on much too long. I needed to say something. "So, tell me about the rodeo."

Immediately, I knew it had been the wrong thing to say. His relaxed posture stiffened, and he sat straighter in his chair. He ran one hand through his short, fair hair and sighed.

"Well, basically, you get on the back of a pissed-off bull and try not to get your ass handed to you for eight seconds. Then you get the hell off and run for your life."

I shook my head. "I meant, tell me why you love it."

"I don't," he said simply.

I frowned. "Really?"

He sighed and leant forward, resting his elbows on the table. A waitress brought us our starters, and he thanked her, calling her ma'am which made me smile, but then he turned back to me.

"What is there to love? I'm thirty-four. I've got a list of injuries as long as you are tall. And I spend half the year away from my family, risking my life."

I prodded a piece of fried calamari with my fork. "So why do it?"

Bowen ran his hand over his stubbly beard. "That's the million-dollar question, isn't it?"

I waited for him to elaborate, not wanting to push him when it was obviously something he had trouble talking about. "I used to love it, you know? Back in the day, it was the biggest rush. Better than any drug you could ever take. And I craved it. I craved that adrenaline high like a true junkie."

He picked up his glass of bourbon, swishing it around making the ice clink before taking a sip. "And then my wife died while I was on tour. And everything changed."

A stab of sympathy caught me in the gut, but his words had me confused. "Why though?"

"Because I should have been home. I should have been home with her and Henry. If I had been, she wouldn't have been working out on the farm and her tractor wouldn't have rolled. But I was off chasing some stupid teenage dream.

Making us great money, but always leaving her and Henry alone."

He looked anguished as he said it. His pain, even years after his wife's death, still evident in the way his voice choked up.

"I'm sure she wanted you to chase your dreams," I said quietly, trying to ignore the red flags and sirens going off in my brain. I felt for him, but at the same time, I knew how it felt to be the woman left at home, raising kids and keeping everything running while somebody else went off and chased the glory. It was hard. And it was lonely.

"Yeah. She did. And that was the whole problem with our relationship. She always wanted the best for me. Always put me, and later Henry, first. And yet I never seemed to be able to do the same for her."

His eyes were full of pain when he looked up at me. "I was a shitty husband to her, Paisley. I didn't deserve her. And she died because of me."

I reached across the table and gripped his hand. "That's not true, I'm sure. It was an accident. There's nothing you could have done to prevent it."

"Nobody knows that. If I'd been home, things might have been different." He sighed hard, finally looking up at me again. "I want to give it up sometimes," he said.

"But..." Because I knew there was a but coming.

His eyes steeled. "I can't. I need to win."

I took a sip of wine, letting his words settle in the air around us. "It's not for the money, is it? It's for her?"

He nodded, relief flushing his features. "Yes, for her. Because if I don't win, then what was the point of me leaving her all the time? What was the point of her death?"

"That's a heavy burden to put on yourself, Bowen." I

squeezed his fingers. And when he looked up, I got lost in his eyes for a moment.

"Tonight is do or die. I've been riding like crap and I'm going to get eliminated tonight if I don't ride well."

I could see in his eyes and the taut line of his mouth just how much pressure he was feeling. "Can I come?" I asked.

He looked surprised. "To the rodeo?"

I stifled a laugh. "No, to the moon. Of course to the rodeo."

He groaned. "It's bad enough you watched my epic fail last round."

"Stop putting yourself down. You had a bad round, so what."

"I've had a bad year, Paisley. I get asked every week if I'm planning on retiring."

"But you can't until you win. Or until you die trying. Right?"

He knocked on the table with a chuckle. "Don't joke, it's a real possibility."

The thought made my stomach churn, but it didn't stop me from wanting to go. "So, can I come or do you have some superstition about people you know watching you?"

He shook his head. "No superstitions. I don't have much family. Just Dad and Henry, really. They don't come because Dad can't take the stress of watching me ride live. I call or text him at the end of every ride to let him know I'm okay, and prewarn him if I got kicked in the spleen or something so he knows what he's in for when he watches it on TV later."

I winced. "Did you really get kicked in the spleen?"

"At least a dozen times. You sure you still want to come? It's probably your last chance, 'cos if I'm bucked off tonight, that's it for my season."

I agreed before I could really let myself think about it. It made me sad to think of Bowen travelling the world, doing something he no longer loved with no one to cheer for him. I already knew from when I'd watched on TV that I was going to be a nervous wreck and I didn't have Stacey there to hang on to this time. But that wasn't going to stop me.

"You can't scare me that easy. I'm in."

$\mathcal{M}$y leg bounced nervously, my foot tapping the clutch of my Land Cruiser without actually pushing it in as I drove Paisley to the arena. She'd gotten changed into jeans and boots and had a scarf wrapped around her neck. With her hair pulled high on top of her head and big hoop earrings, she looked cute as hell. I wasn't sure what I was more nervous about. My rides tonight or being alone with her.

I showed the employee at the gate my pass and parked the car in the staff parking lot. Then I ran around to her side of the car to open her door, but by the time I got there, she was already standing on the pavement. I frowned at her. "You're supposed to let me do that, you know."

Her eyes were full of laughter. "You really are a gentleman, aren't you?"

"Yes, ma'am."

She rolled her eyes, and I grabbed her hand, loving the way her fingers fit between mine. Holding her hand was beginning to feel natural. Though I wasn't sure I'd ever get used to the way my palm tingled with hers pressed against it.

I tugged her arm, and she followed me towards the entrance to the huge arena. She shivered in the cool wind, and without thinking, I pulled her to me, wrapping an arm around her small shoulders and rubbing her arm briskly. Her hand found the small of back and that's how we walked into the rodeo. Me with a woman under my arm. Hell, it had been a long time since I'd done that. I'd never brought anyone to a rodeo before. Not since Camille.

In the tunnels beneath the arena, the first guy I saw was Deacon. I slipped my hand from Paisley's shoulder, finding her fingers again, and she followed me, waiting when Deacon and I hugged and slapped each other on the back. "Deac, this is Paisley. Paisley, Deacon."

Deacon took off his hat and held a hand out to Paisley. She took it with a smile and shook it firmly.

"I'm the best friend," he said with a grin. "Nice to meet you."

I shoved him. "Yeah, we're regular BFFs."

Deacon looked at me in confusion. "I don't have a clue what that means."

Paisley giggled and I rolled my eyes.

"You need to hang out with your godson more."

Deacon grinned at the mention of Henry. "That I do. When are you going to invite me over for dinner then, huh?"

"Come out to the farm and I'll cook you all the damn dinners you want."

Deacon grinned. "Fine. This week? Since we've got a week off between rounds, I'm hanging around Sydney for a bit. So are a lot of the other guys."

"Yeah? Bring 'em."

Deacon seemed surprised. "Really?" He glanced over at

Paisley and gave her his world-famous grin. The one that had won him Bachelor of the Year a few years ago and had his Instagram followers in the hundreds of thousands. "I don't know what you've done to my buddy here, but I like it."

He turned back to me. "I'll tell Johnny, yeah? Maybe Kai and Sunny too? I'm pretty sure they're all sticking around."

"Whoever you like, man. Just bring a sleeping bag. I'll even make a fire so you don't freeze your asses off out there."

Deacon shoved me, but when he spoke, it was to Paisley. "Such a charmer this one. I don't know what you see in him. I hope he doesn't make you sleep outside with the bulls as well?"

Paisley laughed, her cheeks going pink. "Not yet."

Deacon punched me in the arm. "Hey, where's your dad and Henry? I thought you said they were coming?"

I shook my head. "They got a better deal. They're hanging with Paisley's kids."

"Nice. Anyway, I've gotta go get ready." He turned back to Paisley. "I'll see you when I come out to the farm this week, yeah?"

"Uh," she mumbled, glancing over at me.

I wanted to say hell yes, she'll be there. The idea of having Paisley and the guys and their families out at my place for the week sounded amazing. But I didn't want to put her on the spot either.

Thankfully, Deacon wasn't waiting around for an answer. He shoved his hat back on his head and stalked off into the depths of the arena, likely looking for his team.

Speaking of, I needed to be doing the same. "Come on. I'll show you where your seat is."

I led Paisley through the mostly empty stadium, flashing my pass at the handful of security guards we had to get through to find the family areas. They were just regular seats within the crowd, but they were right by the chute.

A couple of the guys' wives and girlfriends and their kids were already sitting there, chatting amongst themselves. I searched the small group, wondering who I could leave Paisley with. I hated leaving her there by herself, though she obviously knew I wouldn't be sitting with her. But I wanted her to feel comfortable. Spotting Isabel's dark mane of hair, I made a beeline in her direction. She'd married Johnny West years ago and never missed one of his rides.

"Isabel," I called, and she looked over from her conversation, her face breaking into a grin.

"Bowen! What are you doing up here?" Then she peered around me to where Paisley stood, then back at me in surprise.

Paisley stepped around me, holding out her hand to the woman. "Hi, I'm Paisley."

Isabel stood, and to everyone's surprise, she pulled Paisley in for a hug. Then grasped her hand and shook it hard. "It's so nice to meet you." Then she turned to me. "You go. I've got her."

I shot her a relieved look of thanks, then turned to Paisley. "You'll be okay?"

She laughed like I was crazy. "Of course. Go do your cowboy thing. I'll be cheering."

"Okay." I paused. I wanted to lean in and kiss her. Just a peck on the lips as a goodbye for now. It felt like the natural thing to do, especially after we'd been holding hands all day. But then I hadn't kissed her at all yet. And I didn't want our first kiss to be some peck. And not with a group full of women and kids staring at us.

She took a step closer, seeming uncertain too, then wrapped her arms around my middle in a hug. Without any conscious thought, I pulled her tight to my chest. For the tiniest moment, I breathed in her scent, pulling it all the way to the bottom of my lungs and letting it linger there. God she felt so good. And it would have been so easy to tip her chin up and claim her mouth. Every inch of me wanted to do it.

Before I could do anything though, she was pulling away, looking flushed. "Go," she whispered. "I'm fine."

I nodded, forcing myself to walk away.

"Oh, Bowen?"

I turned back around. Her hair was backlit by the stadium lights, giving her a glow that made her look almost angelic.

"Yeah?"

"Good luck."

15

PAISLEY

*I*sabel and the other wives and girlfriends all crowded me the minute Bowen walked away. Isabel, with her cat-like green eyes, pounced on me. "Tell all, girl."

"Sorry?"

"Are you two together?" she asked.

I shook my head quickly. "Oh no, no, nothing like that."

"Really?"

"Really." I insisted. "We're just friends. Our boys play video games together."

Isabel's face fell.

"Um, sorry?" I apologised, not really sure why.

She patted my arm. "No, no, I just... Bowen hasn't brought anyone to the rodeo since his wife..."

"Oh."

"It's been a long time, you know? And I was just hoping that maybe he'd found some happiness. He always looks so sad."

"He does?"

"You haven't noticed?"

I thought about it, and sure, Bowen had his sullen moments. And he'd definitely looked sad today when he'd been talking about the guilt and pressure he carried around over his wife's death. But I wouldn't have said he always looked sad. We'd spent a lot of time laughing.

"No," I replied honestly.

Isabel smiled softly. "He's happy when he's with you then." She glanced around the rapidly filling arena before her gaze settled back on me. "I'm really glad to hear that." Her voice was sincere and strong.

Warmth rolled through me. Isabel's words felt like a blessing. And although I knew I didn't need one from this woman I'd only known for a few minutes, I was pleased to have it anyway. She'd known his wife, and maybe somewhere, some part of me felt like a blessing from Isabel was a blessing from Camille too.

We quieted as the stadium darkened and cheered as the men paraded the arena, waving to the crowd. Then they were gone and the announcer was calling up the first rider.

"Bowen Barclay with the first ride of the night, ladies and gentlemen."

I sucked in a deep breath, my nerves threatening to get the best of me. I'd thought I'd have a few rides to warm up and relax a little, but that obviously wasn't to be. A bull was let into the chute and began thrashing around when the gate closed behind him. I jumped as his hooves clanged off the metal, and Isabel grabbed my hand.

"Oh, honey, is this your first time? I should have warned you. It's more intense than watching it on the TV."

I nodded, taking a deep breath to calm my nerves. I tried to block out the noise of the bull, who looked mad as a cut snake. The front row seats might have had the best view in the house, but it also meant I could see and hear everything.

I saw Bowen appear above the chute and watched his team move around him like clockwork. They'd obviously done this a thousand times, each knowing their role and playing it to perfection to get Bowen on the bull safely.

But god, it was hard to watch. Bowen's mouth was pulled tight, concentration etched on his face. He found his seat and worked the rope, wrapping it around his hand and fingers and sliding forward into the correct position. At the last moment, he looked up and his determined gaze clashed with mine, freezing me to my spot. And then his eyes glazed over, and he nodded to his gate man. The gate sprung open.

The bull was huge, his shoulders wide, his body bulky as he kicked and spun his way into the arena. He had none of the grace of some of the other bulls who seemed to spin in almost delicate, predictable circles. No, this bull spun every which way, bucking, then changing directions, bellowing his frustrations and throwing his head around in an attempt to force Bowen off his back.

My lungs sputtered out a breath, and they ached for fresh air, but I just couldn't. Not until he made it.

Bowen's body moved in sharp jerks, his hand up high, well away from the beast's hide. I could see the look of concentration every time the bull spun him in my direction. His every muscle seemed to be pulled taut and I willed him to hang on.

The buzzer sounded, and Isabel and I leapt to our feet, cheering madly. Bowen's head snapped up as if he was shocked he'd made the time. In a flash, he had his hand untangled and was jumping off the bull's back. He landed in the dirt and sawdust that had been laid on the arena floor and sprinted for the sidelines, scaling the barrier. And I found myself face to face with him.

He breathed hard as his eyes locked with mine, and I just grinned stupidly at him.

"Hi."

"Hi, yourself."

His grin stretched ear to ear.

"Bowen, your score." From the corner of my eye, I saw it flashing in lights, but my gaze was glued to his. I couldn't look away.

"Don't care. Come here, Paisley," he commanded, his voice low and rough and full of emotion.

I couldn't have denied him even if I wanted to. I stepped forward, as if drawn by a magnet, and he freed one hand from the railing, using it to grasp my chin. My heart pounded in my chest. My breathing faltered. Then his lips crashed down on mine.

The crowd around us screamed, but I barely heard above the rush of blood in my ears. Bowen's mouth claimed mine in a demanding kiss that seared my soul. I opened for him, letting him in, our tongues clashing and duelling, all while I fought to get closer to him. My fists found the collar of his shirt as he gripped the back of my head, and we tugged each other closer, both of us uncaring that our kiss was being shared by everyone in the arena. It didn't matter. All that mattered was the feel of his hard body around mine, his lips sending sparks across my skin, and the way he made my stomach flip.

When we finally broke apart, we were both breathing hard. Bowen grinned, kissing me quickly on the lips again before he turned around and waved to the crowd once more. Our embrace was being replayed on the big screen, and I went pink with embarrassment.

But when he turned back and gave me a look so hot it

melted my insides, I didn't regret a thing. I'd kiss him a million times over if they were all like that.

There were two things I learned that night. Bowen Barclay could ride a bull with the best of them. And his kiss alone had the potential to make me fall in love with him.

16

BOWEN

$\mathcal{I}$ rode my second bull of the night with a confidence I hadn't felt all season. Instead of forcing my mind to go blank like I normally did, I focussed on Paisley, and the way she'd felt in my arms. When the bull spun to the right, I went with him, remembering the way her lips had opened under mine and the way her breasts had crushed against my chest. When he kicked out, I remembered her skin breaking out into tiny bumps as I'd grasped the back of her neck, holding her to me. Before I even knew what was happening the buzzer was sounding and I was hitting the sawdust, punching the air in victory.

The score wasn't as high as my first ride, but when the numbers flashed up on the screen, I knew it was enough to take out the round. I climbed over the railing, where Paisley was cheering her sweet ass off, and grabbed her hand, dragging her along as I made my way back through the tunnels to the changing rooms. She laughed as she trotted along behind me, and the sound was like pure magic to my already racing heart. Ducking down a side corridor, I pulled her to a stop and closed in on her, finding her mouth in the dim light and fusing it to mine. She let out a little gasp, but then her hands were around my neck, pulling me closer. That little gasp went straight to my cock.

Lifting her back a step, I pushed her up against the wall, grinding my body into hers, getting totally carried away, but her soft moans only encouraged me. Our tongues moved in unison, and my cock ached with the overwhelming sensation of having her body pressed against me. We made out like horny teenagers sneaking kisses behind the football bleachers.

"You were so good out there," she murmured when I broke away to trail feverish kisses down her neck. I pulled back. Her happy smile and well-kissed lips sent a feeling of pride through me.

"Yeah?"

"It was kind of hot."

I chuckled. "You're more than kind of hot."

She bit her lip and damn if I didn't just want to do the same thing. But it wasn't the time or the place. We'd gone from nothing to one hundred in the space of an evening.

"I'm sorry, though. I shouldn't have kissed you in front of everyone like that."

She shook her head. "I didn't mind. I wanted you to."

"That so?"

"The chaps really do it for me." She laughed and ran her hand over my thigh, fingering the fringe on the sides.

"Good to know." I leant in and kissed her again, this time slower, but it didn't do anything to settle the erection threatening to bust through my zipper. Reluctantly, I pulled away.

"So, what now?"

"Well, first, I ring my dad and tell him not to let our kids watch the replay."

Paisley's eyes widened. "How are you going to explain that one?"

I kissed her again, just because I could. "I'm going to tell him that our kids don't need to find out like that, but that I kissed my good luck charm tonight and won the whole damn round."

"I'm good luck, huh?"

I brushed a strand of blonde hair out of her eyes. "You must be. 'Cos standing here right now, kissing you, makes me the luckiest man alive."

She pushed me away playfully. "Charmer."

I pulled her right back in. "I meant it."

Reluctantly, I left her sitting on a bench outside the locker room. Inside, I headed for the locker I'd been given for the night. I jabbed in the combination, stabbing at the buttons, impatient to get back to Paisley. It was only eleven and we were a couple of country kids out in the city. And child-free too. The night was young.

Deacon's booming voice rang out around the locker room and he thumped me on the back hard. "Knew you had it in you still!"

"Just scraped into the next round by the skin of my teeth," I said with a laugh.

"Maybe so, but you did it with style, taking out the whole round. Nice job, man."

"Sorry to steal your thunder." Deacon had been the favourite to take out the competition. He was ranked in the top ten in the world and had been rapidly climbing over the last few years. I couldn't have been happier for him. But that didn't mean I didn't want to kick his ass. With one good night, I was back in the game.

"Hey, I'm grateful for the competition. None of these other assholes come close," he said, deliberately loud so the other guys would hear. He winked at me as a chorus of protests rang out. Sunny threw a boot at Deacon's head, which he somehow ducked, despite having his back to the rookie from the States.

"Sunny, you want to come hang out at the farm this week? Rough it a little instead of sleeping in them fancy hotels?" I called to him.

He nodded quickly, reaching out to fist bump me. "I'm in. I hate the fucking city." I knew that, which was exactly why I'd invited him. Sunny hailed from the middle of nowhere in Texas and felt most at home with wide blue skies overhead and fresh dirt under his boots.

"Nice. Bring Kai up with you too, yeah? That kid needs to get out more." Kai was another American young gun. He was a hell of a rider but the kid spent all his time in his hotel room, studying his rides and going to bed early. It was probably why he was so good. He was a threat to take Deacon's number one spot as well. But at twenty-one, he was also missing out on a hell of a lot. Apart from his friendship with Sunny which predated their rise to the professional levels, he was a loner on the circuit. The dad in me wanted to see him fit in, because he was going to be around for a long time. He needed to make more friends. He reminded me too much of myself in my early years. If I could save him from himself, I would.

"I'll see what I can do." Sunny said. "By the way, did you see the draw for the next meet?"

I shucked off my vest, pushed it into my bag, and shook my head. "That up already?"

"The whole rest of the season is up."

"No lie?"

"Swear on my life. It's posted on the wall outside."

I shoved my arms in my jacket and hoisted my bag onto

my shoulder. "See you during the week? Don't get lost." Sunny had been out to my place a few times before over the last two years so I knew he'd manage the long drive without a problem.

"Let's go check the draw, yeah?" Deacon asked, grabbing his own bag and striding impatiently out the locker room doors.

In the hall, Paisley jumped up when she saw me, and all thoughts of the draw disintegrated from my head. I linked my fingers through hers and pulled her close. I pressed my lips to her temple, breathing in the scent of her shampoo, and was glad I'd decided to change my clothes so the smell of bull and sweat didn't overwhelm her delicate scent. "Hey there," she greeted me, and I bent my head towards hers to kiss her again. I couldn't help it. I was suddenly allowed to do that, and it felt amazing.

"Bowen." Deacon's voice stopped me before our lips touched.

"What!" I snapped, irritated by the interruption.

"You're gonna want to look at this." He tapped his fingers on the paper sheet stuck to the wall and grimaced.

Shit. "Who'd I draw? Just tell me quick, Deac. If it's bad, don't string it out."

"Rampage."

I stilled.

"Is that bad?" Paisley asked with concern on her face. She squeezed my fingers, and it matched the squeezing sensation I suddenly felt around my chest.

"I can't," I choked out.

Deacon clasped my shoulder. "Yeah, you can, man. It's just a bull. And you know you can ride him."

Paisley was staring at me with worried eyes, and despite the fact I could barely breathe, I reached out and smoothed the lines off her forehead. All I could think about was that I'd been riding Rampage while Camille lay dying under her rolled tractor. Images flashed through my head, making nausea rise in my stomach. I took a deep breath and pushed the memory away. I'd always known that at some point I'd probably draw him again, but it had been four years and it hadn't happened. I'd grown complacent.

"Let's go," I said to Paisley, sliding my arm around her back. I kissed the top of her head. "I don't want to think about bulls when I could be thinking about you."

17

PAISLEY

The rest of the weekend whirled by, and all too soon, Bowen was dropping the kids and me off at our door. He helped me carry the luggage in while Henry waited in the car. We still hadn't told the kids about us yet, and we'd managed to keep them away from the footage of our kiss, so we'd been keeping our distance when they were around. Bowen stopped in the doorway after the last bag was unloaded and threw a glance over his shoulder. Henry was watching us with impatience written all over his face. Both he and Aiden had been itching to get home and try out the new games Bowen had bought them at the convention.

Bowen sighed heavily, his gaze hot. "I want to kiss you so badly right now. Sitting next to you for eight hours in the car and not being able to touch you was torture."

God, he knew all the right things to say. I'd never had a man be so open and honest with his feelings and the way he looked at me... Well, if there'd been a chance to rip his clothes off in private, I would have taken it.

"We need to tell them. And then you can do that anytime you want."

Bowen grinned like a kid in a candy shop. "I like the sound of that."

Oh god, so did I.

"Do you want to come out to my place one night this week? A couple of the guys from the circuit are coming out to stay. I'll barbeque and we'll have a bonfire."

"I don't know if Mum will want to mind the kids again."

"Please? I really want to see you again. And I don't want to wait all week."

"You see me every night while we pretend to play video games."

"Not enough."

My eyes dipped to his lips and I had to fight to keep myself from launching at him.

"And if she can't watch them, bring them. Whatever you have to do. Just come."

How was I supposed to say no when he looked so damn sexy, begging me to hang out with him and his friends?

From the corner of my eye, I saw Henry lean on the horn, the blaring noise making Bowen swear quietly under his breath.

"You better go," I laughed.

I walked him to his car and waved as they pulled away. Thank god he'd suggested a midweek date because I already had no idea how I was going to last a few days without seeing him. I wrapped my arms around myself and gave a little squeal of happiness.

I turned to head back to the house, stopping to check the mailbox as I did. I didn't expect anything exciting, since the mailman didn't come over the weekend. It was a relief, really. If he didn't come, he couldn't bring me any bills I wouldn't be able to pay. I sighed, sifting through a few shop catalogues and a brochure for a local plumber. At the bottom of the pile, a plain white envelope with my name printed neatly on the front caught my attention. It had no stamp or postmark, so it had to have been hand-delivered. Flipping it over, there was no return address either. I slowly walked up the path to my door, ripping the envelope open as I went.

Inside was a single sheet of paper. I shut the door behind me, and once I'd dumped the rest of the mail into the recycling bin, I unfolded it.

My fingers started to shake as I read the bold print. Tears built in the backs of my eyes, then threatened to spill over, but I blinked them back angrily. Checking quickly to make sure the kids were upstairs and engrossed in their iPads, I stormed back down, picking up my phone and bringing up the number I wished I could just lose forever.

It rang for ages, and when he finally answered, his voice was lazy, like I'd interrupted him from a nap. Or more likely, he just couldn't be bothered answering my call.

"You asshole!" I whisper-yelled at him, storming through the house and into the laundry. It was the furthest I could get from the kids' bedrooms without actually leaving the house. I shut the door quietly, so they didn't realise I was about to throw down with their father, but it was so unsatisfying. I wanted to slam that door so hard it fell off its hinges.

"Hello to you too, Paisley. I guess you're home from your little trip away."

I could practically hear the disdain in his voice and it only riled me up more. "What? Are you spying on me now?"

I could practically hear his eyes rolling.

"Small town. Word gets around."

Whatever. I didn't have the time or patience to go down that rabbit warren today.

"Why do I have an eviction notice in my mailbox? I've

missed one payment, and I called your office to let them know it would be a little late. You can't evict me for one late payment. It's not legal."

"First. We don't have a contract. And my company owns the house you live in. So actually yes, I can evict you."

My stomach churned with hate. How had I ever been in love with this man? He was a vile human being. Those angry tears were back, and this time, I knew there was no stopping them. "Why?"

"You don't have the income to pay for the rent, Paisley. I know you lost your job."

I bristled. He was spying on me for sure. Or someone close to me was feeding him information. Possibly both. "I'm going to get another one."

"Maybe so, but I need the house back. It's not personal, it's business. I've kept the rent low for you, but I'm getting way under market value. Will you be able to afford five hundred and fifty dollars a week?"

My mouth dropped open. That was more than double what I was paying him now. "Your children live here, do you remember that?"

His voice didn't even falter. "Don't be dramatic. We both know your mother has a big house, with more than enough room for all of you. You'll go there, and I'll get new tenants in. Everyone is happy."

Everyone is happy? He couldn't possibly think that. The only person who would be happy in that situation would be him. He didn't seem to care that he'd be uprooting our entire lives. "I don't know what I ever saw in you." Seething anger curled around me, making me grip the phone so hard I was surprised it didn't crack beneath my fingers.

"Yeah, well, the feeling is mutual."

I hung up before I could let loose with the torrent of rage that burned my tongue. Instead I slid down onto the laundry floor, shoved the sleeve of my jumper in my mouth, and let my tears fall.

18

PAISLEY

*T*he morning after my phone call with Jonathan, Aiden tiptoed into my room. There was no hiding my tear-stained face from him. I'd spent all night crying and worrying over where we'd live and what I'd do for money. He crawled in beside me, suddenly seeming much younger than his ten years, and wrapped his skinny arms around me. We held each other quietly, me hating myself for letting him see me so weak. I knew I was scaring him. He'd found me in the same position when his father had left two years earlier.

"It's not like last time, buddy. I promise." I knew he was remembering how I'd completely fallen apart. I'd sunk into a depression so deep I wasn't sure I could make it out. It had taken months of intense therapy. It was something I'd likely have to manage for the rest of my life.

"I just got some bad news yesterday. But I'm going to work it out, okay?"

He nodded. Then he untangled himself from me and told me he'd get Lily ready for school so I could sleep in. And I let him take care of me. I slept all day. But by the time they got home, I was up, showered, and searching online job listings.

When Bowen rang, I'd already applied for two jobs within the local area. Neither paid quite as much as my previous job did, but out here, you couldn't afford to be picky.

I plastered a smile on my face and answered the video call.

"Hey, gorgeous," he drawled.

"What if my kids had been standing behind me?"

He shrugged. "Pretty sure they already know you're gorgeous."

God. This man.

"I missed you online last night. Everything okay?"

"Yep! Everything's great," I lied. I wasn't about to unload all my ex-husband and financial dramas onto Bowen. Not this early in our relationship. And anyway, hopefully it wouldn't be a drama much longer. I'd get a job, and I'd pay Jonathan's ridiculous new rent for a while, just to prove to him I could, and in the meantime, I'd find myself a new place. I'd leave on my own terms, just to spite him. Asshole.

Bowen looked relieved. "Come out to my place tonight then?"

"Tonight?"

"Mmm-hmm. I want to see you."

"You saw me yesterday."

"The guys are all here already. They got in around lunchtime. Johnny and Isabel are here too. I know she'd love another woman's company. Come for dinner. If you leave now, you'll make it in time."

After spending the day wallowing, a night out in the country air around a bonfire sounded like heaven. "You twisted my arm. Just let me call my mum to come watch the kids."

Bowen coughed, suddenly looking uncomfortable. "Uh, that might be a problem."

"What? Why?"

He held one finger up and said, "Wait." The picture went blurry and I heard a screen door slam. Then there was the sound of voices, and finally, a face appeared on the screen.

"Mum!" I yelled. Then lowered my voice so the kids wouldn't hear. "Oh my god, why are you at Bowen's place?"

She frowned. "I'm not! I'm at Alan's."

"They live on the same property, Mother! And my question still stands, why are you there?"

She laughed and I noticed something was different about her. It took me a moment to work it out, but then I realised her hair was loose, falling down her back in waves. I hadn't seen her wear it out...ever.

"We left the city later than all of you yesterday. It was late by the time we got back, so I just stayed at Alan's place."

My eyes widened. "Mum, you didn't..."

She winked at me. "Oh, but I did."

I closed my eyes. Oh. My. God. My straitlaced mother, who hadn't so much as looked at a man in twenty years, was sleeping with my...my Bowen's father. A man she'd met less than a week ago. And worse. She was telling me about it. I'd apparently walked into a parallel universe.

But as I took in her relaxed face, I couldn't help but smile. She looked happy. That was also a bit of a foreign expression for her. Sure, she smiled and laughed, especially when my kids were around, but I couldn't really say she'd ever looked truly as happy as she did right now. I realised suddenly how lonely her life was. Apart from the kids and me, she really didn't have much to fill her time.

I reined in my surprise and tried to act as if she were my friend instead of the woman who gave birth to me. "Good for you."

"Are you coming out for dinner?"

"You're staying?"

She nodded. I laughed. "Sure, Mum. I'll come meet your new boyfriend, shall I?"

"He's even got this single, handsome son you might—"

I hung up the phone before she could carry on anymore.

I downloaded the map to Bowen's place in Erraville, knowing the internet on my reception might drop out halfway and I didn't want to be stranded in the middle of farm country without a working phone. As it turned out, there were only about three roads I had to take to get from my place to Bowen's. It's just those roads were really, really long.

I pulled into his gravel driveway right before the sun sunk over the horizon. I couldn't even see the house. And as the car trundled along, I prayed I was going the right way. The number on the mailbox had definitely said 678 though, and that was the number Bowen had given me, so I kept driving.

We rounded a corner and drove up a steep hill, and when I hit the crest, my foot fell off the accelerator.

"Holy crap!" Aiden yelled from the back seat, and I didn't even tell him off about his language, because really, holy crap was an understatement. Bowen didn't have a house. He didn't have a farm. Bowen had a ranch. I didn't even know if we called them that in Australia, but the term "farmhouse" was sooooo underwhelming while I was staring at a house that had to have cost millions. The house was single story, but long and wide, with a veranda wrapping around the front. A veranda! Who even had those anymore? But I fell in love with it immediately. Floor-to-ceiling windows and a corrugated iron roof all gave it an expensive yet still country feel. Garden lights dotted the front yard, and as I let the car roll down the hill, I realised fairy lights twinkled in the trees at the back.

Simply, it was magical.

The kids piled out of the car as soon as it stopped, and I tried calling them back, but I knew they'd just go find Henry. And I couldn't stop staring at the house. I got out slowly, closing the door behind me, and just wandered around the side, gazing up at the building and taking in all the little details. It was as if someone had taken an image of my dream house from my brain and planted it right here on the dust-red dirt.

Warm hands snaked around me from behind, and I jumped before Bowen's rumble purred in my ear. "You found me," he murmured.

I turned in his arms and smiled up at him. He was still wearing his Akubra even though the sun had all but lost its battle with darkness. "I did. This place is amazing."

He dropped a quick kiss on my lips then pulled away before one of our kids saw. "Come on, I'll give you the grand tour."

His fingers slipped between mine and I followed him eagerly up a set of steps and through the main door. Inside, the ceilings were high, with exposed beams. The walls were wood panelled, and thick cream-coloured carpet squished beneath my feet. "Living room," Bowen said, pointing, but he didn't slow down for me to take in all the details. "Kitchen."

I almost moaned in pleasure when I took in the huge island bench covered in a dark-coloured stone bench top.

"Bathroom. Guest room. Henry's room. My room," Bowen said in quick succession. He pulled me into his room and closed the door. As soon as the lock clicked shut, his lips were on mine. His hands cradled my face and he kissed with urgency, stealing my breath. I closed my eyes and let my fingers trail over his sides and around to his back, pulling him closer to me. All my worries over Jonathan and the house and my job, and the fact that Bowen was obviously a very rich man, evaporated under the intensity of his kiss. And it was all I could do to mumble "Kids?" as his fingers nimbly worked the buttons on my shirt.

He pushed the plaid material off my shoulder, taking my singlet and bra strap with it, baring my skin to his mouth. He sucked and licked and kissed a trail across my collarbone, and my head dropped back on my shoulders as he tongued the swell of my breasts.

"They're playing outside. Dad and your mum are there. They'll be fine for five minutes."

"Just five minutes?" The words were practically a whine but Bowen's hands were sliding over my breasts and the fact that there was material between his hands and my nipples was maddening. I wanted to rip my shirt and peel off my bra and have him really touch me.

He chuckled into my skin. "Maybe ten."

My shirt fell to the floor, and Bowen's fingers made quick work of my singlet, throwing it in a heap by our feet. I stood in jeans and a bra, with his lips on my neck as he reached around and undid the clasp. I moaned my satisfaction as his lips found mine again, his hands coasting up my stomach and under the cups of my bra. I pulled it off the rest of the way.

I should have been horrified that I was half naked with a crowd of people out in the backyard. I could hear the faint sounds of music and laughter but after my shitty day, all I wanted to do was feel.

Bowen broke away, ducking his mouth to suck one of my nipples, and heat shot straight between my legs. His other hand fondled me, tweaking and teasing until my hips were pressing against him and I was eyeing his bed, wondering if we had time for me to rip his jeans off and straddle him. His hard length pressed against my stomach and my insides felt hollow. I wanted him. I wanted him inside me, filling me, sucking my breasts while his fingers found my clit.

I reached for his fly, but he caught my hand. "I can't," he whispered.

I wanted to cry. I so badly wanted to slip my hands into his Wranglers and feel exactly how thick and long he was. I wanted to drop to my knees and take him in my mouth and taste him.

"Why not?"

"Because I don't want our first time to be a quickie. I want to do this right."

If swooning was a real thing, that's what I did. "What if I want a quickie?" I begged. Because God, I'd take this man in any way, shape, or form I could get him.

He bit my bottom lip gently, drawing it into his mouth, stopping my protests. Then he scooped up my clothes from the bedroom floor and started dressing me again.

I pouted as he threaded my arms through my bra strap and he leaned in, his lips brushing the shell of my ear. "Trust me, you don't want a quickie. You want me to go slow with you. You want me touching and tasting every inch of your body before I slide inside of you."

Well, when he put it like that...

I smoothed my hair back and straightened my clothes, because as it turned out, Bowen was better at undressing me than he was at putting my clothes back on.

"Do I look okay?"

He cast an appraising eye over me, a smug grin spreading over his face. "You look thoroughly kissed and turned on."

I slapped his chest. "Bowen! Seriously!"

He threaded his fingers through mine and unlocked the door. "You look amazing. Just like you do every time I see you. Nobody will even remotely be able to tell I was just considering going down on you."

"Oh my god, stop it." I blushed bright red, but followed him out in the backyard, where a small group of people had gathered. I recognised Isabel's dark hair, and Deacon sat at a fire with a few other guys. They all looked up as we walked out and Deacon wolf-whistled. "Where have you two been, huh?"

Bowen shot him a murderous glare, nodding his head in the direction of our three children playing to one side of the fire, and Deacon gave us a wink that said he knew exactly where we'd been.

Awkward.

"Sorry," Bowen whispered to me. "I'll kill him later."

"I kind of hope you'll be doing something else later," I whispered back, feeling bold.

Bowen rounded on me, his eyes wide. "You want to stay?"

I shrugged. "I'd have to leave early to get the kids to school on time still, but..." I knew I was talking with my hormones, but after the little preview I'd just had, I wanted more.

An all-out delighted smirk spread across his face. "You're staying."

I grinned back, tucking that little secret away in the back of my mind. The feel of his lips all over my breasts and neck and mouth still lingered. There was no way I wanted to go home and spend another night crying over my pathetic situation. It was sad and lonely. I didn't want to feel like that when I could be here, surrounded by people and in the arms of a man who gave me goosebumps whenever he looked at me.

Bowen towed me around the circle of people sitting around the fire, introducing me to the ones I didn't know, and then left me with Isabel.

She elbowed me and moved her head close to mine. "If I didn't know better," she said out of the corner of her mouth, "I'd think you just got lucky."

Heat flushed my face. Dammit. I knew I should have checked in the mirror before we came down here. Maybe Bowen had been telling the truth when he'd said I looked thoroughly kissed and turned on. God. How embarrassing. My mother and Alan were here!

"No, no. No getting lucky." I held my hands out to the fire and avoided Isabel's shrewd gaze.

Finally she said, "I don't know about that. I think Bowen got pretty lucky when he found you. I haven't seen him this happy in a long time."

I glanced back at her. "Really?"

She nodded, flicking her head in the direction of the barbeque where Bowen stood flipping steaks with Johnny, Isabel's husband, and one of the young guys, Sunny. He had a big smile on his face as he laughed at something Johnny said, but he kept shooting little glances in my direction. When he realised I was watching him, he threw me a wink and I wondered how that wink made the man even more attractive. It had to be a sin to be so good-looking.

"So I guess you're his good luck charm, in and out of the rodeo?"

"He said much the same thing."

Isabel picked at a piece of lint on her dress. "They all have them, you know."

"Good luck charms?"

"Yeah. Johnny's is his hat. He always wears the same hat to each and every rodeo. The only two times he's ever been seriously hurt was when he wasn't wearing that hat. So now he's superstitious about it."

I thought about that for a moment. "Bowen doesn't have one already?"

She shook her head. "Not that I know of. And he hasn't had much luck in the rodeo in a long time. Or in his personal life, really. It's no surprise he's latched on to you as quick as he did."

An uncomfortable idea settled in the back of my head. A tiny voice whispering that perhaps Bowen only wanted me around because he somehow thought I'd helped him win. But then I pushed the thoughts away. That was ridiculous. He'd lost the night I watched him on the TV. And anyway, he'd wanted to kiss me long before the night at the rodeo. He'd nearly kissed me that night on my doorstep after we'd spent the night in hospital with Lily. There'd been chemistry between us long before his win. There was no truth to the insecure thoughts running through my head. I knew that tiny voice belonged to Jonathan, and the years of neglect I'd received when I'd been with him. I knew his voice had been stirred up by everything that had happened with him and the house in the last couple of days.

I closed the door on his insidious whispers and focussed

on my cowboy striding across the lawn with eyes only for me.

I couldn't keep my eyes off Paisley. She practically glowed in the firelight. I'd been worried at first that it might be weird having another woman in my house. The same house I'd shared with my wife once upon a time. But as soon as I'd seen her get out of her car, her long blonde hair falling down her back in a loose braid, I'd forgotten all about my worries. My excitement about seeing her had been all I could think of. And then I'd gotten her alone in my room and all thoughts of past lives had evaporated. Paisley was all creamy skin and softness. Her breasts filled my hands, the small nipples hardening under my touch. My dick doing the same behind my fly.

When she'd gone for my pants, I'd had to summon up every ounce of willpower to stop her. But tonight, nothing would stop her. I'd let her do whatever the hell she wanted. After I was through doing a whole list of things to her.

I forced myself to stop thinking about it before I ended up with another boner that I couldn't hide. Wouldn't Deacon and the rest of them have a field day with that.

Instead I filled three little plates full of food for Henry,

Aiden, and Lily, and sent them off to watch a movie while
they ate. Then I filled two adult-sized plates for Paisley and
me. All the while I could feel Paisley's eyes on me. I'd waved
her off when she'd tried to get up to prepare food for her
kids. And she'd sat back down with the beer Isabel had
handed her and watched me with a gentle smile.

When I strode across the yard towards her, her eyes
roamed over me slowly. My body buzzed under her gaze. I
handed her a plate and leant in close. "If you keep looking
at me like that, we aren't going to make it through the end of
dinner." Then I sat down beside her, balancing my own
plate of food on my knees.

Deacon and Sunny were deep in discussion about something to my left, with Kai sitting on Sunny's other side,
quietly listening, only speaking when spoken to.

"What's happening?" I asked.

Deacon sat back in his chair, chewing and swallowing
before he answered me. "Sunny and I were just talking
about heading into Gulgarren Rodeo this weekend, since we
have the weekend off."

I snorted. "You want to go to the little local rodeo that
you aren't even eligible to compete in? On your one week
off?"

Sunny nodded enthusiastically. Kai, behind him, did too.

"What are you going to do there if you can't even ride the
bulls?"

Sunny bounced on his chair like a puppy. "Ride the
Ferris wheel."

Kai rolled his eyes. "More like he thinks he's gonna meet
some pretty young thing and make out with her on it."

It was the longest sentence I'd heard the kid utter
unprompted. I handed him another beer. I liked this Kai
who talked and put Sunny in his place.

"Some of the bulls we're riding in the next few rounds will be there. I want to check 'em out. See how they're performing."

I nodded slowly. "Rampage?"

Deac nodded. "You in?"

"Yeah, man. I'm in. I need to study up on him anyway."

He slapped my hand, and we both went back to our food. The night rolled on, music was turned up, and alcohol flowed. Isabel dragged Johnny up to slow dance in the moonlight, and the two of them ignored Sunny's and Deacon's catcalls. Dad offered his hand to Paisley's mother. Part of me was completely disturbed by their new...friendship. But the other part of me wanted to high-five my old man. He deserved some happiness, and Paisley's mother did seem real nice.

"Come dance?" I asked Paisley, and she nodded. I moved her to the far side of the fire though, out of earshot of the others, while Blake Shelton's "Sangria" filtered through the night sky.

I pulled her into my arms, and she rested her head on my chest as we swayed from side to side.

"Do you all party like this every Tuesday?" she asked quietly.

"Only every other week."

I inched closer, loving the feel of her against my body. She was much smaller than my solid frame, but she fit so perfectly within my arms I was confused as to how she hadn't been there forever. "No, I'm joking. The boys do come out from time to time when we've had rodeos in Sydney. We all ride pro, and tomorrow, we'll all be practicing. But tonight, we can let our hair down. Advantages of not having a nine to five."

"I'm really glad I came. Your friends are great."

"I hope I'll get to meet yours soon."

"You really want that?"

I pulled back, searching her face. A flicker of doubt was quickly replaced by a smile, but I saw it.

"Wait 'til you meet my best friend, Stacey. She's a whirlwind."

"In what way?"

She laughed. "In every way? She's loud, she's crazy. She's always full of big ideas that usually land us in trouble."

"She sounds like fun."

"She is. Unless you're spending the night in jail for streaking through a city street."

I stopped dancing. "You did that?"

She nodded sheepishly. I tucked her head beneath my chin again, a laugh rumbling up my chest. Who knew Paisley had wild side?

"In my defence, I was drunk and nineteen. I wouldn't do it now."

"I wouldn't mind if you wanted to. I've got a paddock over there that could use some nudity."

She shoved my chest. "Stop. I'm sure it's already seen some nudity in its time."

"Deacon does have a penchant for getting his gear off."

The song finished and another country anthem started playing, but Paisley pulled reluctantly away. "We should check on the kids."

I couldn't deny that. I led her back past the fire to the door of the house the kids had disappeared through earlier, and we traipsed through, searching for signs of them. They weren't in Henry's bedroom, but we found the three of them in the living room. Their half-eaten plates of food had been abandoned, and the three lay in a row on the soft carpet in sleeping bags Henry must have pulled out of the linen cupboard. The movie still rolled but the lights were dim and all three kids were sound asleep.

I looked to Paisley in surprise and she pulled out her phone, blanching when she saw the time. "It's ten already! No wonder they crashed." Her mouth pulled tight in a line. "I'm the worst parent ever. They have school tomorrow. They're going to be so tired."

"It's only one day. And there's less than a week until winter holidays anyway."

She nodded, her frown lines smoothing out a little. "That's true."

"What do you want to do? You still want to stay, right?"

She nodded, her face going shy. She was cute as heck.

"I was going to get them some mattresses so they could sleep in Henry's room, but since they're already asleep..."

"The carpet looks pretty soft. Do we really want to risk moving them and waking them up?"

I thought that over for a millisecond. "Hell no."

"Me neither."

"But that means..." I prowled towards her. She didn't back down.

"Means what?"

"Means we can be alone."

"Everyone is still outside."

I walked over to the window and flicked open the blind. Only Deacon, Sunny, and Kai were left around the fire. "I think the other couples all have the same idea."

Paisley scrunched her eyes tight and slapped her hands over her ears. "Oh god, our parents too?"

"They were probably the first to sneak off. They're probably getting their groove on to Barry Manilow right now." I wriggled my eyebrows at her.

She burst into laughter. "I can't even with all of that."

I pulled her into my arms and brushed my lips over hers. "Me neither. Now can we stop talking about my dad boning your mother?"

"Oh my god. I'm dying."

"Get over here and kiss me, Paisley. Or I'll keep saying it."

She was on my lips in seconds. Just the way I liked it.

20

PAISLEY

*B*utterflies rampaged around my belly, floating up through my chest into my brain. All thoughts of anything but Bowen's lips and the heat building inside me disintegrated. He pulled me close, his palms smoothing down my back to my ass and squeezing gently. He was already hard, his erection pressing into me. He groaned.

"Fuck, you feel good."

"I'd feel better naked," I whispered boldly.

Bowen's eyes turned molten, and in a flash, he had me up over his shoulder like a sack of potatoes. He stormed through the house to his bedroom and threw me down on the bed, the soft mattress bouncing beneath me.

"So caveman," I laughed, but sobered as Bowen undid the buttons on his shirt. Each one revealing a little more of his chest and then his abs. I couldn't look away. It was my first glimpse of his body and he was as cut as I thought he might be. My mouth went dry as he shrugged the shirt off and prowled up my body, his broad shoulder muscles rippling as he went.

Lord Jesus. Help me.

The man was too delicious to comprehend. I suddenly couldn't believe I'd spent all night crying because Jonathan was such a prick. He'd never looked at me the way Bowen was looking at me right now. I'd been a stupid, stupid woman to ever let him get in my head. This man right here was who I needed to be concentrating on.

Bowen's legs straddled me, and he pulled my shirt up and over my head in one clean motion as he hovered over me.

"Gotta see those perfect nipples again, Paisley."

I sat up so he could undo the clasp on my bra, but he was too impatient to wait. He shoved the straps down my arms and flipped the cups of my bra, letting my breasts fall free. I was just as impatient to be skin to skin with him, so I reached behind, undoing the clasp myself as he ducked his head and took my breast in his mouth. "Oh," I moaned, arching my back towards him. His mouth was wet and warm and he sucked on my nipples, the sensation shooting right between my legs.

He pushed me back on the bed, his mouth travelling down the underside of my breast to the soft skin of my belly. It wasn't flat and toned like his, but if Bowen noticed or cared, he didn't let on. He took his time, trailing down my skin in soft, slow licks, his tongue running beneath the band of my jeans, so close to my mound it made me ache. He sat up and popped the button on my jeans with one hand, while massaging my breast with the other.

Impatient to get him where I wanted him, I tugged my jeans down, glad I'd worn a simple pair of black underwear. They weren't overly sexy, but they weren't awful either. He pulled my jeans off, one leg at a time, until I was laid out in front of him in only my black briefs.

His gaze rolled down me, lingering on my mouth, my

breasts, my belly, and then finally, the junction of my legs. He reached out, his fingers running underneath the elastic band, so tantalisingly close to where I wanted him. "Jesus," he murmured. "You're like a fucking banquet, all laid out like that. I don't know what to eat first."

I squirmed. I was already wet just from his attention on me, but if he was going to talk like that, I was done for.

He didn't tease me. He yanked my underwear off so quick I heard a seam snap, but then I was naked with my legs spread open and I didn't have time to care about the state of my favourite pair of underwear.

Bowen settled between my legs and in the dim light of his room, his tongue swirled over the skin just above my triangle of pubic hair. He ran his fingers through the short dark blond curls. "I like this," he said into the darkness.

"Yeah? I keep thinking about waxing it off."

"Don't."

"What if I wax it into the shape of a B?"

"For Bowen?"

I raised my head to meet his eyes. "No, for bagel. Of course for Bowen."

He grinned. "You saying your pussy is mine?"

My face heated. "You're embarrassing me with that mouth of yours."

"Maybe my mouth should do other things then."

"Maybe it should."

"Happy to oblige."

"Stop talk—"

His tongue slicked through my centre, making my hips jerk and my mouth snap closed. He did it again, licking through my damp folds and over my aching clit.

"Looks like you stop talking too if I do—" The rest of his words were muffled as I grabbed his hair and held him to me, but I felt his rumble of laughter. And then he got down to business. His tongue swirled around and around my clit and lower, tasting me and teasing me, his rough stubble grazing the insides of my thighs but only adding to the sensation. It felt like he stayed there for hours, leaning his weight on one arm, while the other fondled my breast and his mouth went to town between my legs. I was slick and aching to be filled by the time his fingers moved to my entrance. I opened my legs wider and quietly moaned my encouragement. I wanted him inside me. Not just his fingers, but all of him. But I could already feel the spirals of pleasure building low in my belly and I needed something now. Anything.

Bowen's fingers slid inside me with ease, arching to find my G-spot. I hooked my legs over his shoulders, rocking against him, forcing his fingers deep inside. The cool air of the room washed over my body, but I didn't feel it. My skin was hot, and I needed Bowen to move faster. I rolled my hips, urging him on, and he obliged, stroking that spot inside me over and over again. His mouth landed on my clit, sucking it gently and lapping at it with his tongue. The pressure inside me rose to a crest that I teetered on, but Bowen seemed to know what I needed. He sucked me hard and moved his hand faster until I fell over the edge, into a bottomless well of pleasure. Fireworks shot up my spine as my internal walls pulsed around his fingers. I muffled my cries in his pillow and rode the wave, as Bowen brought me slowly back to earth. When I couldn't take it a moment longer, I pushed him away and took the pillow off my face so I could look down at him.

"Jesus, that was hot, Paisley. The way you were writhing..."

"Got you going?" I asked, feeling boneless but reaching

for his fly. I wasn't done with him. That had only been the beginning. As good as Bowen's fingers were, I knew his cock would be better.

"I nearly came just watching you," he admitted. I could see the evidence of that behind his jeans. His bulge was impressive. I flicked the button of his Wranglers and—

Light poured into the bedroom and the door bounced back off the wall. "Dad?" a little voice asked from the doorway.

Bowen and I both flew into action. He dove across the bed, attempting to block me from view. My first instinct was to get away from the light. I spun towards the far wall. And rolled right off the bed. I landed with a thump on the carpet, cracking my lower back on the bed frame as I went. I swallowed down my yelp of pain. I frantically rolled, terrified Henry would walk around to my side. Then held my breath as I lay there, naked under Bowen's bed. Bowen's confused face appeared briefly as little footsteps padded towards my hiding place and I gave him a wide-eyed look of horror.

"Can I sleep in here?" Henry asked.

"No!" Bowen yelped. His face disappeared and a blanket was tossed down to the ground. I reached out and snagged it, yanking it beneath the bed and over me as best I could.

I wanted the ground to swallow me whole. Had he noticed me in here with his father? It had to be late. Past midnight probably, because Bowen had really taken his time with me. Henry had to have been half asleep, right? He probably didn't notice. Bowen and Henry talked for a minute, but the boy didn't ask any questions about why his friend's mother had been stark naked in his father's bed, so perhaps he'd been too sleepy to really notice what had been going on. I heard Bowen zip his fly and the mattress springs above me creaked as Bowen got off the bed. Shifting to my side, I watched both sets of feet pad out of the room, the bedroom door closing behind them.

Not willing to be caught naked again, I scrambled out from beneath the bed, making sure the blanket was wrapped around me like a cocoon, and searched the darkened room for my clothes.

Sucked to be Bowen. He sure as hell wasn't getting anything more tonight after that little episode. And when he came back, we were going to have words about this little thing called door locks.

"*Y*ou're going to introduce me to all the hot cowboys, right?" Stacey asked as she tucked her arm into mine and practically skipped along the grass. I had to increase my speed just to keep up with her, while dragging Lily along with me. I hoped Aiden hadn't fallen too far behind, because the Gulgarren Rodeo was starting to get full.

Unlike the big one Bowen had taken me to in Sydney, which had been held in a massive indoor arena, this rodeo was more like a country fair. Gulgarren was about an hour's drive from my place in Lorrington, and since I'd promised Stacey I'd introduce her to Bowen's friends, I'd travelled in with her rather than with Bowen and Henry. I hadn't seen Bowen since the morning after our little oral sex session on Tuesday, and my heart was thumping in anticipation of seeing him today.

Stacey led the way through the carnival booths and brightly lit rides with their jangling tunes meant to entice thrill-seeking children. I stopped her once to let the kids go on a swinging chair ride, choking when it cost me fourteen dollars for two tickets. Stacey pouted when I didn't buy myself one, but I mumbled an excuse about motion sickness, and she laid out the cash for her own ticket before skipping off with the kids. She might have hated other people's kids, but she really was good with mine.

When they came off, their faces all flushed and smiling, we finished making our way to the rodeo area, which was a small section of stadium bench seats that overlooked a fenced-off ring.

A sharp whistle caught my attention, and when I found the source, Bowen tipped his hat at me with a grin. My heart leapt into my throat. He hadn't been online much during the week, and I'd surmised he was spending his evenings with his guests. We'd spoken on the phone twice but I'd kind of wondered if the lack of contact this week would change my mind on him. Maybe he wasn't quite as good-looking as I'd thought? Maybe he wasn't quite as rugged. Not quite as kind. Not...sexy.

But oh, he was. That little tap of his hat and I was a goner.

Stacey squeezed my arm. "Who is that?" she hissed as we made our way towards where Bowen was sitting with the other guys and Isabel. Isabel was engrossed in a handheld video game Henry was showing her, and Aiden and Lily took off in their direction.

"Which one?" I asked Stacey.

"On Bowen's right."

"Ah, Deacon."

"Please lord, tell me he's single."

I elbowed her. "Guess it's your lucky day. Pretty sure he is."

"Dibs."

I laughed. "You think I'm going to ditch Bowen for his best friend?"

She lifted her sunglasses and gave Deacon an appraising look. "Have you seen that man? He'd make me want to cheat. If I was ever in a relationship. Which I never am so the point is moot."

I laughed and gave Deacon a quick glance over. He was cute, sure. But he had nothing on Bowen, if you asked me. Bowen didn't need to worry about my eyes straying.

Though that was jumping the gun. We weren't officially anything just yet. I wanted to be, but we hadn't even told our kids. I sighed. I probably needed to have a conversation with him about that. But I also didn't want to be *that* girl, who made a good time into a big deal in her head. Maybe that's all I was? Did he even want a girlfriend? I had no idea.

All five guys stood as Stacey and I approached, and I introduced them all and Isabel. Stacey smiled at each of them though her hand lingered in Deacon's longest. Eventually, she pulled away and plonked herself down next to him. I didn't even bat an eyelid. It was such a Stacey move. I sat next to Bowen.

Bowen leant in and kissed my cheek. "Hey, baby."

His stubble brushed my cheek, tickling my skin, and his rugged, outdoorsy scent swirled around me, but all I could hear was him calling me baby. Why was that so hot? I was instantly ready to jump into his lap and pick up where we'd left off earlier.

But since that would be frowned on in such a public setting, I held myself in check. "So, what did we miss?"

He shook his head. "Nothing major. The guys and I got here early to check out the bulls. Since then, it's been a lot of buck offs. Not much of a show just yet."

"Probably not the calibre you're used to watching, I

guess." I doubted the little local rodeo could compare to the rodeos he'd competed in around the world.

He shrugged. "Still a good time though. I like being on this side of the fences. With my boys. And with my girl." His grin was slow and easy and it made my stomach flip.

"Am I your girl?" I asked quietly.

He frowned. Then his fingers found mine and he threaded them through. "We didn't really talk about it, did we?"

I shook my head.

"Well, for the record, I want you to be my girl, Paisley. I've wanted it since the moment I saw you on that damn TV screen. And getting a little taste of you the other night—"

I elbowed him. "Shh! Someone will hear!"

He chuckled. "I kinda like embarrassing you. I'd kinda like to do it a whole lot more. That...and other things..."

"What other things?" I whispered, unable to stop myself.

He winked. "Things better shown than told. And anyway, you don't like my dirty mouth. So I'll shut up now."

I pouted. "I never said I didn't like it. I just said it embarrassed me. There's a difference."

He nodded, his smile turning into a smirk. "Good to know."

A squeal from Stacey nabbed my attention, and I looked past Bowen to where she sat, my mouth dropping open. Red liquid spread across her pale blue shirt and dripped onto her white jeans. It was like something out of a slasher movie and it took me a second to piece together what had happened.

Deacon jumped up, holding a meat pie and a squeeze tube of tomato sauce guiltily in his hands. "Shit! I'm so sorry. That was supposed to be for the pie!"

Bowen snorted, and I elbowed him sharply, though it

was kind of funny. "Here, Stace," I said, handing her a little package of tissues.

"Let me help," Deacon said, snatching them out of my hand. He began ripping tissues out of the package, but that left him not concentrating on the meat pie he'd taken a huge bite of.

"Deacon!" I yelped, but it was too late. A large glob of mincemeat and gravy filling landed on Stacey's leg.

"Oh my god," I whispered, stifling a laugh. It was like watching one of those old slapstick movies, only in real-life colour.

"What are you doing?" Stacey yelled, pushing to her feet and snatching the tissues from his hand. She swiped at her pants angrily, only succeeding in smearing the mess more.

"Argh!" she huffed, pushing past Bowen and me. We both leant back as far as possible to let her pass without getting the pie mess all over us as well.

I got up to follow her, but she spun around. "Stay, I'll be fine. I'm going to find a bathroom and I'll be back." I sat obediently, knowing better than to argue with Stacey when she was cranky. And what was I going to do anyway? Dab at her boobs and crotch with some wet paper towel?

Deacon, however, was not taking no for an answer. He pushed past us and trailed after her like a scolded puppy dog.

"He's in for it now," I said, finally letting out my laughter. "She's going to hogtie him for that one."

Bowen raised an eyebrow. "Hogtie him? Did you just use a cowboy term?"

I clapped a hand over my mouth in mock horror, and Bowen leant in and kissed the back of my hand. I darted a look at the kids, but they were engrossed in their video game.

"You still didn't answer me, you kno—"

"I've just been informed we have some special guests in the crowd," the rodeo announcer interrupted. "Seems we have a couple of boys from the WBRA competition with us here today! Stand up, fellas!"

"Oh no," Bowen groaned, but I cheered along with the rest of the crowd. Sunny popped right up and started waving, dragging Kai with him, who waved much more demurely. Johnny rose behind them, giving the announcer a salute.

"Bowen Barclay, we see you up there too. Get on down here! Bowen's a local boy, ladies and gentlemen, who's been tearing up the professional scene for the last ten years."

"I'd hardly call it tearing," Bowen grumbled, but I elbowed him and he stood, forcing a smile onto his face. He didn't make any move to head down the stairs, but the announcer didn't seem to be getting the hint that he was less than enthusiastic about being called out.

"Barclay took out the Sydney round this weekend. I don't know about you all, but I want to see a live action replay!" The announcer's over-the-top enthusiasm was practically fangirl level and his excitement was whipping the crowd up. They all seemed oblivious to Bowen's discomfort.

"You did say it hadn't been much of a show yet," I reminded him with a smile. "Do you want to give these people what they came for? If not, we can make up an excuse. Bad back? Emergency phone call? Something to get you out of here."

A gleam appeared in his eye as he looked down at me, indecision flickering in his expression until it morphed into something I couldn't read. Then abruptly he leant across the other guys and called, "Aiden? Lily?"

They looked up at him from their game. "I've gotta go

down there and ride some bulls. But I need to ask you a very important question first. Okay?"

They nodded, their faces serious.

"Can I kiss your mum for good luck?"

Lily beamed at him and nodded enthusiastically. Aiden crinkled his nose like that was the most disgusting thing in the world, but shrugged and said, "Do what you gotta do."

I stifled a laugh, but whispered to Bowen. "What about Henry?"

He gazed down at me. "I already told him you were mine. He's cool."

My heart stopped. "You did?"

He nodded.

"You better get down here and kiss me, Bowen Barclay."

He pulled his hat off and placed it on my head. "If you say so."

He tilted my chin and dropped a searing kiss on my lips. I had to catch his hat and hold it to my head with one hand as his mouth claimed mine. The crowd around us cheered and I could hear Aiden fake gagging, but I didn't care. I grasped his face, his stubble prickling my palms. "Yes, I'll be your girl," I said against his lips, answering his question from earlier.

I felt more than saw his smile. And then he was gone, bounding down the stairs and jumping the fence with athleticism that told me he'd done that a million times before.

"You're really lucky, you know?" a voice said from behind me, and I turned to face a young woman two rows back who was watching me intently.

"Me?"

She nodded, but then her gaze focussed on Bowen. "He's one of the good ones."

My smile faltered. There was something in her tone that made me uncomfortable. I opened my mouth to answer, but before I could, Sunny interrupted.

"Hey! Addie, right? We met at the pub last time I was out here, you remember?"

Addie turned her attention in his direction, and I gratefully turned back around, happy to be excused from the awkward conversation. What had all that been about?

Stacey and Deacon returned, and I welcomed the distraction. Stacey slumped down next to me. Her light-coloured clothes were still smeared with stains, only slightly better than when she'd left.

"I hate cowboys," she said grumpily.

I put my arm around her shoulders. I couldn't say I felt the same. I was pretty sure I felt quite the opposite, in fact.

22

BOWEN

"That bull is an asshole. You named him well," Sunny complained as he climbed the fence of my training ring. He shook out his hand, clenching and unclenching his fingers a few times.

"You okay?" I asked.

He nodded, and I slapped him on the back. I had a couple of tough bulls, and some that were a whole lot easier. It was a gamble, practising on the ones that liked to buck. But practising on ones who didn't wasn't really practising. The guys had all voted for the big guns, so that's what I'd given them. But Sunny was right. Udder Pucker was an asshole. And Sunny was nursing an old hand injury, so I was concerned.

"That hand gonna be okay for Saturday?"

Sunny grinned. "Hells yeah, it'll be fine. I'm keen for it. Though I'm a bit worried with you all of a sudden performing."

"One good ride doesn't mean I'm suddenly back."

"You rode like a badass on the weekend. And that bull

was no country fair crap. He gave it to you good. And you held on."

I shrugged. "Ain't getting paid nothing to hold on to that one."

"Maybe not, but you win this weekend and you'll be back in the game for sure. Prize money is big."

I nodded. I already knew all that. I'd calculated exactly how many rounds I had to win to make the finals.

"Bowen," my dad yelled from the back of the house.

I twisted, and he waved me in. So I bumped knuckles with Sunny and left him watching the other guys get their asses handed to them by my ill-tempered little buddy and trotted across the stretch of dirt and grass.

Dad held up my phone, then tossed it to me. "I answered it. It's Brad Pruitt."

I gave my dad an exasperated look and he shrugged, putting on his Mr Innocent face. He was an asshole too sometimes. He knew I couldn't stand the head of the association and would have avoided his call if I'd been given the opportunity. Not much I could do about it now.

"Brad. What's up?"

"You, my friend," he drawled in his American accent.

I shoved my free hand in my pocket, feeling impatient with his cryptic answer. "How so?"

"Your ride last week. Fucking magnificent. Haven't seen anyone ride like that all season."

I should have been filled with pride. Brad was an older guy who grew up with the sport. If he said I'd ridden well, it was a compliment most guys would have been frothing over. But something was holding me back from getting excited. Brad didn't call just to tell me I was good. He rang when he wanted something.

"I'm training, Brad. Get to the point. What do you want?"

He chuckled. "Fine, fine. I wouldn't want to keep my star rider from his bulls. I want to talk about your new girlfriend."

Surprise nearly made me drop the phone. "Paisley? Why?"

"Because women are the hot new market in bull riding. They love this cowboy shit. They eat it right up."

"Still not seeing what that has to do with Paisley."

"Have you looked at your kiss video on YouTube? It's got a million views."

"What kiss video?" But before he even filled me in, I knew what he had to be talking about. I'd kissed Paisley right in front of everyone at that first rodeo. In front of a crowd, and in front of TV cameras. Of course it was on bloody YouTube.

"You need to take that down," I growled.

Brad chuckled, making my blood boil. "Not a fucking chance. It's gone viral anyway. People are lapping that shit up."

I sighed. "Seriously? Who fucking cares if I kissed someone after my ride?"

"Women! Bowen. Women care. I've had PR on it. They're spinning the two of you as this romantic fucking affair. The woman you randomly plucked from the crowd and kissed after your comeback ride—"

"Hey, hold up. She wasn't random. I knew her." He was sort of right in that I hadn't kissed her before that night, but he didn't need to know that.

"Yeah, that's not the story we're selling. But..."

Out of the corner of my eye, I could see the guys looking in my direction and I lowered my voice. "But what?"

"You're bringing her to the event this weekend, right? In Melbourne?"

"What do you care?"

"I want you both to do an interview. Actually, a few interviews. We've had a slew of phone calls about the two of
you."

"No."

He sighed. "Come on, Bowen. Don't be a prick. It's good
for the sport. People are invested in the two of you. It's
romantic and all that bullshit."

"No."

"We'll pay you. Both of you."

The word "no" was on the tip of my tongue again. I
didn't give a shit about the money. Once upon a time I'd
loved doing all the interviews that came with the job, but
ever since Camille had died, I'd refused them all. I didn't
want to talk about my dead wife. Those nosy fucks could
piss right off. But who was I to make decisions for Paisley?
Especially when she didn't have a job. I knew she wouldn't
take money from me, but maybe this was a way of giving her
some without actually giving it to her.

"How much?"

"A grand."

"Make it two, plus you pay for her flights and accommodation, and I'll ask her."

"Deal."

Shit. That had been too easy. I should have asked for
more.

"Bye, lover boy."

I hung up without replying.

I stalked through the house to my bedroom, closed the
door behind me, and sat down on the neatly made bed. I
couldn't help the corner of my mouth lifting when I replayed
the memory of Paisley rolling off the bed and hiding

beneath it, completely naked. Every time I'd walked in this room since that night, I'd remembered and smiled. And then gotten hard over it. If she came with me to Melbourne, that would be a whole weekend I could spend naked with her. Damn, that sounded good. Plus, there was the charity ball afterwards... The invitation was still sitting on my kitchen bench. I'd planned on ditching it, but that made me feel like an asshat. All the other guys would be going, and it would be for a good cause. I knew my sponsors would have a hissy fit if I didn't attend. Maybe Paisley would want to go...

I brought up her number and waited while it dialled.

"Hey," she breathed, and just from her tone I knew she was happy to hear from me. She was always smiling. Always happy. She was a ray of sunshine and I gravitated towards her warmth like I'd been stumbling through a snowstorm. I was a lucky to have her. And I knew it.

"What are you doing?"

"Studying."

"How's it going?"

She sighed. "I'm a bit behind actually."

I frowned, but then she added in a rush, "It's no big deal though, I'll catch up."

My frown smoothed over. "Good. Because I have a proposition for you."

"Is it sexual?"

I lay back on the bed, tucking one hand beneath my head. "Could be."

"Tell me more then."

"Tell me what you're wearing."

"What do you want me to be wearing?"

"Black," I replied immediately. "Black lacy underwear. And cowboy boots."

She laughed, but the sound was husky. I wondered if she was getting as turned on as I was.

"And if was wearing that, what would you do?"

"I'd tell you to touch yourself. To reach your hand down into the lace between your legs. I'd tell you to run your fingers over your clit, then lower. I'd ask if you were wet."

Her breath hitched. "Then what?"

"I'd undo my belt buckle." I reached down with my free hand and did it. "And then I'd unzip my fly, and take out my cock..." After following my own orders, I ran my hand down my length, flicking my thumb over the precum there and hissing as my palm rubbed over the sensitive head. "And then I'd ask if that turns you on."

"And if I said yes?" Her voice was breathy.

"Are you touching yourself right now, Paisley?"

"No!" She laughed abruptly, and then she sobered. "If I wasn't sitting in my pyjamas, surrounded by textbooks and job application forms...and it wasn't 1 p.m. on a Thursday, I might have."

She went quiet for a moment, then asked curiously. "Were you?"

"Yes," I replied honestly.

There was a moment of loaded silence.

"Shit. That's hot."

I grinned. But then I tucked my cock behind my fly, even though it killed me to do so. I'd need to do something about that later, no doubt. But for now, I had something to ask her. I sat up.

"Listen, my boss just called."

"You don't have a boss."

"The head of the association. He's kinda my boss."

"Fair enough. What did he want?"

I quickly explained the proposition, then waited for her to mull over the offer before she replied.

"So, I'd get an all-expenses weekend away in Melbourne, with my hot new boyfriend, and they'd pay me two grand."

"Essentially, yes. Don't know about the hot boyfriend bit though, he's a B minus at best."

She laughed. "I'm in. The kids are on holiday and due to go to their father's place anyway, so it works out perfectly."

"So you're coming? Just like that? I get a whole weekend of you, alone, with no ten-year-old to walk in and interrupt us?"

"Looks like it. I'll need to bring my books to study in our downtime though…"

"Deal. I can help you study. I'm a very good student."

"Okay, stop. You've gone from sexy to corny. You've crossed the line."

I grinned. Fuck, she was a good time. I loved the way she always gave me shit. The thought sobered me. I'd known her for less than a month, yet I could already name a bunch of things I loved about her. I hadn't even slept with the woman. My dick hadn't even gotten near her, and yet, here I was, creating a mental list of everything I loved about her.

I locked the thoughts up tight, not willing to say them out loud. But they required further analysis, for sure.

Maybe by the end of the weekend I'd have more of an idea about what to do with my out-of-control heart.

23

PAISLEY

*W*hen Stacey appeared in my bedroom doorway on Friday after the kids had gone to school, a mountain of textbooks, clothes, shoes, and accessories were threatening to bury me alive.

"Oh thank God, you're here." I bounded off the bed and grabbed her arm, yanking her into the room. She stumbled after me in her ever-present heels.

"What on earth happened in here? Were you robbed?" She cast a wide eye around my bedroom before her gaze settled on me again.

"What? No. I know it's a bit of a mess, but—"

"A bit of a mess is a bit of an understatement," she mumbled.

I threw a pen at her and winced when it bounced off her forehead. "Sorry. But quit judging my housekeeping skills and get in here and help me. I need you to pack for me."

"For the dirty weekend away?"

I rolled my eyes. "It's not a dirty weekend away."

She folded her arms across her chest. "As if. The minute

you two are alone he's going to be ripping your clothes off. You lucky cow."

I blushed at the thought. She was probably right. At least I hoped she was. Because the idea of getting naked with Bowen was all I could think about lately.

"Well, I'm never going to get naked with anyone if you don't help me pack!" I wailed. "I've got a mountain of work to do on this assignment. It's already overdue and I'm going to flunk this module if I don't get it in before I leave. And then there's another four assignments that need doing after that—"

Stacey held up a hand. "Right, right, I get it. You've been too busy fawning all over your cowboy and now you're behind."

Guilt washed over me. I'd told Bowen I wasn't that behind on my studies, but I really was. I hadn't planned on going to Sydney with him. I hadn't planned on spending a night at his ranch, nor had I planned on losing a whole day of study when we went to the local rodeo. Not to mention the countless hours we'd spent pretending to play video games when I should have been hitting the books. Or all the wasted hours I'd spent daydreaming about him.

I shook it off. "It's fine," I insisted to Stacey. "I'm just not used to making room for another person in my life and I let some stuff slide. I'll get used to the new schedule, and everything will be fine."

"Good. So you study, and I'll pack. I'm better with clothes than you are anyway."

I couldn't argue with that. I put on some noise-cancelling headphones and dove into my assignment, furiously typing as the clock ticked by. Bowen was picking me up at lunchtime for the drive to the closest airport, which was really little more than a landing strip. I had to get this assignment turned in before then. So I lost myself in a world of palliative and end-of-life care. What a great topic to get me in the mood for my weekend away.

I jerked when Stacey tapped me on the shoulder, pulling one headphone off my ear.

"Bowen's downstairs."

"What?" I gaped at her, then frantically looked at the time. Noon on the dot. "Crap, where did that time go?"

Stacey shrugged. "You were pretty engrossed in what you were doing. I think I could have danced around in nothing but nipple tassels and you wouldn't have even noticed."

I choked on a laugh. "Wait, do you own nipple tassels?"

She laughed. "Perhaps I packed them for you."

"Oh my god, my bag."

"Don't stress. You've got everything you need. Trust me." She held up my small suitcase, then placed it on the floor, swivelling the handle towards me.

I hugged her, grateful she was always around when I needed backup. "You're a lifesaver."

"Don't forget to hit send on that assignment."

"Right." I glanced over it and stifled a sigh. It probably wasn't my best work, but it would hopefully at least get me a pass. I hit the big green send button and closed my laptop, looking up at Stacey with a grin.

She grinned back. "Go get 'em, tiger."

———

A small plane sat waiting for us on the runway at the airport, and we made a short flight to the major airport where we switched onto a commercial flight. Bowen let me have the window seat, and as soon as we were both settled, he reached across the armrest and squeezed my thigh. Then left his hand resting there. He didn't seem to think anything of it, but I stared down at it, the sight setting off butterflies in my stomach. He ordered us both a drink, all the while never moving his hand from my leg. And I loved the feel of it there. Loved that little bit of possessiveness he'd begun to show around me. His hand on my thigh was a clear sign to everyone around us that I was his. And I liked it. I wanted to be his. In every way.

When the hostess came back with our drinks, and Bowen passed me my wine while he thanked the hostess for his glass of bourbon. His thumb started up a kneading pattern on my leg and I pretended to look out the window, so he wouldn't see the effect he was having on me. His touch made me restless. I shifted in my seat, which only succeeded in giving his fingers more room between my thighs.

"You okay?" he asked, leaning in so his breath brushed over my neck. I wondered if he was deliberately trying to turn me on and just doing a good job of acting innocent.

I didn't dare look at him. I knew my eyes would give away that I was thinking about throwing a blanket over us and letting his hand slide high between my thighs to touch the parts of me that were beginning to throb. Being alone with him for the past few hours had my libido hyped up.

My nipples hardened beneath the cups of my bra just at the thought of being completely alone with him later, and I fought to keep my breath steady. "Are you a member of the mile-high club?" I blurted out.

His ice rattled in his drink as he looked around us, and it was only then that I realised my words had come out squeaky and kind of loudly. The woman across the aisle from us gave me a dirty look, and I bit my lip to fight back the laughter that suddenly felt ready to explode. "Shit, sorry," I whispered, leaning into him. "That was so loud."

He kissed the side of my temple, pausing for a moment before lowering his lips to my jaw, then brushed them over my mouth. They were gone all too soon though, and I instantly missed their presence. Daring the wrath of the woman across the aisle, I leaned in and kissed his neck, feeling the stubble prickle. I swirled my tongue over him and sucked gently.

"What's going on with you?" he asked with a chuckle.

I shrugged. "I don't know."

"Pretty sure I know. Want me to fill you in?"

I saw the challenge gleam in his eyes. I couldn't back down from it. "Sure."

I immediately knew it was a mistake. He shifted his body so his back gave us some semblance of privacy, his fingers wandering higher on my thigh. My inner prude screamed at me to stop him, but the buzz from the wine I'd downed kept my mouth shut tight.

"Are you thinking about all the things I'm going to do to you once we're alone in that hotel room?" he whispered.

I shook my head. "No." I'd meant for it to sound sassy and cheeky but instead it came out breathy, relaying exactly how turned on I already was. My nipples ached and all I could think about was the way Bowen had rolled and teased them in his bedroom.

"No? Maybe you're thinking that you can't wait until we're alone. Maybe you're thinking of how I could slip my fingers beneath your skirt and trail them up between your thighs? About how you'd shift in your seat, spreading your legs just enough that I could get beneath your underwear and feel how wet you are. Then I'd stroke your clit until you were fighting back moans before I fucked you with my fingers. And I bet you're wondering how I could do it without any of these people even knowing."

I didn't say anything. Game over. He was better at this than me.

"I'm closer, aren't I?"

He had no idea.

He chuckled. "I think you like my dirty mouth more than you say you do."

I squeezed my thighs together. I couldn't deny that one.

His lips pressed against my neck and my head lolled to the side without an ounce of encouragement from me, my body giving him better access without me giving it permission. His tongue traced a slow pattern down my skin until a tiny whimpering sound escaped my chest.

"Shh," he murmured. "Don't make a sound or I'll stop."

I didn't want him to stop. Not ever.

"Your nipples are hard, Paisley. My cock too."

I glanced over at his lap and could see the bulge of him straining against the fabric of his jeans. "Do you want to know what I'm thinking?"

I did so badly but I was also scared if I made a noise he'd stop. So I just nodded. "I'm thinking about following you into that tiny plane bathroom and dragging your underwear over your ass and down your legs. I'm thinking about looking at you in that mirror while I plunge into you from behind. I'm thinking about rubbing your clit and feeling you pulse around me. And I'm thinking about all these people hearing you scream my name."

His words were barely more than a murmur, and so close to my ear that it would have been impossible for anyone else to hear, but god, I was both dying of embarrassment and so horny I was considering doing it.

Bowen abruptly turned around, and I realised a hostess

was standing there, smiling at us with a knowing look on her face. Bowen shifted a magazine over his lap and I flushed hot.

"Could you two put your seatbelts on, please? We're landing in a minute. The sign is on."

She pointed to the seatbelt sign and I wondered where the hour-long flight had gone. Apparently, I'd completely missed it while I was in a Bowen-and-his-filthy-mouth haze. Not that I cared.

We clicked our seatbelts on, both of us staring straight ahead at the seats in front. I didn't know about Bowen, but I was struggling to get myself under some sort of control.

"Probably better that we got interrupted," Bowen said casually.

"You think?" I wasn't so sure about that. Given a few more minutes, I might have run for the bathrooms just to get myself some relief.

"Don't get me wrong, on the way home, I'm doing everything I just said."

I coughed. "You are?"

He gave me a smirk that set my lady parts on fire. "That and more."

Jesus Christ.

"But now I get to take you back to the hotel. And at the hotel, I'm going to make sure you can't stay quiet. Even if you wanted to."

24

BOWEN

"*D*id you want to order your—"

"No," I barked impatiently.

"Oh, won't you be—"

"No."

The polite mask the receptionist wore slipped for a moment, betraying her true feelings towards my rudeness, but she quickly schooled her features back into her fake smile.

"Okay, well, room service hours are five in the morning till 11 p.m., and you just dial seventy on your room phone. We have a really nice..."

My leg bounced up and down impatiently as the woman droned on and on until I felt like screaming that I didn't give a shit about all of this. When she finally handed me our room keys, I snatched them out of her hand and practically ran for the lifts, dragging an apologising Paisley along behind me. The lift opened, and after making sure Paisley was safely inside, I jabbed the close door button repeatedly. I willed them to hurry up before some other poor fool got on, because I didn't think I could keep my hands off Paisley another second.

"Man, you're an asshole when you're horny. That poor receptionist is going to give you all the surcharges," Paisley chuckled.

But then the lift doors were shut and I was pushing her up against the wall and claiming her mouth the way I'd wanted to do for hours. She opened immediately, our tongues searching for each other urgently. The bell on the elevator binged before I was ready for it to, and we stumbled out, not even checking if we were on the right floor. We were a mess of hands and tongues and aching, dangerous need. When had I ever wanted a woman this much? I broke away just long enough to check the door numbers and swipe one of the keys through the lock. The door sprung open, and I pulled Paisley through before shutting us inside. Unable to take my eyes off her, I walked backwards towards the centre of the room where I couldn't see it, but knew there had to be a bed.

"Bowen! The—"

She didn't have a chance to say bags. My foot rolled on the suitcase one of the bellboys must have brought up to the room, my arms pinwheeling as I stumbled backwards. But for all my coordination on the back of a bull, three pieces of ill-placed luggage was my downfall. I landed on my ass with a thump, blinking up at a stunned Paisley in surprise at my sudden, newfound seat.

Paisley's mouth dropped open, and in the next breath, exploded with laughter. "Oh my god," she cried, her hands covering her mouth, but her shoulders continued to shake. After a moment of shock, I joined in.

"Well, fuck. That kind of just ruined my sexy persona, huh?"

She sobered, shaking her head slowly. "No. It just makes me like you more. And you're still pretty sexy from my point of view."

I propped myself up on my elbows, watching as she stalked across the room, toeing her shoes off as she went. She paused at my boots, and I waited, letting her run the show. Her fingers trailed up the outsides of her thighs gathering up her skirt as she went, exposing long, creamy white legs. She pulled the skirt down and stepped out of it. I let my gaze wander, desperately wanting to run my hands up her legs towards the place I really wanted to get at. But then I was distracted by her slowly undoing the buttons of her shirt. First the top, which exposed her delicate collarbones. Then the second, which exposed the swell of her cleavage. The third and fourth showed me a lacy black bra and her soft but flat stomach.

"You strip teasing me, Paisley?" I groaned, my eyes glued to where her fingers unfastened the last button, revealing matching black lace covering her pussy. The long shirt dropped off her shoulders, pooling around her elbows. She straddled my legs, walking closer until she stood before me, her pussy at perfect eating height. She trailed her fingers through my hair, and I groaned at the sensation, my scalp prickling as she gently tugged my head back so I was looking up at her.

"Maybe I am."

Fuck me. Her sudden confidence was hot as hell. I'd let her have her fun teasing me, but I was ready to do some teasing of my own. Without warning her, I hooked my fingers around the scrap of lace and yanked it down her legs. She gasped as the cooler air hit her skin. I took in her neat folds, her already gleaming slit, and my cock ached to get in on the action. But so did my tongue.

I leaned forward, reached around, and grasped her ass cheeks while my tongue darted out to taste her. Immediately, she stepped out of her underwear, her legs widening and her grasp on my hair tightening. I pulled closer to me and ran my tongue through her wetness, groaning at the taste of her.

Manoeuvring her over my face, I pushed her legs wider, my chin nestling right between her thighs, giving me full access to the centre of her. She moaned, and the noise made every sensation in my body heighten.

"I'm a fucking idiot," I murmured between licking and sucking at her clit. "I should have got you alone the first night I met you. How did I wait this long? You're so fucking sexy like this, Paisley. You have no idea."

Her fingers fisted in my hair, holding me to her as her legs began to tremble. I slid a finger inside her, immediately searching for that spot that would send her over the edge. I stroked in and out of her, hitting it over and over, before adding another finger.

"Oh!" she cried, her legs buckling. I withdrew my fingers, replacing them with my tongue, and gripped her thighs to steady her as the sweet taste of her orgasm burst across my mouth. She wobbled again, and I licked her slowly until she pushed my head away, unable to take any more. I stood, gathering her up in my arms, then laid her out on the bed. She still wore her lacy black bra, her cleavage spilling over the tops of the cups, but she was completely bare otherwise. I struggled to keep my eyes from the shining evidence of her orgasm that glimmered between her slightly parted legs. My dick strained at my pants, eager to get in on the action, and the look on Paisley's face was pure blissed-out happiness.

God, she was beautiful like this. Relaxed. Happy. And with a look on her face that said "Come here," I was the luckiest man alive.

Standing at the end of my bed, unable to look away from her, I pulled off my boots and shirt, and Paisley raised an eyebrow at me. "Now who's the one strip teasing?"

I chuckled, undoing the button and zip on my jeans and letting my aching cock spring free. Paisley's gaze lowered, and I gave myself a stroke just to see what she'd do. Her eyes darkened. "Get over here."

She didn't need to tell me twice. Not when she was on the bed with her thighs open, waiting and wanting. I grabbed a condom from the wallet in my jeans pocket and rolled it on. Then I slid between her legs, notching myself at her entrance and listening to her hiss of pleasure with satisfaction.

"Jesus, Bowen. You're so thick."

"I'll go slow," I whispered, meaning every word. She was dripping wet, but I didn't want to ever hurt her.

She gazed up at me with molten eyes. "Don't."

She lifted her hips and I sunk deep within her with a long groan. God, she was so ready for me. So hot. I withdrew, savouring the sensation, before plunging back inside her tight warmth.

"Bowen," she whispered.

I searched her eyes, making sure she was okay, and seeing reassurance there, I leant in and fused my mouth to hers. Our tongues moved as slowly and leisurely as our hips, exploring every inch of each other, until pressure began building at the base of my spine, and her whimpers turned needy. I reached between us, finding her clit again, this time with my fingers, and rubbed, slow, hard, and then faster circles on her nub. Her back arched, her moans growing louder, and I was suddenly glad I hadn't tried this in a plane bathroom. She was loud, and I liked it. The whole plane truly would have heard the way her breaths came in quick bursts and her moans echoed around the room. I increased the speed of my thrusts, matching the punishing pace I set on her clit.

"Jesus!" she yelled.

"Try again," I rasped into her neck.

"Bowen!"

Her walls clamped down on me, urging me on as I pumped in and out of her, no longer worried about hurting her. Pure manly pride roared through me as I came inside her, hot, thick liquid spurting from deep inside me, releasing an ache that had been building ever since I'd first heard her singing. She writhed beneath me, taking everything I had to give and more, draining me dry. I silenced her cries with my mouth, kissing her hard, and feeling more for her in that moment than I'd ever thought I'd feel again. Our bodies moved in sync, slowing down, until I pulled from her body.

"You're still wearing your bra," I realised with a frown.

She looked down in surprise, like she'd forgotten it was there. "Oh, yeah."

"Sit up."

She did as I commanded, and I reached around her, unhooking the clasp and peeling the lace from her body.

"That's better."

She play pouted. "You didn't like my underwear?"

I shook my head. "I fucking love that underwear. But I love you better like this."

We both paused for a moment, hearing the word "love" come out of my mouth. Shit. Not wanting to examine what had made me say that, I ignored it and started kissing a circle pattern around one of her perfect pink nipples.

It had just slipped out. It wasn't like it meant anything. I told myself the lie over and over, as I worked Paisley's body into her third, but not last, orgasm of the day.

25

PAISLEY

*B*owen's skilled lips had evaporated every thought in my head for a good few hours, and it wasn't until I was alone in the shower later that I'd really processed his words. There'd been an I love you in there. It had been mixed in with other words, and he'd just kept on like it had been no big deal. Maybe it was just an after-sex high talking, but my stupid, traitorous heart was doing backflips all the same.

I was falling for him. I knew that. I'd been falling for the man a little more every time I'd seen him. But it was way too early to be considering feelings like that. Especially when I had two little people at home I needed to protect. I couldn't just fall head over heels in love with a man I'd known for less than a month. Those sorts of feelings needed more time. And Bowen hadn't meant it like that anyway. He'd said he loved me naked. That was not the same as being in love with me. I shook my head, washed the last of the shampoo out of my hair, and told myself to quit acting like some lovesick fool.

Through the screen of the shower, I watched the bathroom door open and Bowen stride in. My gaze dipped over his glorious body. The man was cut, all lean muscles, tight and toned from hours of manual labour and his rodeo training. And that cock...it was like nothing I'd seen before. He was big in every sense of the word. Long and thick, and he'd shown me that he knew exactly what to do with it. When my gaze reached his face again he was smirking. "Want to go again?"

His dick was already thickening, despite the two rounds of mind-blowing sex we'd just had. But I grabbed the shower door as he reached for it on the other side. "Nope," I said firmly. "You stay on that side of the glass or we aren't going to make it to the interview tonight."

I could practically see his ego increasing as he stood there. But it was true. Even though I was already missing the fullness of him inside me, we did actually have responsibilities here this weekend. There were things we were obligated to do, beyond screwing each other into oblivion.

"What if I just stand here and watch then? That okay?"

I frowned at him. "You're *just* going to watch?"

He held up three fingers like he was a Boy Scout. "I solemnly swear."

"Fine." I lathered up some conditioner in my hair, piling it on top of my head, then squirted body wash into my hands, running it all over my body.

A strangled noise came from Bowen's direction. When I looked over, his cock was thick and hard again, and he was gripping a towel rack as if he needed it to stand.

I snorted. "You okay there?"

"Fine," he gritted out.

I squirted another dollop of body wash into my hand and slowly spread it over my breasts and down across my stomach, this time keeping eye contact with Bowen while I did it.

"You sure you're fine?" I teased. "This was your idea, you know. You wanted to watch."

"I might have made a mistake. This is torture."

As much fun as I was having teasing him, everything inside of me ached for him again. God, the man had barely been out of me thirty minutes, and I was already ready for more. Who was I kidding? I was just torturing us both. I pushed open the door. "Get in here."

I didn't need to tell him twice.

After he'd spun me around and taken me from behind, we actually did get clean and dressed. We rode the elevator down to a conference room where the WBRA had set up a small backdrop and some lights. A group of people milled about the room, some with large cameras, others with notebooks or microphones. Bowen's fingers tensed around mine.

"There's a lot of people here," I whispered to him.

"I know," he gritted out. "More than I agreed to."

I forced a smile as people began realising we were in the doorway. "Not much we can do about it now. Let's just do it, so we can go back to the room."

He raised an eyebrow.

My mouth dropped open. "You can't be serious. Bowen, I need to be able to walk tomorrow, you know!"

He slung an arm around my shoulder, pulling me in close and kissing my hair. A flash went off, and I blinked in the brightness. "We could just stay horizontal all day instead..." he whispered.

I elbowed him because a large man was striding towards us, well within earshot. If he heard us though, he pretended he didn't.

"Bowen!" The man's big voice boomed around the room.

The two of them shook hands, though Bowen didn't smile. Then he turned to me. "Paisley, this is Brad Pruitt, creator and owner of the WBRA."

Brad grasped my hand, giving me a fake smile, and kissed my fingers. I pulled my hand away gently and smiled at him, even though I was cringing on the inside. "Great to meet you, you little superstar!"

I gave Bowen a wide-eyed look of panic but he just rolled his eyes as we were ushered into two seats in front of the backdrop. I turned and studied it for a second before I elbowed Bowen. "That's you," I said, pointing to the bull rider on the backdrop.

Bowen blushed pink beneath the brim of his Akubra. He'd dressed the part of the cowboy, even though it was evening and we were inside. In the city there was absolutely no reason for him to be wearing a hat. But it was part of his "branding" apparently, so I hadn't given him shit about it. Not much anyway.

Brad stepped in and introduced the first reporters, a man and a woman from Channel Nine News. Bowen watched as Brad walked behind the reporters and crossed his arms over his broad chest, apparently planning to stay and watch the show. Bowen sighed before he turned back to the reporters. "Channel Nine?" he asked. "I'm surprised y'all are interested in bull riding."

The woman smiled warmly, and a little of my nerves settled. "Oh, we're very interested. You two have gone viral." She turned her attention to me. "That kiss was so romantic, wasn't it?"

I smiled genuinely this time. "It was a good one."

"So, he's a good kisser?"

Bowen squirmed next to me, but I just laughed. "Very."

"And how does it feel to be the woman who inspired Bowen Barclay out of his riding slump?"

My smile faltered. "Oh, I don't know about that. I think I just happened to be there when he found his form."

The man piped up, focusing in on Bowen. "But you have to admit, Bowen, your season has been a disaster. You were on the verge of disqualification. Is she your good luck charm?"

Bowen tensed beside me. I was suddenly uncomfortable too. Why was everybody calling me his good luck charm? Isabel had said it. Bowen himself had called me that. And now this guy? A tightness spread across my chest.

"Maybe she is," Bowen said calmly. "All I know is I'm lucky to have her."

The woman reporter, who was hanging off Bowen's every word, practically swooned. It made me a little jealous to see another woman looking at my man like that but at the same time, I could hardly blame her. He was 100 per cent swoon worthy. I focused my attention on her; the guy gave me a bad feeling, but he had more questions to ask.

"You'll need to win the next several rounds to make the finals. You think you have that in you?"

Bowen nodded without hesitation. "I've still got a few rides left in me."

"No thoughts of retirement? You're mid-thirties. Got a few injuries behind you and a son at home. Most guys might have given retirement some serious thought by now."

Bowen bristled. "I'm not most guys." There was an edge of aggression in his voice that made me squeeze his fingers. His attention shifted from the reporter to me and I gave him a reassuring smile. The stiffness in his posture relaxed the tiniest amount.

"So what keeps you riding?"

"I need to win."

The reporter raised an eyebrow, obviously catching the scent of a story, and I just prayed Bowen was seeing where this was going too. "Why's that? The money?"

Bowen huffed out a laugh, but it sounded cold. "The money doesn't mean anything."

"No? For the glory then?"

Bowen shook his head. "I've got my reasons, but they're personal."

The reporter looked thoughtful for a moment. Then switched his line of questioning. "This is the first time you've been seen with a woman besides your wife."

"I'm not here to talk about my wife." Bowen's voice was like steel, and he trembled slightly.

"You've never spoken about her, not since her death. The coroner's report said she died the night you won the Newcastle Invitational Rodeo. How did that make you feel?"

"Hey—" I interrupted, because that was a shitty thing to ask, but Bowen answered at the same time.

"How did that make me feel?" Bowen seethed. I bit my lip and squeezed his hand again, but this time, he dropped my fingers. He shifted forward on the edge of his seat towards the reporter. "My wife died a horrible, painful, tragic death while I was winning that damn rodeo. How the fuck do you think I felt?"

The reporter gave him a cocky grin, obviously loving that he was riling Bowen up with his completely disrespectful and insensitive questions.

"I think I'd feel like a pretty big asshole."

Bowen pushed to his feet, and I jumped up after him, shooting a panicked look at Brad for help. Bowen looked ready to punch this reporter in the face, but Brad just stood there, leaning against the wall like he didn't have a care in the world.

The reporter, who seemed to have no regard for his own life, kept on needling. "So why keep riding then? You say it's not for the glory, but I think maybe it is. Otherwise, why not leave? Why not retire and be home with your son? He lost his mother while you were on tour, and you don't ever seem to bring him with you. How does he feel about you continuing to ride?"

Bowen exploded across the space, his fist slamming into the side of reporter's face. His partner screamed, scrambling away from the commotion.

"Bowen!" I yelped, reaching for him again, but his fist was already flying, ready to connect with the reporter once more.

"Brad!" I yelled, looking to big man and wondering why the hell he wasn't over here, breaking this up. Brad grinned widely, and I realised in that instant that this was exactly what he wanted from Bowen and me. He wanted headlines however he could get them. Bowen exploding about his wife's death would be all over the place within an hour.

Bowen dragged the reporter to his feet, his fingers fisted in the man's shirt. Blood poured from his nose, which was almost certainly broken. Bowen shook him hard, then with barely an inch of space between them, he seethed, "You don't speak of my wife. Or my son. Ever again."

"You're insane," the man said, shoving Bowen away. To my relief, Bowen let him go, but his eyes blazed, watching as the reporter backed out of the room, not daring to turn his back on Bowen.

I couldn't blame him.

The people remaining in the room were quiet, their mouths pulled together in tight lines of disapproval.

Everyone except Brad, who was still grinning like he'd won the lottery. Bowen sank down in his chair, slumping over with his elbows on his knees, his head cradled in his hands. Brad pushed off the wall, starting up a slow clap. "Well, that was fucking newsworthy!"

Bowen glanced up wearily, opening his mouth to speak, but I beat him to it.

"Get out," I said quietly.

Brad turned to me with a raised eyebrow. "Excuse me?"

"I said, get out." I turned to the other people in the room. "All of you, get out."

Brad shrugged and strode out the swinging doors. The other reporters skittered out after him.

I sank down beside Bowen and pressed my fingers into his thigh. Eventually, he looked up at me, guilt and remorse written all over his face.

"I'm sorry."

I gave him a tight smile. "Probably not me you need to be apologising to. I think you broke that guy's nose."

He dragged in a breath. "Shit."

We sat side by side in silence while I wondered what the hell to do now. We were scheduled to do interviews for the next few hours, but I guessed that was over. I doubted any of the reporters would want to talk to him now.

"Come on," I said, suddenly exhausted. I pushed to my feet and held my hand out to him. He took it, and I pulled him up.

"I don't know what happened," he confessed. "One minute I was answering questions and the next..."

He looked so anguished and full of pain that I rubbed his arm and shushed him. "Stop. You don't need to explain to me. I get it. The guy was looking for a reaction. He got one. Not saying you couldn't have handled it better..."

Bowen nodded, his expression still guilt ridden. He pushed open the door and held it, letting me go ahead.

On the other side, two uniformed officers were waiting, one with a pair of handcuffs hanging from her fingers. "Bowen Barclay?"

My stomach sank.

He nodded slowly.

The female officer grasped one of his hands and twisted it behind his back. He let her.

"Bowen Barclay, you're being arrested for assault. Anything you do or say..."

The woman's words blurred as the room around me became a buzz of noise. Camera flashes went off and people held phones up to capture the action.

And I watched helplessly as the man I was falling for was escorted to the back of a waiting police car.

26

BOWEN

"*B*owen Barclay?"

I lifted my head and focused bleary eyes on the police officer standing in front of the holding cell. "Yeah?"

"You made bail."

I pushed to my feet feeling worse than I did the time a two-thousand-pound bull stepped on my chest. Every muscle in my body fought against movement. I just wanted to slump back on the rough wooden bench of the holding cell and pretend that the last few hours hadn't happened.

The uniformed officer indicated I should follow him, and at the front of the police station I signed some papers, nodding numbly when I was told I'd receive my court date in the mail. What a fucking joke I was. I was going to have to stand in front of a court of people and admit that I'd completely lost my cool and assaulted someone like a hot-headed teenager. My face flamed with the shame of my actions, and I shuffled towards the glass doors.

"Bowen," a voice called.

My upper lip curled in disgust. "What do you want, Brad?"

"I bailed you out."

"I hope you aren't waiting for me to say thank you."

"I'm not that stupid."

Could have fooled me, but I held my tongue.

"You gonna be right to ride tomorrow?" He looked at his watch. "Or rather, later today? It's already past midnight."

My temper flared. "That's all you really care about, isn't it? That I do your interviews. Ride your bulls. Make you money?"

Brad's usual smirk hardened into something darker. "You knew what this was when you signed up for it. You wanted the glory."

"I didn't want all this."

Brad folded his arms across his broad chest. "So quit then. No one is forcing you to do anything. I'll accept your withdrawal from the competition right now."

My blood began to boil in my veins. Fuck him. He knew I couldn't quit. And he knew why.

"You knew Camille. You remember once you said she was like a daughter to you? What happened to that?"

He shrugged. "That's still true. She was a great girl."

"Then you tell me how the hell I quit. I hate this fucking sport. Every damn day I risk my life. Risk never seeing my son grow up."

His eyes bored hard into mine. Then abruptly, his expression changed back to his regular casual arrogance. "It ain't my fault you're chasing ghosts, Barclay. I sleep just fine at night. If you don't, then that's between you and the big guy upstairs."

I shook my head, disgust souring my mouth. "I'm done with this."

Brad let out a laugh. "I'll take that to mean you're done with this conversation. Not that you're done with rodeo. 'Cos we both know you're a junkie. And like a true junkie, you're gonna keep coming back until it kills you."

I ground my teeth together and pushed through the glass doors of the police station. My steps were quick, but not quick enough. When I hit the road, I broke into a jog, desperate to put space between me and Brad. Or perhaps I was just trying to put space between me and the words that hung in the air. *You're gonna keep coming back until it kills you.* I hated that for once, Brad Pruitt was probably right.

*T*he hotel suite was dark and silent when I slipped in sometime around 2 a.m. It was so silent that for a moment my heart stopped while I tried to determine if Paisley was even in the room. As my eyes adjusted to the darkness though, I saw her slight frame huddled beneath the covers of the bed we'd spent hours in not all that long ago.

Her shoulders rose and fell in a rhythmic movement, so even though she faced away from me, I surmised that she was asleep. I'd run the whole way back from the police station, which had been further than I thought and left me with burning lungs and blisters on my feet but I deserved the pain. It had only spurred me on.

I stalked silently to the bathroom, closing the door softly before turning on the shower. I didn't bother waiting for it to warm up. Instead I let the cold spray pour down over my heated, sweaty skin and wash away the grime. I'd already spent hours beating myself up while I'd sat in that police holding cell. I was physically and mentally exhausted, and I let my mind go blissfully blank as I stood there beneath the spray.

Eventually I turned the water off, dried myself with a towel hanging from a rail, and tucked it around my waist. I padded back out into the room where Paisley slept and just watched her for a long moment. Her golden blonde hair fanned out around her head, but even in sleep, her face didn't look relaxed. There was a frown between her eyebrows and tension in the set of her jaw.

A new round of guilt slammed me in the gut. I'd put that expression on her face. She'd been so relaxed and happy this afternoon, and in one moment of hot-headed anger, I'd completely blown that up for her. She didn't need that. She had enough stress at home with two small kids to raise alone and a douchebag ex.

Something squeezed in my chest. I didn't want to lose her. She'd been in my life such a short amount of time, and it wasn't nearly long enough. I wanted her for dinners and birthdays. I wanted the chance to wake up next to her in the mornings and see her soft and sleepy. I wanted long nights of making love.

And I wanted her by my side when I won the championship title.

I dropped the towel and crawled into bed behind her, surprise ricocheting through me as I moulded myself around her bare skin. She stirred when I locked my arms around her and pulled her to my chest.

"You're back?"

I kissed her naked shoulder. "I'm back."

"You're okay?"

"Mmm." A delicate vanilla scent wafted around her, and I pressed my lips to her neck.

"That feels good," she whispered. "Don't stop."

My kisses trailed to the sensitive spot behind her ear, and then turned open-mouthed as they trailed back down her neck, sucking and gently grazing her with my teeth. This hadn't been the welcome home I'd been expecting. I'd been expecting anger, yelling, or perhaps for her to not be here at all. I'd royally fucked up and I'd expected to have to grovel, beg, and whine my way back into her good books.

But for now, at least, I'd take what she was offering. Her ass pressed back against my dick, and I reached around to cup her breast. She filled my hand so perfectly, her nipple responding immediately to my touch. My cock thickened, and she shifted so my length ran between her thighs.

I hissed at the wetness pooling there. I grabbed a condom from the bedside table, hastening to get it on, before dragging my hand down her stomach and finding the junction of her thighs. She moaned, opening her legs as my fingers found her clit, and my dick slid into her from behind.

"More," she whispered, and I picked up the pace, rubbing her while I pumped into her.

She moaned her approval, but that only made me want more. I flipped her to her stomach, pulling her hips up to meet my cock, and slammed into her harder still. She pressed her face into the mattress, stifling her moans and reached out for the bars of the bedhead. Her slender fingers wrapped around them, giving her leverage to push back against my thrusts.

My balls ached, clenching with the need to release, but I wouldn't let myself come. There was an agony in the pleasure that I deserved, that I revelled in. I ran my hand down her spine, before reaching around to tweak her nipples, and then her clit. I could tell she was close, but something seemed to be holding her back too. I slowed my punishing pace and pulled out of her, even though it nearly killed me to do so. I nudged her until she was on her back, needing to connect with her. She went, but twisted her head, looking off to one side, not meeting my eyes.

My heart stopped. "What's wrong?"

She shook her head. "Nothing." She reached for my cock, jutting out from my hips, still glistening with her moisture and hard as rock from delaying my orgasm. But as much as I wanted her hands, her mouth, her pussy wrapped around me, I moved away.

"Paisley, look at me."

She dragged her gaze to meet mine.

"Talk to me."

She shook her head, reaching for me again, and this time I couldn't resist. My dick ached so bad, it was easier to slide into her warmth than to push her to tell me something I was sure I didn't want to hear.

But as I slid in and out of her in long, slow strokes, I couldn't take the tortured look in her eyes. "Tell me. Please," I whispered, the words coming out brokenly. I kissed her lips, barely a brush, but sparks flew at the brief contact.

"Do you still love her?" she asked softly.

I stilled. "Yes."

She bit her lip and looked away again.

"Paisley," I said with more conviction this time. "Ask me if I'm *in* love with her."

Hope flashed in her eyes. "Are you?"

"No. I'm not."

She let out a long, shaky breath laced with relief. "Okay." Then she reached up, locking her fingers around my neck and pulling my head down to meet hers. She kissed me, soft and slow and sweet, until my hips picked up the pace again. When her body clenched around mine, she came not with a shout, but with whispered words in my ear, her fingernails in my back, and I let go of everything I'd been holding back.

Almost everything.

The three little words I wanted to say still sat trapped on the tip of my tongue.

27

PAISLEY

When I opened my eyes, Bowen was gone. I blinked in the dim light of early morning, then pushed myself up, taking the sheet with me, and cast my gaze around the room. Empty. The bathroom door was open, and the air around me was silent apart from the dull noises of people moving around in the hall outside.

A piece of paper on the pillow beside me caught my eye. Sitting next to it was a shiny silver credit card with Bowen's name on it. I picked them both up, turning the card over in my hand before reading the note.

Gone to train. Rodeo starts at 2. I'll send someone to pick you up. The afterparty tonight is kind of formal. A charity thing. Will you be my date? Take my card and buy whatever you need this morning. PS—can't wait to see you.

I read the note twice and sighed. Part of me was giddy over the last little bit. I couldn't wait to see him either. But the melancholy feeling from last night hung around me like a black cloud. Flashes of making love with Bowen in the early hours of this morning burned through my brain. I wanted him. I wanted him so badly I hated it. He'd sworn he wasn't still in love with his wife, but he'd gotten so worked up when the reporters had brought her up, he'd spent an evening in jail. An insidious voice in my head said I was falling in love with a man who was never going to love me the way I loved him.

And I'd been there before. I'd loved Jonathan with all of my heart. And he'd loved his job. And where had that left me? With a broken heart and two small children to raise alone. I wouldn't make the same mistakes twice. I couldn't.

Vowing to guard my heart better, I wandered into the bathroom, took a long shower, put on some makeup, and got dressed. I ordered breakfast and scrolled through Facebook while I ate it. By the time I finished, it was almost 9 a.m. Bowen's note and credit card sat on the table in front of me. I debated whether it was a good idea for me to even go, given my new vow to back off a little with him. But what was the alternative? Stay here in the hotel room by myself? The sensible side of my brain said I should do exactly that. I should stay in and study. My books had sat in a bag on the floor by the door since we'd gotten here. But how often did I get the chance to get dressed up and go out? Never. And I hadn't vowed to stop seeing the man. I'd just promised to stop falling for him so fast. And I could always study on the plane on the way home tomorrow.

I grabbed the card and my purse from the table and strode out into the hallway, pulling the door closed behind me.

"Boo," a voice said behind me.

I whipped around, grinning when I laid eyes on Isabel. She hugged me quickly, her fruity perfume floating around her perfectly put together outfit. I eyed her skinny jeans and heeled boots and wished I had half her style.

"Bowen training?"

I nodded. "Johnny too, I suppose?"

"Yep."

We walked side by side towards the elevator. "Hey, are you going to this afterparty tonight?"

Isabel raised a flawlessly plucked eyebrow at me. "Afterparty? You mean the WBRA charity gala?"

"I guess so. Is it a big deal?"

Isabel shrugged. "Depends on your definition. But it's pretty formal. Tux and ball gown sort of caper."

I cringed internally. "Really? Bowen only just told me about it."

Isabel rolled her eyes. "Typical man. They have no idea that we actually need time to get ready for events like that."

I bit my lip, my anxiety rising. "What are you doing now? I don't have anything to wear, and I've no idea where to even start. Bowen gave me his credit card..."

Isabel grinned wickedly at me. "Did he just? That calls for a shopping spree!"

I frowned. "I don't want to spend his money though. That doesn't feel right."

"He trusts you, Paisley. He knows you aren't going to go crazy. And he invited you, last minute, I might add, to a pretty swanky event. You have nothing to wear. You need a dress. What's the alternative? I mean, you could pay for it yourself, but he offered so..."

I made up my mind quickly. "Will you come with me? Please? I'm not good with fashion. I'm a jeans and T-shirt girl."

Isabel linked her arm through mine as we exited the lift and strode through the lobby. "You're speaking my love language, sister. Did I ever tell you how Johnny and I met?"

I shook my head.

"I used to work in a department store. Come on, I'll tell you as we walk. It's a good story."

---

*T*wenty minutes later, Isabel had filled me in on her whirlwind romance with Johnny and we were standing in the women's section of a large department store in the middle of Melbourne. Isabel swirled around me like a tornado, pulling dresses from racks and piling them into my waiting hands. When I could barely see over the pile of silky material, she pushed me towards a changing room.

I dumped the dresses on a bench, and pulled off my outer layers of clothes, folding them neatly before sucking in a breath as I took in the first dress. It was long, black, and delicately beautiful. I slipped into it, pulling up the zipper as far as I could before tugging the change room door open to let Isabel zip me up the rest of the way.

I chanced a glance in the full-length mirror and my heart rate picked up.

"Hoo boy, Paisley," Isabel drawled like a true cowgirl. "Do we even need to try on the other dresses? Bowen is going to keel over and die when he sees you in that."

A smile flickered at my lips as butterflies picked up in my belly. "You think?" The dress was truly stunning. It plunged low in the front, showing off my cleavage, and had a thigh-high split that showed more leg than I'd ever thought I'd want to show. I took a deep breath and closed my eyes for a moment, imagining Bowen's reaction. I snorted on a laugh because the Bowen in my imagination stared for a long moment...then said something dirty.

"I'd love to know what you're thinking right now, but I'm sure my innocent ears can't handle it," Isabel laughed.

I grinned at her. "You have no idea."

"Oh, it's like that, is it?" She whistled softly. "Ah, new relationships where it's all kissing and sex, and nothing else matters. You enjoy that bubble."

I smoothed out a barely existent wrinkle in the fabric. "I know, it's just..."

"Uh-oh. Trouble in paradise already?" Isabel frowned at me in the mirror.

"No, no. It's not like that. I really like him. It's just..." I sighed as Isabel waited for me to continue. "Did you know his wife?"

Isabel's eyes flickered with something indistinguishable. "Camille? Yeah. I knew her."

I waited, but when she didn't expand, I probed a little further. "I'm not like her, am I?"

Isabel took my hand and squeezed my fingers. "No, sweetheart. You're not like her."

I let out a long breath. "I didn't think so."

"Paisley, that's not a bad thing though. Camille was...I don't know. She was difficult to like sometimes."

"But she and Bowen were some golden couple, weren't they?" I asked.

"Depends on who you talk to. They grew up together and were high school sweethearts. Yeah, lots of people called them the perfect couple."

My shoulders slumped. "I thought as much."

"But you ask the other boys who've been on the circuit a long time. They weren't all sunshine and roses. They fought. A lot. They'd have rows that would last for weeks."

"Oh?"

Isabel passed me a pair of heels to try on. I did as instructed. I didn't want to gossip, but I was dying to ask more. This was insight into Bowen's past I hadn't heard from anyone else.

"You're different, Paisley, but not in the negative way you think. I haven't seen Bowen this happy in a long time."

"You don't think he's still in love with her?"

Isabel paused. "I'm not sure he ever really was. Or at least not since they were teenagers."

Isabel pulled off her own delicate gold chain and placed it around my neck, and we both studied my reflection in the mirror. "You know, you really don't need to compare yourself to a ghost. She's gone. And she's been gone a long time. If you're worried that Bowen can't move on, I think you're worrying unnecessarily."

I fiddled with the chain around my neck, distractedly. "I don't know about that. He thinks he has to win the championship buckle for her."

"What? Why would he think that?"

I knew a crease had formed between my eyebrows. "I don't know. A misplaced sense of guilt perhaps? But now I feel this pressure for him to win...and if he doesn't that it's somehow my fault."

Isabel looked at me like I'd lost my mind. Perhaps I had.

"Everyone keeps calling me his good luck charm. What if I...suddenly stop working or something?"

Isabel laughed, and I tried to smile back. She leant in and hugged me. "Paisley, you're worrying about nothing."

I forced my smile to widen. "Yeah of course. Ignore me. I'm just in my head. It's silly."

"All you need to think about is how Bowen is going to react when he sees you in that gown. If you two don't make the gala tonight, I'll know why."

I gazed into the mirror and pushed away my doubts and

fears about Bowen's wife and being his good luck charm. Isabel was right. Bowen was going to love this dress.

And I was going to love the way he took it off me afterwards. I could do this thing with him without losing my head. Or my heart.

*B*owen didn't climb the fence and kiss me when he won the Melbourne Invitational Rodeo. But he did glance up at me from under the brim of his Akubra and give me a wink that had me rubbing my thighs together in anticipation.

"Girl, you got it bad," Isabel laughed from her seat beside me. And I groaned. She was right. But there was something about watching Bowen out there on the back of a bull, and completely dominating the competition, that was the biggest turn-on. One look from him, and all my earlier fears disappeared. He didn't look at me like a man who still harboured feelings for someone else. Or like a man who was only with me because he had some idea stuck in his head that he needed me to win. Even if he had kissed me before his rides, all the guys did that with their wives and girl-friends. Bowen just looked at me like a man who wanted a woman. And those looks made my heart pound.

My phone buzzed in my pocket, and I sighed as I pulled it out. Jonathan. Again. I'd cancelled his calls at least a half a dozen times during the rodeo. I'd sent him a text asking if the kids were okay, and he'd confirmed they were fine but that he needed to talk to me about other "pressing matters". I'd told him it could wait until Monday and put my phone away. I wasn't prepared to deal with him when I was out with Bowen. Whatever his pressing matters were, if they didn't involve the kids, then he could speak to me during business hours. I was so thoroughly sick of being at his beck and call and getting nothing in return but hurt and heartache.

Truthfully, that wasn't all I was worried about. The video of Bowen punching the reporter was already gathering views. I just hoped Jonathan didn't see it. If he had...well, I wasn't in the right frame of mind to deal with any of that tonight.

Bowen drove us back to the hotel, chatting happily about stats and prize money and how many more rounds he'd have to win or place at in order to qualify for the finals. It seemed like a lot to me, but who was I to doubt him? It's not like I knew the first thing about bull riding.

In the hotel room, Bowen stripped off and got in the shower while I redid my makeup in a rapidly fogging mirror. My gaze kept drifting to the shower though. After a few moments of watching Bowen soap his abs, I gave up on my makeup and just turned around and gawked at him.

"You could just get in here, you know," he said after a moment. He didn't look up from his task, but I could see the hint of a grin tugging at the sides of his face.

I grasped the sink tighter to stop myself from doing exactly that. "Nope," I said reluctantly. "I need to get dressed." Forcing every muscle in my body, I turned and left the bathroom and a deliciously sudsy Bowen behind.

The main room, with its lack of naked Bowen, was bitterly disappointing in contrast.

I pulled my dress from its garment bag and slipped into the silky material. Then sat on the edge of the bed to pull on my heels. Bowen opened the bathroom door just as I was standing up again and smoothing out the wrinkles in the back of my dress. Steam billowed around him and water still dripped down his chest.

His gaze took me in, roving ever so slowly over my body, my temperature rising with every second he stared at me. "You look beautiful," he said quietly. There was something soft and reverent in his voice that wasn't normally there when he was joking around or talking dirty. And while I had come to admit that I kind of did like his dirty mouth, I liked when he looked at me like this even more. Looks like this told me he cared about me.

Looks like this could convince me he might love me.

My breath hitched, and I turned away, overwhelmed by the expression on his face. If that was love I saw in his eyes, the whole "slow down, get a little space" thing wasn't going to work.

I grabbed his suit from the hanger and held it out between us like a shield. "You should get dressed. We'll be late."

Bowen glanced at the clock on the wall and did a double-take. "You're right." His gaze turned hot again. "I really wish you weren't, because if we had more time..."

I laughed. "Should I wait in the hall for you then? If this dress is too distracting for you?"

He shook his head. "It's not just the dress. It's the woman inside it."

Oh lord. My knees tried to buckle, and I was sure I was going to end up a puddle on the floor. I picked up my purse and looked back over my shoulder as I grasped the door handle. "I'm waiting in the hall. I think it's safer. For both of us."

Bowen rolled his eyes but let me go. In the hallway, I leant against the cool beige wall and tried to get my libido under control. We still had one whole night left together and most of the next day to just be us. The promise of spending those long hours in bed with him made me tingle. I'd get as much of him now while I could, because once we were home, alone time would be rare again. And having sex with Bowen and losing ourselves in the physical meant I didn't have to think too much about the emotional, and whether I was falling too fast. Or not fast enough. Or really, what I was feeling at all. It was all so confusing.

Three people came out of the room next door, dressed to the nines, and I raised a hand in greeting when I recognised Kai and Sunny. A vaguely familiar dark-haired woman trailed them, and I fought to place her.

"Paisley," Sunny drawled in his true American accent. He pulled me in for a hug, and I returned it. He was like an overgrown puppy dog, tall and kind of lanky and always radiating positivity. I suddenly wondered if that's where his nickname came from. It suited him. The man was like a sunbeam on a dark day. You couldn't help but be happy when you were around him.

Kai, on the other hand, stood quietly behind his taller friend. "You look handsome," I told him and smiled as his cheeks bloomed pink. It was the most reaction I'd seen out of him in the whole time I'd known him.

Sunny turned back and grasped hands with the woman who was with them. He tugged her forward, and my eyes widened as our gazes collided.

"Paisley, have you met Addie?"

She was the woman from the rodeo. The one who had

sat behind us and told me I was lucky to have Bowen. "Uh, sort of. Not officially." I stuck my hand out and she took it, shaking it gently. She looked different tonight. Her long hair cascaded down her back in perfect waves and her dress was a deep, shimmering blue that set off her dark skin. Black makeup ringed big brown eyes. She somehow looked younger and more innocent while still being a complete knockout all at once.

"It's nice to officially meet you," the woman said softly. Then stepped back linking hands with Sunny again. He looked proud as punch to have her on his arm.

The door beside me opened, and Bowen's cologne hit me before I even saw him. I sucked the scent in greedily. I had no idea what he wore but damn, I liked it.

He stopped abruptly in the doorway when he realised I wasn't alone. His eyes locked with Addie's and widened in surprise. "Ah, hey." He leant in and kissed her cheek, then shook hands with the two guys. Addie stiffened and looked down at the floor. My gaze darted between her and Bowen, and I wondered at the weird tension between them.

Sunny seemed to notice it too. He gave Bowen a strange look then said, "If we're all here, let's go then, huh? I hear there's an open bar!"

He held his hand up for Kai to slap, but Kai just looked at him then kept walking towards the elevator. I stifled a grin as Sunny shrugged, no doubt used to his best friend's quiet demeanour, and followed after. Addie trotted along with him.

Bowen and I trailed behind, his arm draping over my shoulder. "I'm really glad you're here, you know. I normally hate this event. But it might actually be fun this year."

I kissed his cheek. "Of course. I'm super fun. Just ask me."

Bowen laughed, his arm around my neck pulling me tighter, and he kissed the top of my head. From the corner of my eye, I saw Addie watching us, her expression unreadable. My smile fell. I might have been super fun, but I was suddenly worried that I might not have been the only one Bowen had been having fun with.

———

*T*he charity event was much like I expected it to be. Lots of round tables with white linen cloths in a large square room. A stage at the front had a microphone on a stand. I sat squished between Bowen's and Deacon's broad shoulders. Sunny sat in the middle of Kai and Addie, while Isabel and Johnny were over on Bowen's right.

It was a happy little group, with Isabel pouring wine from a bottle that sat in the centre of the table, chilling in an ice bucket. Waiters roamed the room with finger foods. Sunny practically accosted them whenever they appeared. The rest of us were lucky to get one with the way he wolfed down the delicious little morsels. Bowen chatted with Johnny, which left me gazing around the room until Deacon tapped me on the shoulder.

"Can I ask you a question?" he asked quietly, darting a look over my shoulder at Bowen.

"Sure." I settled my full attention on him, intrigued by the sudden seriousness in his expression.

"Your friend..."

"Stacey?" I asked.

"Yeah..."

I smiled, remembering Stacey's initial interest in Deacon at the rodeo. Before the meat pie incident anyway. "You want her number?"

He gave me wry grin. "Maybe? Would that be alright?"

"You going to spill meat pie filling all over her again?"

He winced. "Is she still mad about that?"

I patted his arm. "Oh, Deacon. You've got your work cut out for you. She's gonna eat you alive."

"Not if I eat—"

I threw my hands over my ears. "Oh God! Please stop. You're as bad as Bowen."

Deacon reached across me and punched Bowen in the arm.

"What the hell was that for?"

"You dog."

"You're both dogs," I interrupted with a laugh. I turned to Deacon. "If I give you her number, can we just stop this conversation?"

Deacon held out his phone. "Deal."

I punched in Stacey's number then shook my head as he snatched his phone back and immediately started texting. I tried to sneak a peek over his shoulder, but he gave me a look and sat back in his seat, shielding the phone from my view. I rolled my eyes, but then Bowen squeezed my thigh and I turned my attention back to him.

"Hey, I've got to do a thing in a minute," he said close to my ear.

"Oh?"

"I do it every year. It's an award. It's in Camille's name, so I'm always the one to present it."

Surprise punched me in the gut. And though it was childish and immature, I found myself a little dismayed by Camille's name coming up yet again.

"You okay?" he asked.

I nodded vigorously. "Of course." It was mostly the truth. It was ridiculous to be feeling weird about a woman who had been dead for four years. But she was still so ingrained in his life. I almost felt like the other woman. When Bowen got up to present the award, I quietly excused myself and made a beeline for the ladies' room.

The door swung open and I groaned internally at the sight of Addie standing at the bathroom sinks, reapplying her lipstick in the mirror. Shit. There was no leaving without embarrassing myself.

She glanced over at me. "Escaping?"

I sighed and went to stand beside her. I could hardly deny it. "Sort of. You?"

She shook her head. Then shrugged. "Maybe."

"How come?"

"I don't think too many people at that table like me."

I frowned, but a trickle of guilt rolled down my spine. It wasn't that I didn't like her. It was just...uncomfortable. And I wasn't even really sure why. "I'm sure that's not true."

She rested one hip on the bathroom sink. "Bowen can't even look at me."

I'd noticed that. I was almost scared to ask my next question. I bit the bullet. "Why?"

She looked down at the sink. "He didn't tell you?"

My stomach sunk. My earlier worries at Bowen's avoidance of Addie came crashing back. "Tell me what?"

"We had a thing."

My face must have betrayed the way I felt inside, as if someone had poured cement into my stomach. Because Addie quickly rushed to add, "No, no. It wasn't recent. It was long before you came along."

That eased a smidgen of the heavy feeling in my gut. But still.

"You kinda hate me now too, huh?"

I sighed. She looked young and miserable, and my heart

went out to her in a motherly sort of way. And I was big enough and mature enough to know that Bowen had a past before me. I reached out and squeezed her fingers.

"Of course not... You don't still have feelings for him, right?"

She shook her head quickly. "No, no. I never really did. It was just a one-time thing. I do envy you though. The way he looks at you."

"Sunny seems to like you."

She smiled softly. "I like him too. But I think Kai hates me. And that might be a deal-breaker for Sunny. He and Kai are pretty close."

"Kai looks like he hates everyone. There's a reason they call him Frost."

"I hope so."

I quickly checked my makeup in the mirror. "You ready to go back out there and face the music?"

"Yeah. Thanks, Paisley."

"For what?"

"For not freaking out about the Bowen and me thing. It really wasn't a big deal. And I like Sunny. I don't want there to be a weird awkwardness between you and me. The wives and girlfriends in the WBRA need to get along, you know? There's so much travelling around with them, and staying in hotels and parties and everything. We're going to practically live in each other's pockets during the season."

"Is that what happens? They all travel with the men?" I frowned. I knew Isabel travelled with Johnny, but I hadn't really had much to do with any of the other wives and girl-friends.

She nodded. "Isn't that exciting? Getting to see the world with the man you love by your side?"

She was looking off into the air dreamily, and I was glad

she wasn't paying enough attention to see the smile fall from my face. She was a lot like I'd been at the same age. I was sure I'd worn that same look as I'd stared at Jonathan while his business went from strength to strength. While I'd followed him to parties and functions, always being the dutiful wife and the gracious hostess.

Always pushing my own desires aside so he could chase his dreams.

A buzzing in my purse pulled me from my memories, and I shuffled through the contents until I found my phone. My thumb was poised to hit the cancel button, assuming it was Jonathan again. But I pulled myself up just in time, realising it wasn't Jonathan after all.

"Hey, Mum," I said gratefully when I answered the call. It was like someone wrapping a warm blanket around me. I don't know how she did it, but she seemed to have some sort of sixth sense about when I needed her. And hearing her familiar voice right now was exactly what I needed. "How's your weekend been?"

"Paisley."

The tone in her voice made me still. "Yeah?"

"You need to come home. Immediately."

*P*aisley's fingers had been curled into fists for hours. From the moment she found me at the charity even, wide-eyed and breathless, to the moment we'd gotten off the plane back home. I reached across the centre console, taking one hand in mine and smoothing open her fingers. Little half-moon indentations marked her palms.

"You doing okay?" I asked, steering with one hand through the dark, quiet country streets.

"Nope."

"Didn't think so."

She stared blankly through the windscreen, and I put her hand down in her lap when her house came into view, using both hands to pull into the driveway. Before I'd even stopped the car completely, she threw open the door and ran for the house. I yanked up the park brake and took off after her, catching her easily with my longer strides. Her fingers fumbled with the house keys in the dark, her hands trembling, and eventually, I gently took them from her and pushed open the door.

A gasp escaped Paisley's throat.

"Son of a bitch," I murmured, taking in the completely empty space. She took a small step into the living room, and I followed. She moved stiffly, numbly, from room to room, but there was nothing left in any of them. Her furniture and clothes and kids' drawings that had filled these rooms just two days ago had been removed without a trace.

It was as if Paisley had never lived here.

"How can he do this?" Paisley whispered.

My blood boiled beneath my skin as I took in the shell of the house that had once been her home. "He can't. This is ridiculous. You must have some rights."

A single tear dripped down her face as she turned to me. "He's taken everything I have."

"We'll get it back. I promise. I'll fix this." I was ready to storm over to her ex's house, kick his damn door down, and pummel the shit out of him. The gutless wonder.

Paisley seemed to pull herself together, straightening her shoulders. She looked me dead in the eye with a new determination. "No. I need to do that. Can you drive me to his place, please?"

I nodded, holding the door open for her. She cast one last long look around her house. "I guess this will be the last time I stand in here. He's ruined this house for me now. Everything here is tainted with Jonathan and his selfishness."

I didn't say anything as she walked out the door. We went back to my car and I drove her the short distance to her ex's house. The house he lived in only made my anger spike. His house was new and easily triple the size of the run-down cottage he'd left Paisley and his children to live in. The man obviously wanted for nothing, while Paisley scrimped and saved then gave the lot to her children.

Paisley stared up at the big house for a long moment, her anger vibrating through her, her small frame shaking.

"You don't have to do this, you know. We can just go to the police..."

But I wasn't even sure she heard me.

"Wait here." She got out of the car stiffly and strode across the lawn to the shiny wooden door of her ex's house. Paisley thumped on the door, her fist beating against wood, the noise ricocheting around the sleepy neighbourhood. A light in the upstairs window flicked on, and I pushed open the car door, ignoring her instructions. No way in hell was I letting her confront this guy at three in the morning without some sort of backup.

I leaned against the brick wall a few steps behind her and folded my arms across my chest. The door swung open, and I had to fight the urge to launch myself at the man who stood there. He was tall and lanky, wearing boxer shorts and a hastily thrown on robe he hadn't bothered doing up.

"What the hell, Paisley? It's 3 a.m.! You're going to wake the kids up!"

"*What the hell, Paisley?* Seriously? Is that all you have to say to me after you emptied my entire house?"

"My house actually. And we can talk about this in the morning." He tried to shut the door, but Paisley wasn't having any of it. She shoved it open and pushed her way into his entryway with a strength that surprised me. And obviously Jonathan too, because he took a step back and let her.

"We can talk about this now."

"I tried calling you."

"You can't just come into my home and steal all my belongings, Jonathan! Whether you call me or not!"

He rolled his eyes, which only made me clench my

fingers tighter. "You were squatting in my house, Paisley. You haven't paid rent in weeks. I told you to move out, and you didn't. I'm well within my landlord rights. And here." He reached over to a bowl on a side table in the foyer. He pulled out a small brass key and dropped it into Paisley's hand. "All your things are perfectly safe. I had a professional team pack them and store them in a storage facility. You can collect them anytime you like."

Paisley stared down at the key in her palm, before her fingers slowly closed over it. "Where am I supposed to go, Jonathan? You've just taken your children's home away from them. I don't understand why you're doing this."

"I told you. I need the rent money. You can't afford it. It's not personal. And the kids have a home here."

Paisley's mouth dropped open. "You don't seriously think you're keeping the kids full-time?"

Jonathan eyed me over Paisley's shoulder, and I realised a low growl was coming from my chest. I was practically vibrating with the need to feel the satisfying connection of my fist against his jaw.

"I don't mean to keep them from you. But you said so yourself. You've got nowhere to go. Are you going to live in your car with two children?"

My resolve broke. I launched myself across the space, ready to throw this clown up against a wall. But Paisley stepped in front of me and gave me a look that clearly said, "Don't you dare." And I pulled myself up short. Though it killed me inside.

"You'll be hearing from my lawyers," Paisley said quietly, with a steely determination lacing every word. "And I'll be back to get my children at the regular time this afternoon. I'll have a place sorted by then."

She spun on her heel and strode back to the car.

I stared Jonathan down until he closed the door. And then I followed Paisley. I got in the driver's seat without a word and quietly started the engine. Paisley just stared, with unseeing eyes, as I reversed out of the driveway, and drove away from Jonathan's house. As we turned the corner, a sob burst from her chest, the sound so gut-wrenching and full of absolute misery that it tore straight through my chest.

PAISLEY

*B*owen pulled the car over on a side street halfway to his house. Tears streamed down my face, and my chest felt hollowed out. Everything ached. My throat, my skin, my heart. My entire body felt shredded by everything Jonathan had taken away from me. My home. My children. He'd taken my whole damn identity with one fell swoop. Pain burned through me like a wildfire, leaving nothing but devastation in its path.

I barely registered the slam of Bowen's car door through my sobs, but then my door was opening and he was pulling me from his ute with strong arms and holding me together while I fought the urge to fall apart.

He held me, cradling my head to his chest, the other hand pressed against my lower back. He spoke slowly and softly into my hair and I breathed in his scent in the darkness of the country road. There was nothing above us but clear winter skies and nothing around us but acres and acres of farmland. And in that moment, it was easy to pretend the rest of the world didn't exist. If I just concentrated on his fingertips brushing over a bare patch of skin at my back. Or the way his heart thumped beneath my ear. I could forget my problems if I just focussed on his words, his lips in my hair. Nothing else mattered. Nothing else existed but him and me, and an open sky.

I stifled a sob and looked up at him with tear-stained cheeks. "Bowen..."

"Shh," he whispered. "It's okay. I know."

I shook my head, because he couldn't possibly know, but then his lips pressed down on mine. His touch was soft and sweet, and I closed my eyes, realising that he did know. He knew what I needed even when I didn't.

I tilted my head back, opening for him, as my fingers snaked around his neck and held him to me. Our tongues tangled and my heart swelled, the feeling making me breathless. Making me crave.

I reached for the button on Bowen's jeans, praying he wouldn't play the gentleman who didn't want to take advantage when I was feeling down. I wanted him to. I wanted more, more of his hands, his touch, his lips, his heart. I was selfish and greedy, but I didn't care. I wanted it all. I just wanted to feel. Feel something other than the pure anguish that was threatening to split me in two.

Bowen's lips dropped to my neck as I fought to get his jeans and boxers down his thighs. I palmed his cock, eliciting a hiss from him as I stroked his length. His kisses turned sloppy as I flicked the zip on my own jeans, pushing them down my legs.

"Jesus, Paisley," he gritted out.

"Don't ask me if I'm sure. I'm sure."

"I wasn't going to. I was going to ask if you were ready."

He spun me around, pressing my front down over the hood of the car. There was a crinkle of a condom wrapper, a second's pause, and then he slammed into me from behind.

I cried out as his thick length filled me so deliciously. He was warm and hard, and I thrust my hips back, meeting each stroke, taking him deeper and deeper each time.

I held on to the cool metal of the car, the cold air caressing my ass, at complete odds with slick heat emanating from the place Bowen and I were joined. The slap of our skin, my moans, Bowen's mumbled words of passion all swirled around me as an orgasm built deep within me. I reached between my legs, finding my clit and rubbing it hard as Bowen's palm slapped my ass cheek. Surprise shot through me, but it didn't sting. Instead I found myself clenching around his cock, an orgasm barrelling down on me like a freight train. "More," I panted, surprising myself, and was rewarded with another stinging ass cheek.

"Oh God," I moaned, rubbing my clit rapidly. "Oh God!" I jerked as I came apart, colours and noise rushing in, swirling around me, taking me higher. Bowen groaned behind me as he found his own orgasm, his fingers biting into my hips in the most delicious way, and I rode him out, pushing my hips back, demanding more and more as I pulsed and clenched around him, until he had nothing left to give.

"Paisley," he said, his voice hoarse. "Paisley, stop. I'm done. I'm so done." He turned me around and kissed me gently as he pulled up my jeans then did them up for me. Then he did the same to his own. I leant on the car, feeling boneless and sated, watching as he tucked himself behind his denim.

When he was finished, he put his arm around my shoulders. I rested my head on his chest, and we stared up at the wide, open sky until the sun peeked over the horizon.

"What do I do now?" I asked quietly. I no longer felt like

crying. And for that, I was thankful. Crying wasn't going to get me anywhere. What I needed was a plan.

Bowen kissed the top of my head. "I've got an idea. Let me show you something."

I nodded and followed him back into the car, willing to let him lead.

owen and I watched the sunrise as we drove towards his property. In the light of day, with Bowen beside me and the delicious ache from our rough and ready sex still throbbing between my legs, a calmness washed over me.

The car bounced over the gravel road, but he took a turn-off I hadn't noticed the last time I'd been here. The road meandered over a hill and away from the main house, the scrub thick on either side of us.

"Where are we going?" I asked curiously.

"Right there." Bowen pointed, and I redirected my gaze past him, my mouth dropping open in surprise.

"You have another house out here?"

Bowen pulled to a stop in the small clearing. The yard was overgrown, and the house looked a bit run-down. It was obvious no one had lived there for a while.

"It's the original house on the property. Camille and I lived here pre-Henry. While we built the main house."

He got out of the car and jogged around to my door, opening it and offering me his hand. I took it and climbed down. We slowly made our way to the door, and Bowen had to shoulder it open. He looked at me guiltily. "I haven't come down here in years. I'll oil that for you."

I blinked at him in surprise as we stepped into the small

house. The furniture was all covered with dust sheets and it smelled musty, but sweet, pale yellow, early morning light filtered through the grimy windows, bathing the space in warmth.

"What do you mean for me?"

Bowen shrugged, going pink. "You need a place. Fast. I have a place."

I shook my head. "Bowen, I can't."

"Paisley, you can."

"It's too soon."

"I'm not asking you to move in with me. You're here. I'm over there. You do your thing. I'll do mine. We're neighbours, sure. But that's all this is."

I stared at him sceptically. "Neighbours? That's it?"

A sly grin spread across his face. "Neighbours who like to get naked and use their tongues to—"

"Bowen!"

He laughed. "Sorry, sorry! Just getting in one last chance to make you blush before we're surrounded by kids again."

I shoved him, sending him into a lounge covered in a dusty drop sheet. I coughed as Bowen wiped off his hands on his jeans and wrinkled his nose. He sneezed, then winced at me. "We've got all day to clean this place up. You can start, and Dad and I will go get your furniture. We can move this old stuff into my shed."

I hesitated.

"Say yes, Paisley," he murmured, coming up behind me and wrapping his arms around me. "Can't you see yourself living here?"

I nodded before I could stop myself. Because I could see myself living here. I could see a safe place for my children, with tons of room for them to run around. I could see a cute home, with space for me to have privacy with my children, while still just being around the corner from Bowen.

"How would the kids get to school?"

"There's a bus into Lorrington every morning and afternoon. Or they could do the distance education program with Dad and Henry. It's really good. Henry is doing so well with it."

"I still need to find a new job though. There's probably not many jobs out here..."

"That's true. But I might have an idea about that too, if you aren't picky on what you do..."

I shook my head quickly. "I'm not."

"Some folks I know run a restaurant on their property out here. They've got a B & B style set up and they're getting pretty busy. I know they need someone to wait tables. Clean rooms. That sort of thing."

"I'm interested."

"Yeah? Okay, I'll call them later. Set you up with an interview. And in the meantime, you live here, rent-free."

"Bowen, no..."

He held up a hand. "Just let me help. Please? You can pay all the rent you want once you get that job."

I took in his earnest expression. He was practically pleading with me. And I was holding out? Why? I had nowhere else to go, besides my mother's house. Or Stacey's. But neither of those were very good long-term solutions. My mother and I would kill each other and while it would be fun for me to live with Stacey temporarily, I knew the kids would drive her insane in about five minutes flat. She loved them. In small doses. Living with them would be too much.

And Bowen was offering me my own space. I sighed.

"Are there snakes?"

He chuckled behind me. "Yes. But they're generally more scared of you than you are of them."

"I doubt that."

"And you call yourself a country girl."

I laughed. "Shut up. I never called myself that."

"I'll deal with any snakes. How 'bout that?"

I paused again. "Teach *me* how to deal with them. How about that?"

He didn't hesitate for a minute. "Deal."

"Okay, then."

He dropped his chin to my shoulder, his lips by my ear. "Is that a yes?"

I nodded, a small smile flicking at my lips. "Fine. It's a yes. Thank you."

Bowen let out a whoop of joy and smacked my ass again.

I frowned at him. "What's with that by the way?"

He feigned innocence. "What?"

"The ass smacking?"

His grin turned devilish. "Oh, you mean the ass smacking that you begged me for?"

My cheeks heated. The ones on my face. Though my ass cheeks still tingled from earlier too.

"I did not beg."

I totally did. But I didn't have to admit it.

Bowen's hand cupped my ass and squeezed it. "Oh baby, but you did. How about I take you back into one of these rooms and make you beg for it some more?"

"I won't do that," I protested indignantly.

"You already admitted you liked my dirty mouth, Paisley. I get a whole lot dirtier than that. Just you wait and see."

Despite my protests, I found myself following him back to a bedroom, my ass cheeks tingling in anticipation.

31

PAISLEY

*D*ust was an insidious little bugger. Ridding the little house on Bowen's property of it turned out to be a huge task. Running on exactly no sleep, I went through several vacuum filters, a whole roll of cleaning cloths, and two bottles of disinfectant. Mum and Alan made an appearance at about 10 a.m., looking thoroughly loved up. It was almost sickening the way they looked at each other with such fondness in their eyes, their gentle little touches, and stolen kisses when they thought we weren't looking. If I hadn't been so happy for them, I would have vomited over the sweetness.

Mum rolled up her sleeves and got busy with a duster while I cleaned out the bathroom. Alan and Bowen and Henry went into town with the little key Jonathan had given me and loaded as much of my stuff as they could onto the back of Bowen's ute and a trailer he used for transporting bulls. When 4 p.m. rolled around, an hour before I was due to pick Aiden and Lily up, I stood back and almost wept with relief.

"It looks like a different house from this morning," Mum

said, casting a critical eye around the room. She caught my gaze and squeezed my arm. "The kids will love it out here."

"You think?" I asked hopefully.

She nodded. "What's not to love? Fresh air. Peace. Quiet. Good-looking men..." She cast a glance at Alan, who huffed and looked at the ground, but the smile tugging at his lips told me he enjoyed my mother's compliments.

"We should leave," Bowen said as he clumped back into the house with another load of kids' toys. "I don't want you to be late."

I caught his hand as he walked past. "Actually, I think I'm going to go by myself. This is going to be a big change for them. I think I should tell them alone."

Bowen frowned. "You sure?"

I nodded.

He smiled softly. "Okay. I'll have dinner ready when you get back."

I grinned at him. "That's very neighbourly of you."

He tipped his hat at me before pulling me in and kissing my lips gently. "See you soon."

I grabbed my car keys and waved to Mum and Alan, who were sitting on a newly cleaned porch swing, and got in my car. Out on the road, I turned the music up and sang along loudly. I was tired. Exhausted really, but adrenaline over facing Jonathan again had me twitching and pushing my foot down harder on the accelerator. In a break between songs, I realised my phone was ringing, and I grabbed it from the centre console, turning it to speaker so I could still drive with both hands.

"Paisley? It's Ken Debartlo, I'm one of the officials at Open Universities Australia. I just wanted to talk to you about your coursework. Is now a good time?"

I groaned internally, because it was really the worst time,

but when was there ever going to be a good time? I had a feeling I knew exactly what he was going to say, and I might as well rip the Band-Aid off.

"Now's fine."

"I've been reviewing your coursework. You've always been a good student, but you've missed your last two assignments. You have another due by midnight tonight, which we haven't received from you yet either."

I winced. "I know. I'm sorry about that. I've just had some personal issues lately..."

I could practically hear the disapproval in his breathing.

"Do you think I could get an extension? Just a few days?"

He sighed. "I'll give you an extra two days for the assignment that's due today. And an extra two weeks to catch up on what you've missed. But you also need to keep up with any new assignments issued in that time."

Relief coursed through me. "Of course. Of course. Thank you. I really appreciate it."

"You need to do better, Ms Ackerly. I don't like to see students fail, especially since you've already done two years of the course."

"I won't fail. I can't. I need this. I can do better, I know that."

"See that you do."

I hung up feeling like a ten-year-old who'd been scolded. My cheeks flamed. How embarrassing. It wasn't like me at all to get behind. Or to do badly on an assignment. I was a perfectionist through and through and the thought of failing my final year made me feel sick. I'd been living in a Bowen bubble. It was time to pop it. That was for sure. It would be harder to do than ever now, living so close to him. But I threw the phone on the passenger seat, vowing to talk to Bowen about it after dinner.

Pulling into Jonathan's driveway, I sucked in a deep breath, squared my shoulders and checked my reflection in the rear-view mirror. I had dirt smudged across one cheek, which I scrubbed off furiously, then smoothed my hair before getting out of the car.

I knocked on his door this time, unlike earlier in the day where I'd pounded it like it was a piece of meat. Little footsteps rang out from inside, and the door swung open.

"Mummy!" Lily yelled, launching her little body into my arms. "You're here! I missed you!"

I breathed in her little girl scent, hugging her until she squirmed to be put down. "Missed you too, baby girl."

Aiden stood behind her, watching, and I tugged him in for a hug. He was stiff for a moment, but then he relaxed, his arms wrapping around me.

"Mum?" his muffled voice asked.

"Yeah?"

"You're smushing me."

"Oh, right. Sorry." I stepped back. Then changed my mind and pulled him to me again. "On second thought, I'm not that sorry."

He giggled into my shirt, and then I let him step away. "Go get your stuff and say bye to your dad, okay?"

The two of them ran off upstairs right as Jonathan appeared. He was fully dressed this time.

"Where are you going?" he asked, leaning against the wall and shoving his hands into his pockets. "I need to know the address."

"I'll text it to you," I said through gritted teeth. I really didn't want to look at the man right now. Or ever again, really. But I knew that was impossible.

"If you're just going to your mum's place, you don't need to text me. I remember."

"It's not my mum's."

"Stacey's then?"

"No. I got my own place."

Jonathan raised an eyebrow. "In one day?"

"Not like you gave me much of a choice, did you?"

"You're moving in with him then? The boyfriend?"

"Jonathan, it's none of your business, but yes. I mean sort of. It's his house but it's just me and the kids living there. We're completely independent from him."

He frowned. "Hardly independent if he's your landlord and your boyfriend."

"It's not like that." But I heard the uncertainty in my own voice. And Jonathan did too.

"If you say so."

My fingers clenched into fists. "Kids, let's go. You'll see your dad in two weeks, as normal."

They thundered down the stairs, and Jonathan's expression changed instantly. He high-fived Aiden and Lily hugged him round the legs. He didn't bother walking us out.

I followed the kids to the car, buckled Lily in, and sat in the driver's seat before twisting round to smile brightly at them both. "Guess what! We're going on an adventure!"

The two of them cheered as I turned back around and stiffly put the car into reverse. Jonathan's taunts echoed in my ears. Moving into Bowen's place had seemed like the ideal situation. I'd have a house of my own, he knew people who could get me a job...I'd have everything I needed. But a sinking feeling settled over me. And I couldn't help wondering if this was the exact same adventure I'd already been on once before. Just wrapped up in a prettier package.

32

PAISLEY

*B*owen's friend's restaurant wasn't like any I'd ever seen before. We sat outside beneath stars and fairy lights, a bonfire crackled off to one side, and tall gas heaters were scattered in amongst tables set with white linen and shining silver cutlery. In the middle of our intimate table, Australian native flowers sat in a jar, tealights circling the centrepiece. A dozen other couples and a few small groups were scattered around the open space, the quiet hum of their conversations and low jazz music swirled around me. I was cosy, tucked into a thick jacket and scarf, with the warmth of a heater on my back. And in complete awe at what these people had created in their own backyard.

"This is kind of amazing," I whispered to Bowen, and he nodded.

"Isn't it? They do horse riding lessons here during the day, and they've got cabins down the back of their property. Ryker said they're almost always booked out. And then they do this pop-up restaurant thing every week now. So I guess it's not pop-up anymore?"

"It's so busy."

"Yeah, they've developed a bit of a reputation. The food is good. And all handmade from local produce. You're gonna love it."

My mouth was already watering. My stomach growled as a man, several years younger than me by the look of it, approached our table. A young woman in a wheelchair followed him. Bowen stood up and shook hands with him, and I smiled at the woman, sticking my hand out. "Hi. I'm Paisley."

She took my hand eagerly. "Gemma."

Bowen turned to us. "Sorry, babe. Paisley, this is Ryker. Ryker and Gemma own the place."

I was a little surprised at how young the couple was to have such a thriving restaurant, but Ryker shook his head. "It's Gemma's parents' property. Her mum and I co-own the business."

"And I'm just the hired help," Gemma laughed.

Ryker kissed her cheek. "You're a bit more than that."

She shrugged. "I help out when I'm here. But I have a part-time job in Sydney too, so I travel back and forth a lot. Which is where you might come in, Paisley."

I nodded eagerly. "I just want to work. I'm happy to do anything. And I'll work hard and be reliable."

Ryker nodded. "That's really all we need. It'll be a lot of cleaning cabins mostly. We have ten of them down in the back paddocks now. But it's too much work for just me. Gemma's mother helps out with the restaurant a lot, but she doesn't want to be working full-time. She's semi-retired. And while Gemma is a whirlwind, and she has the horses and lessons side covered..." He smiled at me. "Sorry, I'm rambling. Basically, we just need another set of hands."

I held my hands up and wriggled my fingers at him. "I've got a set if you're willing to let me use them."

We grinned at each other. I liked the younger couple immediately. I got the innate sense that they would be good people to work for.

"You're hired. You can start Monday."

Relief swept through me. With a job, I was back on the right track. Or, at least, I was on the side road on the way back.

"It's going to be great to have you here. I'm looking forward to getting to know you better." Gemma's smile was genuine.

"And it should work out nicely for all of us. Gemma is always home on weekends, so you'll still be able to travel around with Bowen to his rodeos." Ryker turned to Bowen. "You've been killing it lately, man. They said you might have a shot at the title?"

Bowen shrugged modestly. "Maybe. We'll see."

Ryker slapped him on the shoulder. "We'll leave you two to eat. But it's real good to see you finding your form again. Lucky you found Paisley, huh? You were shithouse without her."

Bowen found my fingers beneath the table and squeezed them. "Luckiest man alive."

*I*n the car on the way home, with bellies full of delicious handmade pasta and organic sauces, I stared out the window at the night sky, replaying the evening in my head. One thing in particular kept repeating over and over again in my head.

"What's up, babe? You're super quiet tonight."

"How many rodeos are in a season?" I shifted my weight so I was facing him.

He glanced over at me. "Depends. Twenty-five? Thirty? Something like that."

"Thirty."

"Yeah, why?"

"No, I just...that's more than half the weekends in a year. That's a lot of time to be away."

He didn't look over but his fingers tightened ever so slightly on the steering wheel.

I rushed to clarify. "I'm just wondering how I fit into all of that."

He jerked the wheel to the side, pulling the car up on an embankment and setting the handbrake. Then unclipped his seatbelt before he turned to face me. "You can come with me. You and the kids. And Dad, if we need to be away for a while for the US leg of the tour."

My eyes widened. "The US leg of the tour?"

"Well, yeah...you didn't know there was an international competition?"

I shrugged. I mean, it made sense what with Kai, Sunny, and Johnny coming from America. I just hadn't really thought it through. Probably a bit naive of me.

"It's pretty cool, really. We get to travel around with a great group of friends. You like Isabel, right?"

I nodded. "Of course, she's great."

"And you'll get to know the other wives and girlfriends in time. There's a real sense of family within the group. You and the kids will fit right in."

An uncomfortable weight settled on my shoulders. "That does sound nice," I said, choosing my words carefully. "It's just..." I looked down at my hands.

But Bowen's fingers were quick to lift my chin. "Hey," he said, leaning in and brushing his lips over mine. "It's okay. Whatever is bothering you, you can tell me."

I bit my lip, not wanting to disappoint him. "I can't just be your groupie, Bowen."

A frown creased the space between his eyebrows, and he recoiled slightly as if the word offended him. "I don't expect you to be my groupie..."

I sighed. "Okay. Bad choice of words. But I can't come to the rodeo this weekend. I know I'm your good luck charm and all that, and everyone is expecting me to go, but I've got an assignment to do, and we only just got back from Melbourne...and Sydney before that..."

"Why don't you just bring your stuff with you? Do it on the plane?"

I shook my head. "I tried that, remember? And you spent the whole plane ride whispering about what you wanted to do in the plane bathroom."

He sighed. "Look, Paisley, I'm sorry—"

"No, please don't apologise. I liked it. You know that. But me getting my assignments done just doesn't happen when you're in the room. You're kind of distracting, you know?" I smiled and ran my finger down his stubbled jaw.

A hint of a smile loosened his frown lines, and I leaned in and kissed him, not wanting to bring down a nice night by arguing. My tongue ran over the seam of his lips and after a moment of hesitation he opened, our tongues meeting. He grasped the back of my neck and I fisted his shirt, pulling him closer to me. We kissed until we were breathless, in the moonlit interior of the car, and my heart pounded when he pulled away.

"What?" I panted.

He shook his head. "I'll be fine at the rodeo without you. I don't care what everyone else says, you aren't the reason I'm winning again. Or maybe you are, but I don't need you there. I just need you in my life. If you've got an assignment to do, I want you to stay home and do it. Your course is important. *You're* important."

I searched his face. "You sure?"

"Absolutely."

He turned the key in the ignition and the engine started up again. He'd be fine. Of course he would be. He'd been doing this thing a lot longer than the last few months since he'd met me. I didn't have anything to do with how he rode.

33

PAISLEY

On Friday morning, I kissed Bowen long and slow before waving him off on his way to the airport. I spent Friday night alone in our new little place with the kids, and after I'd put them to bed, I'd spent three quiet hours studying. Saturday morning was more of the same. The kids ran off to the main house to play with Henry, who'd stayed behind with Alan, and I got comfy on the lounge, with a stack of textbooks, my laptop, highlighters, pens, and Post-it notes spread out on the coffee table in front of me.

I flicked on the TV to the sports channel and muted the sound, taking notes for an ethics in nursing module, while I waited for the rodeo to start. I got so engrossed in my studying that I missed the first ten minutes, and with a start, scrambled to turn off the mute button as Sunny's smiling face waved to the crowd. I grinned. It was still kind of weird to know these guys, then be watching them on the TV.

I cheered when Sunny held on for his eight seconds and dismounted safely.

"Bowen Barclay up next after the ad break, ladies and gents."

A tingle of anticipation shot through me, and I ran to the kitchen to grab a bowl of popcorn, figuring I'd been studying all morning. I could at least take a snack break while I watched my man... Just because I'd stayed home didn't mean I didn't care about how his ride went. And I wasn't missing a chance to see his ass in chaps either.

The arena filled the screen again, the ad break finished, and butterflies took flight in my belly. The camera zoomed in on Bowen hanging over the top of the chute. He handed his rope to Jimmy while the announcer yammered on in the background.

"Bowen Barclay has had a phenomenal comeback this season, Jerry. Just a few weeks ago, he was on the brink of being dropped from the competition due to a series of poor performances and buck offs."

The other announcer chuckled. "Yeah, but then he went and found himself a lady..."

I wrinkled my nose and rolled my eyes towards the ceiling. Oh, great.

"His new girlfriend definitely seems to have helped him turn a corner. We're told she's not here tonight though for the first time since that crowd-pleasing kiss where he found his mojo again. A lot of people have been whispering about her not being here tonight. What do you think her absence is going to do to his state of mind?"

I groaned and threw a piece of popcorn at the TV screen. "It's not going to do anything to his state of mind, you morons! He's a grown man!"

My finger hovered over the mute button, but then the screen switched back to Bowen again, now on the back of the bull. The bull thrashed in the pen, and I gasped as

Bowen slipped to one side, his spotter yanking his vest to the left to keep him upright.

"Oooh, Rampage is in a mood tonight. And these two have never gotten along."

My mouth dried. "Oh no. No, no, no."

With all the drama going on lately, Bowen's bull draw had completely slipped my mind. He hadn't said anything about him riding Rampage *this* weekend. If I'd known that, I would have gone for sure. I knew how that bull messed with his mind, but I'd been too involved in my own dramas and getting caught up on schoolwork that I hadn't even asked him which bull he'd drawn. I felt sick with guilt, and my heart hammered in my chest as Rampage settled enough for Bowen to get the rope around his hand.

"Barclay's just been put on the clock by the judges," one of the announcers called and I squeezed the edge of the popcorn bowl so hard I was surprised the glass didn't shatter.

"Please, please, please," I murmured, shifting to the edge of my seat. I stared up at the screen, knowing that being put on the clock, given only a minute to nod and get your ride underway or be disqualified, was going to stress him out. "Don't rush it..."

Rampage stilled, and Bowen took the moment. He nodded sharply and the gate flew open.

Rampage stormed the ring like he was possessed. He spun to the right, and I cried out, knowing it was Bowen's weaker side, but he held on as Rampage bucked and kicked. The bull was a powerful machine, twisting and turning, his thick flanks glistening beneath the bright arena lights. His horns were deadly, flashing beneath spotlights as he threw his head around in sharp jerks, fighting desperately to unseat Bowen. But Bowen held on. The seconds counted down, and Bowen's form grew sloppy but hope rose in my chest. He was going to do it! He was going to make. Six... seven...eight! Eight! I stood and cheered in unison with the crowd, relief lifting the vice that had been gripping my chest. My phone rang, but I didn't even glance at it. I couldn't wait to see him yank off his hat and throw it into the crowd. He was going to be so happy, and I was thrilled for him. He just had to get off first.

He yanked hard on the rope but nothing happened.

He didn't jump off like he usually did.

My grin slipped from my face. Rampage dipped his front quarters, and Bowen was thrown forward, his head connecting with a vicious snap to the side of the bull's horns. And then he went limp. He slid down Rampage's side, his body being thrown around like a rag doll, but his hand caught firmly in the ropes.

"Oh my god," I whispered, watching in horror.

"He's out!" the announcer yelled, panic in his voice. "Barclay is knocked out and held up. This is not a good situation."

The bull fighters, with their painted faces, danced around the bull, each of them desperately trying to get to the ropes that held Bowen's unresponsive body captive.

A sob broke through my chest as the bull spun and kicked, knocking one of the fighters to the ground and stepping on him. Another made a desperate lunge for the bull, leaping to loosen the rope, and Bowen's hand slipped out, his body crumpling to a pile in the dust.

He didn't move.

The crowd went silent. The bull fighters distracted Rampage, moving him away from Bowen's body until the bull gave one final bellow of disgust and trotted out of the ring like he didn't have a care in the world.

Then all hell broke loose. The announcers screamed for the medics, and a team of men circled Bowen's body, shielding him from the TV camera. Tears poured down my face. And all I could do as I stood there, watching the man I loved leave the arena on a stretcher, was pray he wasn't dead.

The cameras went back to the announcers, as I stood in shock. My phone kept ringing, and eventually I grasped it, looking at the screen. Bowen's handsome face in his cowboy hat filled the small screen, making me gasp.

I fumbled with the phone, stabbing at the buttons with shaking fingers until I got it to answer. "Bowen!" I yelled. "Are you okay?"

Deacon's voice was grave on the other end. "Paisley, you need to come. Now. It's bad."

My chest tightened, squeezing until it threatened to explode. "Is he alive?" I whispered.

Deacon's voice was barely a murmur. "I don't know."

34

BOWEN

*T*hick grit coated the backs of my eyelids, stinging my eyes until I forced them open. Bright light made my eyes ache, but that just meant it matched everything else in my body. Pain radiated through my skull, and a wave of nausea hit me like a freight train. I struggled to sit, but nothing happened. My body wouldn't move. Strong hands rolled me to my side as I vomited, and I dimly became aware of people yelling my name.

"Bowen!" Deacon's face swam into view, only to be replaced a second later by faces I didn't know, and my head swam in confusion. But I waited and when Deacon's face appeared again, I choked out the one thing I wanted most. "Paisley?"

"Yeah, she's coming, man. I called her. You hang in there, okay? Don't you fucking die."

Die? I wasn't going to die.

Fuck. Was I?

The last thing I remembered was adrenaline mixed with fear pulsing through my veins and that eight second buzzer sounding like songs from the angels. Sweetest sound in the world. Then nothing, until now.

"He's in and out of consciousness," someone yelled as sirens pierced through my skull, and I tried to force my lips to speak words and not just moan about the pain ricocheting round my body.

"You with me, Bowen?"

"Doc?" I was no stranger to the team doctor, who everyone just called Doc. I actually had no idea what the guy's name was.

"Yeah, it's me. You got knocked out. Anything besides your head hurting?"

I groaned. "Everything?"

He frowned. "I thought that might be the case. Try to stay awake, okay? We're getting you some help."

"Sure thing," I mumbled, squinting as there was suddenly two of him. A laugh escaped my chest, though it hurt so I stopped abruptly. "Stay awake. Got iiiiiiiitttt."

Everything went black before I could remember what I was supposed to be doing.

35

PAISLEY

*N*umb from head to toe, I chased Alan and Henry through the swinging hospital doors and tried to process the blur of white and the crowd of people around us. I was dimly aware of Isabel taking my hand and leading me to a seat in the waiting room, but I don't think I even managed to get a coherent word out until Deacon squatted in front of me and put his hand on my knee.

"Paisley? You okay?"

I shook my head and grabbed his fingers. "Is he...?"

Deacon's mouth tilted in a half smile. "Doctor said he's the luckiest man alive."

A sob tore from my throat. "He's alive?"

He nodded. "His head is a bit messed up. He's got a severe concussion, but they scanned his brain and they said he'll be okay in a few days. Everything else is superficial."

I let out a long, shaky breath.

"He wants to see you. He hasn't shut up about you since he came to."

"No, no. Henry and Alan should go in."

"They already did."

"What? When? We just got here?"

Deacon squeezed my hand gently. "You've been here for an hour, Pais."

He exchanged a concerned look with Isabel. "Is she in shock? Should we get the doctor to have a look at her?"

I shoved his hand away. "Stop. I'm fine. Where's his room?"

Deacon still looked doubtful, but he stood and took my hand.

"I'll be right here when you're done, babe." Isabel's smile was tight, and I thanked her before letting Deacon lead me away.

We walked in silence down a long corridor with nurses and patients and family members bustling around, then past a sign that read Intensive Care.

I gaped at Deacon. "You said he was okay! Why is he in intensive care?"

"It was just a precaution. They're going to move him once they have a bed in the regular ward."

"Oh, okay. Sorry."

He gave me a quick hug. "He's just through there. I'll wait here until you're done."

I hugged him back. "Thank you."

He pushed the door open for me and held it as I walked through. It closed behind me with a click. Bowen lay in a bed covered in a white hospital blanket, his head bandaged and one of his eyes completely black and swollen. I gasped as I moved closer and saw more bruising down his neck and disappearing beneath his hospital gown, only to reappear on his forearms and hands.

He didn't stir, but his chest rose and fell steadily and there was a regular reassuring beep that came from the monitor he was hooked up to. I bit my lip as I sunk into a chair beside his bed and felt the guilt flow through me like a tidal wave. A lump rose in my throat, choking me, and I tried to stifle my sobs but it was useless. I should have been there. I'd let him ride that damn bull without me in the crowd. Good luck charm or not, I should have been there to support him when he needed me. The guilt hacked at my heart, at my lungs, the weight of that feeling pressing down on me until I thought I'd break in two.

I gripped his bruised fingers, then quickly let go when he stirred, scared I'd hurt him.

"Paisley?" he murmured, not opening his eyes.

"Hey, hush. It's me. I'm here. Go back to sleep. You're okay."

"Gotta tell her..."

I frowned.

"Gotta tell Paisley..."

That lump in my throat doubled in size. Was he supposed to be this out of it? Was this normal? I looked around for a doctor, but the room was completely empty.

Bowen's face creased. His eyes opened.

"Tell me what, Bowen? I'm here."

His gaze was unfocussed, and he closed his eyes again, but words still fell from his lips. "Tell her I love her. So much. She's everything."

My heart broke. It split right down the middle with how much I loved this man, and how much I desperately wanted him to be okay. I opened my mouth to tell him I loved him too. Because I did. Oh, how I loved him. I think I'd started falling for him from the very first time I'd seen him on my TV screen. But nothing came out. I tried to force my lips to move. To tell him everything I felt for him, but that crushing pressure kept me silent. He was bruised. And broken. And until that moment, when I'd seen him lying on the dirt floor,

I hadn't realised how much of my life had become about him. My heart and soul were twined around his. And now I was just as broken on the inside as he was on the outside. I didn't know how to see him like this and still keep breathing.

He would be alright.

This time.

But what about next time? And the time after that? How could I ever let him go to a rodeo without me again? How could I ever watch him ride a bull and know that in a split second it could end with me sitting by his side in a hospital bed again? Or worse, I'd be sitting in the front row as they lowered his coffin into the earth.

A shudder ran through me as Bowen drifted off again. I couldn't. I couldn't do it. The pressure was too great. I had to protect myself. Protect my heart. And protect my children. Aiden's face when I couldn't get out of bed for weeks after Jonathan left flashed in my memory. I couldn't do that again. I couldn't ever get so lost in a man that I could be so wrecked by his leaving. Whether that be the way Jonathan had left, or the way Bowen surely would if he kept riding bulls. My kids deserved more from me than that.

I stood on shaky legs, and with one last look over my shoulder at the man who owned my heart, I walked away.

Better to do it now while I could still stand on my own two feet.

36

BOWEN

2 months later

*D*eacon handed me a beer, and I clinked it against his own before twisting the screw cap off and pocketing it. The cold liquid ran down my throat, washing away the dirt I'd swallowed coming off the back of one of my training bulls.

"Kid is good," Deacon said, nodding towards where Kai was riding Big Bugger, the bull that had just thrown me.

"He makes it look easy."

"That he does."

"You've got this year in the bag, but next year, Kai might have you beat."

"Yeah, maybe. We'll see. I don't think anything is in the bag just yet."

Deacon rolled his eyes. "You're top of the leaderboard. Unless you ride like shit for the finals, you're gonna take the title."

I shrugged, a flash of blonde hair across the yard catching my eye. I fought the urge to turn my head, but it was a losing battle. My gaze landed on Paisley, and she bit her lip as our eyes locked. Every muscle in my body stiffened as she approached.

"Uh, hi. Sorry. I don't mean to interrupt. I'm just looking for Aiden. Is he around here?"

I nodded towards the house, not trusting myself to speak around her.

"Um, okay. Thank you."

She stared at me for a long moment, looking like she wanted to say more, but then sighed and headed towards the house. I forced myself back to the ring before I ran after her, threw myself at her feet, and begged her to take me back.

I ground my finger against a splinter in the wooden fence, focusing on the pain as it pierced my skin. Anything was better than the sting of Paisley's rejection. Even two months on, that wound was as raw as ever. I couldn't imagine any amount of time passing would heal it.

"Shit, man. I hate seeing you like this." Deacon sighed.

I glanced at him. "Like what?"

He gave me an exasperated look. "Like someone ran over your puppy. All heartbroken and shit. It's been months, man."

I steeled him with a look. "I'm fucking in love with her, Deacon. And she doesn't love me back. What do you want me to do? Just get over it? I'm not like you, never being with anyone long enough to form a proper attachment."

Deacon looked like I'd punched him in the gut, and I softened a little. "Sorry. That was out of line."

"Nah, it was the truth. Can't get mad at you for that. But you gotta move on. Or rather, she does. This ain't right, her still living here, you seeing her every day. Pining away like the pathetic fuck you are."

He punched me in the arm and laughed. I knew he was joking, trying to make light of the situation, but nothing about the last two months without Paisley was anything I felt like laughing about. I missed her. So damn much. She was so close in that little cottage on the other side of my property. I still saw her almost every day, as she went to her job, or picked her kids up at the bus stop, or if she came to my place, looking for Aiden. Yet the gap that had opened between us had been like an ever-increasing chasm that I couldn't cross, no matter how hard I tried.

"I don't want her to leave. She already tried. I told her not to."

Deacon gaped at me. "What? Are you a sucker for punishment? She broke up with you, Bowen."

"I can't just kick her out because it rips me in half every time I hear her voice. I'm not gonna be like her asshole ex."

"Then what are you going to do?"

I gave him a hard look. "I'm gonna win the goddamn championship title." That was all I could do. It was all I had left. I'd done nothing but train and travel to rodeos for the past two months. If I was concentrating on winning, I wasn't thinking about Paisley.

He sighed. "You think that's gonna make you feel better?"

"About Paisley dumping me on my ass? No. Probably not. But that's irrelevant. The title is for Camille. Not me."

Deacon groaned.

"What?"

"What are you doing? I loved Camille, man. She was like a sister to me. You know that. But you avenging her death like some ancient warrior is just over the top."

"I'm hardly avenging her death."

"Aren't you? 'Cos from where I'm standing, Paisley broke

up with you because she can't handle the pressure of being in Camille's shadow. And if you aren't willing to let her go—"

"Wait, what? What are you even talking about?"

"You think it was easy for her to watch you nearly die, all because you're obsessed with winning for your dead wife?"

He may as well have punched me in the gut. But then I shook my head. That didn't make sense. "That's not what she said. She said she just didn't feel as strongly as I did... and that we were moving too fast. She was too reliant on me, too wrapped up in me, and she needed time and space for her studies and her job. She basically said she didn't have room for me in her life, Deacon."

"Or maybe that was just her polite way of saying that you didn't make room in your life for her."

I toed a clump of grass at the edge of the ring. But Deacon wasn't done. "She felt like she had to follow you around, just to see you. Everything you did together was on your terms. Did you ever do anything she wanted to do? Did you even have any idea that she was falling behind in her course? Do you know how devastated she was that she was supposed to be your good luck charm and the one time she took some time for herself, you nearly died? Man, if you look up 'pressure' in the dictionary, pretty sure there's pictures of all that."

I stared at him as pieces all started clicking together. "How the hell do *you* know all this?"

He smirked at me, then turned back to watch Kai and Sunny in the ring. "Stacey told me."

I rolled my eyes. "Cheater. Here I was thinking you were super insightful."

He laughed. "Not a chance." Then he sobered. "I think she's in love with you too, you know."

Hope flickered in my chest. "Did Stacey say that?"

He shook his head. "No, that one is an insight from me."

"I hope so," I said quietly. "I want her to be. I thought she was...and sometimes I catch her still looking at me like she used to..."

"So do something about it. You obviously aren't willing to let her go. Make room for her. Show her that she has nothing to do with whether you win or lose and that the pressure isn't on her."

"How the hell do I do that, oh wise one?"

He shrugged. "Seems pretty obvious to me, oh dumb one. Quit."

"What?"

He sighed, turning to me again. "You hate bull riding, Bowen. You've hated it ever since Camille died, and you've been forcing yourself for years. I've known you my whole life. You think I don't see the difference in you?"

"Fuck off. You're insane. I'm on top of the leaderboard. I'm what? Two rides away from the championship title? And you tell me to quit?"

"What's more important? Her? Or winning?"

"It's not just about winning and you know that." I ran my hands through my hair, feeling like screaming. "It's gotta mean something, Deacon. Camille's death. She can't have just died because I was off chasing pipe dreams."

He shoved me, hard this time. Hard enough to make me blink at him in surprise. I was even more shocked at the angry expression on his face. "Dammit, Bowen. I'm so sick of hearing you talk like that. She didn't die because you weren't there! It was an accident! It happens! It fucking sucks, but it happens. And it had nothing to do with you. She was her own person. Just like you were yours. And now you're going to throw away something that made you real fucking happy because of a memory."

I just stared at him, not knowing what I was supposed to say in response. In the ring, Kai and Sunny stood quietly watching us.

Deacon gave me a disgusted look and pushed off the fence. "I'm going to get another beer."

I watched him walk stiffly back to the house, wondering who the hell that was, and what he'd done with my best friend.

37

PAISLEY

"Are you going to tell Bowen we're here?" Stacey asked the question as casually as ever while she pretended to study her nails.

"Nope," I said firmly, peering down from the back of the stadium at the empty arena. "Why would I do that?"

"Uh, because you're in love with the man? And because we drove all the way to Sydney to be here for the finals just in case you really are his good luck charm?"

I glanced over at her and sighed. "It doesn't matter. It's not always enough to just love someone, Stace. It was all just too much."

Stacey rolled her eyes. "I call bullshit, Paisley. You didn't even give the man a chance. You backed off when it all got too intense. You got scared it was you and Jonathan all over again. But you've watched every single one of his rides since you broke up. You've secretly dragged me to three of them. And now we're all the way here in Sydney for the finals. You say it was all too much pressure, and that you couldn't watch him get hurt again, but from where I'm sitting, you can't help it. Sounds like love to me."

I folded my arms across my chest and frowned at her, but she waved her hand in my face. "Nope. Don't give me that look. I'm right, and you know it. You say you don't want all this, but you've spent the last two months doing all the hard yards, all the watching and holding your breath with your heart stopping until you know he's okay. And none of the fun, sexy stuff that should go along with it."

I opened my mouth to defend myself but then abruptly shut it.

Stacey smirked. "I'm right, aren't I?"

I picked up my hot dog and took a bite, chewing it slowly so I didn't have to answer her.

Stacey shot me one last knowing look which I pointedly ignored.

"Do you know which bull he drew for this round?"

"Yeah, Party Time."

Stacey squinted. "Who the hell names these bulls anyway? They all have such stupid names."

I shrugged. "The owners, I guess? But at least it wasn't Rampage. I couldn't watch him ride that bull again."

"Has he ridden Party Time before?"

I nodded. "Yep, I researched it when I saw the draw. He rode him for the eight seconds once last year. And twice the year before. He got low nineties both times."

Stacey's eyes brightened. "So he's got this in the bag then, right? No sweat?"

"I really hope so. For him." I sighed. "And for Camille too. I know how badly he wants to win it in her memory."

Stacey slung her arm over my shoulders. "You're a better woman than me, you know? You've got a compassion most people don't."

"You'd do the same for someone you love."

"Ha!" Stacey pointed at me, like she'd caught me in some sort of trap. "You do still love him. You admitted it."

The dimming lights in the arena stopped me from bothering to try to deny it. It was probably written all over my face anyway.

The finals were like nothing I'd seen before. Fireworks and pyrotechnics lit up the arena as the announcers called out each rider.

"Deacon Ashford," the announcer drawled as Deacon ran out into the middle of the ring.

Stacey stood and screamed, waving her arms in the air. We were way too high in the nosebleed section for Deacon to hear us, and I just stared at her in shock.

When they called the next rider, she sat down as if nothing had happened.

"What the hell was that?" I asked with a laugh.

She shrugged. "Nothing. I know him. I cheer for all the guys like that."

"Uh, no you don't. They just called Sunny's and Kai's names and you barely looked up from your phone."

Stacey waved her hand around dismissively. "Shh, you're going to miss Bowen."

I let the subject drop because she was right. When they called his name I clapped, but my heart was beating too loudly in my chest for me to do anything else. I felt frozen to the chair, my muscles stiff with anticipation.

"Who's riding first?" Stacey asked.

"Kai, Sunny, Deacon, Johnny, then Bowen." I rattled off the order I'd memorised. "There's other guys in between, but they're the ones you know. Bowen, as leader, goes last."

Stacey groaned. "That's kinda torturous."

I gave her a tight smile. "I know."

Kai looked quietly confident as he mounted his ride in

his usual calm and collected manner. A motherly sort of pride washed over me when he rode like a seasoned veteran and came away with a score in the low nineties. Sunny and Deacon both nailed their rides too, but their scores were lower, in the high eighties. They both looked pleased, though it put them out of contention for a place. Johnny was bucked off and looked fuming mad as he stormed down the tunnels. My heart ached for him and I sent Isabel a message of commiseration. I was staring blankly at my phone, waiting on her reply, my leg bouncing in nervous anticipation when they called Bowen's name. My head snapped up, and I grabbed Stacey's hand. My heart pounded so hard I thought I was going to have a heart attack. I couldn't remember the last time I'd felt so much anticipation.

The big screen zoomed in on Bowen's face as he stood to one side of the chute, preparing for his ride. He adjusted his gloves and tugged down the brim of his hat. He rolled his head from side to side, loosening tension, and I dug my nails in Stacey's palm.

"Ow, girl. You touch your man like that? You kinky—"

"Shh!" I whisper-yelled at her. "Stop. I can't concentrate on you and him at the same time."

Stacey good-naturedly mumbled something under her breath but whatever it was I wasn't listening. I was zeroed in on Bowen. He shifted his weight from side to side, then took a step towards the chute. When he had one foot on the rung, my breath caught. This was it. This was his big moment. One ride. Eight seconds to glory. Eight seconds to prove to the world what he was made of.

"Please, please, please," I murmured under my breath.

Bowen's fingers gripped the rungs, readying himself to climb over. I bit my lip, waiting for him to swing his leg over the top bar and climb down onto Party Time's back.

But he didn't move.

"What's he doing?" Stacey hissed. "Did he forget to pee or something?"

I elbowed her sharply as Bowen lifted his head. The camera zoomed in as the announcers speculated over what was going on.

Bowen stepped back and said something to Jimmy, and then to the guy who spotted him. Jimmy started talking furiously, shaking his head, and I squinted at the big screen, desperately wishing I could read lips.

"Something is wrong," I murmured. My stomach rolled and I hated that I wasn't down there behind the chutes. Hated that I wasn't there backing him up, ready to give him a reassuring smile.

"Bowen Barclay seems to have some sort of problem; we're just waiting on word from his team as to what's going on," one of the announcers said. "Don't forget, this is the last ride of the season. And the ride that will determine this year's champion. This is not a ride he wants to screw up."

"I don't understand," I said, looking around in confusion. Why wasn't he getting on? The crowd was silent, the cameras following Bowen as he skirted the chute and then climbed the fence, dropping down onto the dirt of the arena floor. A ripple of confused conversation spread around the arena. He strode across it with confidence rolling off him, a small smile tugging at his lips until he reached a high platform at the far end where the judges and announcers sat. One of the announcers stood to meet him, Bowen taking the handful of steps two at a time.

The man shook Bowen's hand, then Bowen pulled him in and said something in his ear. The announcer shrugged. My gaze darted between the big screen TV that had a close-up of the two men's faces and the actual spot where they stood.

"Uh, well, this is unexpected, but Bowen tells me he needs to make an announcement."

"What is he doing?" I asked Stacey, but she looked as baffled as I felt.

The announcer handed Bowen the microphone and he pulled off his hat. His hair was tousled like it always was, but he was still impossibly handsome to me. The fine lines around his eyes, the gentle lift of his lips, the stubble that adorned his strong jaw... All the features of the man who made my heart beat quicker every time I saw him. I really did love him. With everything I had.

"Thanks, Jerry," Bowen said when he took the mic. He ran his fingers along the sides of his jaw. "Listen, I'm sorry. I know this isn't what you all paid to see. But I won't be riding tonight." He paused. "Or ever again. I'm announcing my retirement."

Jerry the announcer's mouth dropped open as shocked and surprised cries rang out around the arena. Some people booed.

"Ohhhh wow. Do you think..." Stacey said beside me, but I was already on my feet, pushing past the people sitting next to us and heading for the aisle.

"Where are you going?" Stacey cried, but her voice got lost in the pounding determination in my head.

"You do realise you're just one ride away from taking the championship?" Jerry the announcer was obviously having a hard time understanding what was going on.

As was I.

I reached the end of the aisle as Bowen took back the mic. "I know. But I've realised there's more important things in my life. Things I need more than I need this title. Actually, if I'm truthful with you all, trying to win this title has been holding me back for years. I thought I needed it. But the truth is I need *someone* more than I need that belt buckle."

Oh no. No, no, no. He didn't mean me. He couldn't. But I increased my pace and jogged down the stairs, rapidly moving towards the man who was making the biggest mistake of his life.

And I had a sneaking suspicion he was doing it for me.

Jerry clapped Bowen on the back. "Well, I've got to say, this isn't something I've ever seen before. Are you sure?"

Bowen laughed and nodded.

I ran faster, taking the last few steps until I reached the fence that separated the crowd from the ring. I grasped it tightly. "Bowen!" I yelled, my voice echoing around the ring.

Everyone around me stared. From the corner of my eye I saw two security guards start to move in. But then Bowen turned in my direction. His gaze clashed with mine, his eyes widening in surprise.

"So what are you going to do now?" the announcer asked, oblivious to the silent war Bowen and I were having with our eyes. I knew mine screamed, *What are you doing!* While his were calm, and said quietly, *Don't worry, I've got this under control.* But he didn't. I didn't know why he was doing this, but he was going to regret it. He'd wake up tomorrow and regret everything he'd said in the heat of the moment tonight. I had to make him see sense.

Bowen leant in. "Actually, there's only one thing I want to do, Jerry." His gaze bored into mine. "I want to ask the woman I love a question."

The air punched from my lungs. Bowen strode down across the ring, his boots sinking into the soft dirt. Security guards appeared at my side and I braced myself to be thrown out, but one took me gently by the arm and led me to a gate that opened onto the arena floor. I glanced at him in a daze as I stepped through, the dirt flattening beneath my boots. The crowd around me went wild and I looked around at the smiling, cheering faces who were all fixated on me and wondered what the hell was happening.

But then Bowen was at my side, and I turned to him, my daze suddenly wearing off. "What are you doing!" I hissed, pushing his shoulders.

He took a step back.

"You can't retire before you even finish the competition!"

But he just smiled easily at me, like he didn't have a care in the world. He reached out, running a palm down my arm until he reached my hand. He linked his fingers through mine and took a step closer so I had to tilt my head back to look up at him. "Yeah, Paisley, I actually can. I just did. It's not what I want."

I shook my head. "Of course it's what you want! You've been waiting for this for years! Did a bull kick you in the head?"

He cupped my face between both his hands. I closed my eyes briefly at the familiar touch, desperately wanting to sink into him, but I couldn't. He wasn't mine to sink into anymore.

"You're what I've been waiting for, Paisley. Not this. I don't need any of it. Not the crowds or the money or the risking my life every night. It's not what I want. I just want you. Only you. Forever."

My mouth dropped open, and tears welled behind my eyes. "I can't let you do this. You have to finish. You'll hate me."

"I could never hate you. But I hated myself for letting you go. For letting you push me away. I get it. I acted like

Jonathan. Focusing more on myself and my career and my goals than I did on what you need, but I'm not as stupid as I look. I know when I've let a good thing slip away, and I'll be damned if I'm going to let it be you."

He took a deep breath and dropped to one knee. If I thought the crowd had gone wild before, this time they went completely insane.

"Paisley Ackerly. Will you please marry me? No more bulls. No more leaving you alone. No more travelling. I'll be home every night. Every weekend. You'll have all the time in the world to finish your studies, and then to work wherever the hell you want. And I'll be right there supporting you every step of the way."

"But...what will you do? Bull riding is your life."

He shook his head, his expression so calm and full of confidence. "*You're* my life. You and Henry, and now Aiden and Lily too. I'll open a bull riding school. Or I'll farm cattle. Or I'll work at McDonald's. I don't know. I don't care what I do, as long as you're by my side."

A tear spilled down my cheek. "You're insane."

"Insanely in love with you."

I choked on a laugh. "Insanely corny."

He winked. "You gonna answer my question, Ackerly? 'Cos I've been down here a long time."

My breathing shuddered and I dashed away my tears. "Yes!" I replied through tears and smiles. "Yes, Bowen. I'll marry you. Anytime, anywhere."

With a whoop of joy, he pushed to his feet and swept me off mine in a spinning hug. My arms came around his neck and I breathed in his familiar scent, letting it fill the Bowen-shaped hole that had opened up inside of me ever since I'd walked away from him. When I pulled back, he kissed my lips gently.

"I love you," I whispered. "I've loved you for such a long time and it killed me not to tell you. I just had to protect my heart."

He placed his hand over my chest. "I want to be the one who protects your heart, Paisley. Now and forever. You just have to trust me."

I nodded, pressing my lips to his again. "I do. I love you."

"Love you too, darlin'."

I didn't even give him shit about slipping into his cowboy drawl. Our kiss was slow and sweet, and like all of our kisses, it took my breath away. I was panting when we finally broke apart, my cheeks heating as I realised we were still in the middle of the arena, with thousands of people staring at us.

I turned to Bowen in a panic. "I'll marry you, Bowen Barclay. And you can retire, if that's what you really want. But you've got to go ride that bull tonight."

He shook his head. "I don't need to do it anymore. I've made my peace with Camille's ghost."

I grabbed his shirt and pulled him closer, my lips landing on his again. "Then do it for me. Or do it for yourself. But don't give up on your dreams just yet. You've got one more ride in you, right?"

He stared down at me for a long time, checking, assessing, convincing himself that what I said was the truth. But I meant every word.

"Go get 'em, cowboy."

38

BOWEN

*L*aughter surrounded me, drinks flowed, and the championship buckle sat securely on my belt. I trailed my fingers over the ridged edges absently, my other hand wrapped around a rapidly warming beer. I'd barely been able to take a swallow between a constant stream of congratulations and well wishes on my win. And my engagement.

Paisley's arms snaked around my middle and I grinned down at her, pulling her against me and dropping a kiss to her mouth.

"Say it again."

"I love you, Bowen." She pressed up on toes and deepened the kiss. Not caring who was watching, I followed her lead, taking everything she was willing to give.

"One more time," I said against her lips.

She rolled her eyes and shoved me playfully. "I'll tell you a thousand times when we're alone. How 'bout that?"

"Mmm," I groaned. "Let's go be alone now then."

"Hell no," Deacon interrupted, appearing as if out of

nowhere. "We need to celebrate that ride! A ninety-three earns you a beer on my tab."

Paisley's friend Stacey materialised beside her, her gaze flicking to Deacon briefly, but she didn't address him. She leant in and kissed my cheek instead. "Congratulations, Bowen. You really were something."

A low grumbling sound came from Deacon, and I cast a curious glance at him, but he had his gaze fixated on Stacey, who was still steadfastly ignoring him.

Deciding to leave that one alone, I waved to Johnny and Isabel, who were pushing their way through the crowd followed by Kai, Sunny and Addie in tow.

"Gang is all here!" Sunny declared. "That means shots, right?"

He didn't wait for any of us to reply, simply pushed his way towards the bar, leaving Kai and Addie standing next to each other. I didn't miss the way they both abruptly turned in opposite directions—Addie to talk to Stacey on her left. Kai to talk to Deacon on his right. So obviously Sunny was the glue in that unhappy little threesome. Kai and Addie looked awkward as hell.

I shook hands with Johnny and let Isabel wrap her skinny arms around me in a congratulatory hug.

"Sorry about your ride, J."

Johnny shrugged. "Not my time. Maybe next year."

I flicked my head over at Kai. "Dunno about that. Frost over there is coming up fast. He well deserved second place tonight."

Kai went pink and looked down at his boots. Deacon punched him in the bicep. "You're gonna have to get used to that sort of talk, kid. You're what, twenty-two? You got a whole lifetime of people telling you how good you are. Learn to own it."

Kai, in his usual quiet demeanour, didn't answer.

Addie glanced over at him and looked as if she wanted to say something, but Sunny's arrival with a tray of shot glasses put a stop to that. He passed them around, pushing them into each of our hands before dumping the tray on a nearby bar table. He held his shot glass in the air. "To Bowen, for finally getting his shit together and not only taking out the title but taking home the love of his life. Well done, old man. Well deserved."

"Oi, ease up on the old bit, young'un."

Sunny ignored me.

"To Bowen and Paisley!"

"To Bowen and Paisley," everyone else cheered, and the nine of us clinked our glasses, and downed the liquid. The burn warmed me all the way down.

"I'm going to go dance with the girls." Paisley brushed her lips against the stubble of my cheek, and I watched her gorgeous backside sway away and disappear into the crowded bar's dance floor. Stacey, Addie, and Isabel all followed.

One glance around at my friends and I realised they all wore identical expressions on their faces watching the women walk away. I chuckled. "Should we just go follow them? Instead of standing here staring?"

"Fuck yeah," Deacon said, already on the move. Johnny and Sunny nodded, pushing through after him. I glanced at Kai. "You coming, bro?"

He shook his head. "You go though. I'm going to get another drink."

"You sure? Plenty of young ladies out there, and you're on the pretty side. I'm sure you'd find one willing to warm your bed."

The younger man cast one long look over at the dance floor but shook his head. "Not tonight."

I clapped him on the shoulder, knowing there was more he wasn't telling me, but the thought of getting Paisley in my arms, her luscious body pressed against mine as we danced, was too much to resist, and I left Kai to his drinking.

On the dance floor I wrapped my arms around my fiancée from behind and groaned quietly as her ass pressed back against me, her arm coming up to the back of my head. I lowered my mouth to her neck and kissed her gently as we swayed.

For the next hour, the nine of us danced and drank and talked bulls and wedding dresses. With alcohol coursing through my system, I was light as a fucking feather.

And growing hornier by the minute.

"Can we get out of here now?" I whispered into Paisley's ear sometime around 1 a.m. "I want to take you back to the hotel and spread your legs and devour your sweet pussy until you scream my name."

For once, she didn't turn pink or elbow me or tell me to stop. She simply pulled my mouth to hers and seared it with her kiss. I was cross-eyed when her mouth moved to lick up the side of my neck. Her lips brushed against my ear. "And after I've screamed your name, I'm going to bend over the bathroom sink and watch in the mirror as your cock sinks deep inside me—"

I grabbed her hand. "We're leaving!" I yelled to the others.

"Hey, but—"

"No! Gotta go." I had her halfway out the door, around the corner of the bar, and up against an alley wall in seconds. I kissed her hard, grinding my swollen dick between her legs, desperate to unbuckle myself and set my cock free to find home.

Her laugh tinkled out across the night, and I stepped back and grinned at her. "I love you," I said with a conviction I felt right to my soul. "I love every fucking thing about you, Paisley. I love your heart, your soul, how kind you are, and how you always put others first. But..."

She raised an eyebrow. "But what?"

"I really fucking love your mouth when you talk like that."

She tipped her face up to mine. "Then take me home and talk dirty, cowboy."

EPILOGUE

ADDIE

I was ready to leave. The bar which had been full of rodeo folk and fans had begun emptying about an hour ago, but a handful of us had been keen to carry on the party. Sunny had bought more shots. We'd danced. We'd talked and laughed with Johnny and Isabel until they'd left too, following after Paisley and Bowen.

Sunny had kissed me and I'd let him because it felt nice to be wanted by someone. His kisses didn't set my soul on fire, but not every kiss had to. Kissing him was fun. It was nice. He was big and strong and eager to please. And I was young and drunk and on a high to be out of my sleepy little hometown. So I'd kissed him back. He was a nice guy. I liked him a lot.

When his lips had trailed off mine, my eyes had fluttered open, my gaze colliding with Kai's. I sucked in a breath at the intensity of his stare. He was incredibly handsome, in a brooding, intense sort of way. In the sort of way that could consume you, if you let it. Our gazes held while I tried to decipher what the look meant, but he looked away.

"Can we go?" I asked Sunny. "I'm getting tired."

He nodded. He linked his big, warm hand around mine and I smiled at his back. He really was a gentleman. There weren't too many of those left in this world, I knew that. So what if he didn't give me that buzz I craved? Nice outweighed a buzz any old day. He would make a good, solid, steady boyfriend.

"Kai, time to roll."

Kai nodded, abandoning his bottle of water. "Keys. I'll drive."

Sunny waved him off. "I'm fine."

Kai frowned. My eyes drew to the pinched lines between his eyebrows.

"You've had twice as much to drink as I have. I'm driving."

Sunny rolled his eyes and slung his arm around my neck. "Fine, Dad. You drive then." He tossed him the keys and Kai caught them easily. I didn't say anything.

"Are you guys going back to the hotel?" Stacey asked. "I came with Paisley, so now I'm stranded."

Kai nodded curtly.

"Me too," Deacon cut in, his voice slightly slurred. "Way too fucking drunk to drive. I'm gonna leave my ride here."

Stacey gave him an exasperated look but didn't say anything. I eyed the two of them curiously, wondering what the dynamic there was.

"Come on then."

We followed Kai to the doorway, and Stacey groaned loudly as we all stopped abruptly under the little shelter over the door. "When did it start raining? I didn't even notice."

"A while ago," Deacon declared. "Was raining when I went out for a smoke."

"You smoke?" Stacey asked, wrinkling her nose in disgust. I let out a giggle.

Deacon shrugged. "When I drink I do."

Kai ignored them and darted out into the rain. I gripped Sunny's hand harder and raced after him, being careful not to slip on the wet pavement in my heels. Kai beeped Sunny's car and slid into the driver's seat.

"Here, babe, you sit in the front. I don't want you having to sit next to Deacon and his obnoxious cigarette smell." Sunny held the passenger-side door open for me, but I shook my head rapidly.

"No, no, that's fine. I don't mind. I can sit in the back." I glanced through the open doorway at Kai, who was strangling the steering wheel with his fingers. Body rigid, he stared straight out the windscreen into the dark night.

"I insist." Sunny swiftly picked me up off my feet, and before I could even yelp, he placed me down on the seat next to Kai and slammed the door.

"Sorry," I said quietly to Kai, not really knowing why I was apologising but feeling the need to do it anyway.

"What for?"

I didn't answer, because I didn't know.

The back doors closed with thumps and I twisted to see Stacey squished between the two broad-shouldered men. She shivered, rainwater dripping from her hair down her face, and when Deacon put an arm around her, she snuggled into his warmth without her usual smart-ass comment. Kai reversed the car out of the parking spot and steered us out on the road.

The car was quiet, except for the occasional chatter of Stacey's teeth and Deacon's murmured words of comfort.

Sunny's hand squeezed my shoulder. "You okay?"

"Mmm-hmm." I shot him a smile.

Kai glowered some more as rain pelted the windscreen. I sighed, suddenly sick of his stony expression. Sick of feeling uncomfortable around him. And just sick of his mood in general. "Kai, is there a reason you hate me so much?"

Kai glanced at me sharply. Deacon coughed in the back seat uncomfortably.

"He doesn't hate you, babe. That's just his face."

I shook my head, staring at Kai's profile intently. "No, I think it's more than that. I think it's—"

Headlights blinded me and the sudden explosive noise of crumpling metal rang through my ears. I barely had time to register that we'd been hit by another car before my head smacked off the side window, sending pain splintering through my body. The car spun in dizzying circles. Kai frantically hauled on the wheel trying to get the car under control again. I opened my mouth, but fear cut off my voice.

From behind me, Stacey screamed but all I could see was the looming traffic light, and my side of the car spinning as if in slow motion directly towards it.

"Fuck!" someone yelled, and I briefly registered the crunch of metal against metal as the passenger side of the car wrapped around the pole.

The pain in my head cleared, only to be replaced by fogginess and a sudden heaviness I didn't know how to explain. I heard someone yell my name and vaguely registered Kai's panicked eyes and his deep growl pleading with me to stay, before I closed my eyes and succumbed to the fogginess, letting the entire world go black.

THE END

heck out Ride Dirty, Cowboy (Dirty Cowboy, #2) on Amazon!

ALSO BY ELLE THORPE

The Only You series

*Only the Positive (Only You, #1) - Reese and Low.

*Only the Perfect (Only You, #2) - Jamison.

*Only the Truth - (Only You, bonus novella) - Bree.

*Only the Negatives (Only You, #3) - Gemma.

*Only the Beginning (Only You, #4) - Bianca and Riley.

*All of Him - A single dad anthology, featuring Only the Lies. Only the Lies is a bonus, Only You novella.

Dirty Cowboy series

*Talk Dirty, Cowboy (Dirty Cowboy, #1)

*Ride Dirty, Cowboy (Dirty Cowboy, #2) - Preorder now!

*Sexy Dirty Cowboy (Dirty Cowboy, #3)

*25 Reasons to Hate Christmas and Cowboys (a Dirty Cowboy bonus novella, set before Talk Dirty, Cowboy but can be read as a standalone, holiday romance)

Add your email address here to be the first to know when new books are available!

www.ellethorpe.com/newsletter

ACKNOWLEDGMENTS

Want to know something funny? When I finished the Only You series, I felt really lost. I'd spent two years writing it (maybe more actually), and then it was finished and I really had no idea what to do with myself.

I needed to write another series, obviously. But which one? There were so many ideas, and yet choosing one to dedicate the next year to felt really overwhelming.

So I (foolishly) decide that I'm going to give writing clean romance a go. Yep. No sex. No swearing. And hey, maybe I'll throw a prince in and make it a royal romance?

Sounded fun. So that's what I did. In the first draft of this book, Bowen was actually a very clean cut prince named Nathaniel lol. How we got from that, to Talk Dirty, Cowboy, I'll never understand. But I'm glad I did. Because I'm really proud of this book, and I hope Bowen's filthy mouth made you grin.

There's a little nod to that original storyline hidden within the book. Did you catch it? Let me know at elle@el-lethorpe.com. I love hearing from you guys!

Anyway, on with the list of people who make my books possible.

A big thank you to all my readers, bookstagrammers and bloggers, who support me by reading, telling their friends and writing reviews. I know it doesn't seem like a big deal to pass on a recommendation to a work colleague, or to jot down "This book was great!" on an Amazon review, but it really does help!

Thank you to Jolie Vines, Zoe Ashwood, and Beth Attwood who make up my stellar editing team. And an extra thanks to Jo and Zoe for being my author besties too!

Thank you to Shellie, Ally, Karen, and Alyssa who always amaze me by dropping whatever they're doing and reading my early drafts whenever I email them and not-so-casually say, "Hey, I've got this book...want to read it?"

Thanks to my hubby who didn't think it all that weird when I made him drive me two hours each way on a Saturday night so I could do real life rodeo research. Thank you also for not caring that this cover has been my screen-saver for months. He's got nothin' on you, babe. ;-)

And thank you to my gorgeous kiddos who laid on my bed behind me while I created this cover and told me it was awesome. I think the three of you are pretty awesome too.

Love, Elle x

ABOUT THE AUTHOR

Elle Thorpe lives on the sunny east coast of Australia. When she's not writing stories full of kissing, she's a wife and mummy to three tiny humans. She's also official ball thrower to one slobbery dog named Rollo. Yes, she named a female dog after a dirty hot character on Vikings. Don't judge her. Elle is a complete and utter fangirl at heart, obsessing over The Walking Dead and Outlander to an unhealthy degree. But she wouldn't change a thing.

You can find her on Facebook or Instagram(@ellethorpe-books or hit the links below!) or at her website www. ellethorpe.com. If you love Elle's work, please consider joining her Facebook fan group, Elle Thorpe's Drama Llamas or joining her newsletter here. www. ellethorpe.com/newsletter

facebook.com/ellethorpebooks

instagram.com/ellethorpebooks

goodreads.com/ellethorpe

pinterest.com/ellethorpebooks

9 780648 381464